I0618069

SMART PHONE

A Mystery Adventure

Josh Eber

For author/publisher contact info:
https://SmartPhonetheBook.com

Front / Back Cover: Mibl Art
Chapter Art: Cleanpng, Kissclipart, J. Eber

Library of Congress Control Number: 2024918855

ISBN: 978-0-9660188-0-6 (paperback)

1. Young Adult Fiction / Mystery & Detective / General
2. Young Adult Fiction / Action & Adventure / General
3. Young Adult Fiction / Action & Adventure / Travel

To my parents, Eleanor and Joe,
for unlocking my world,
and to Birdie, Chris, and Cory,
for always making it shine.

Also, thanks to BJ for the
decades of unwavering support,
and Alex Trebek for a
lifetime of Daily Doubles.

BOOKS BY JOSH EBER

• For Young (and not-so-young) Adults:

Smart Phone, A Mystery Adventure

• For Young Readers:

Just Call Me MAX! (MAX-IS-ME Adventures)

MAX Saves A World! (MAX-IS-ME Adventures)

First Day

"It's not where you go, it's who you meet along the way."

The Wonderful Wizard of Oz
L. Frank Baum, 1899

"The whole is greater than the sum of its parts."

Aristotle, circa 340 BC

Table of Contents

In 2009, Barack Obama was president; Toys "R" Us was a thriving global giant; Alex Trebek ruled the dinnertime airwaves on *Jeopardy!*; seven-year-old Billie Eilish hadn't published a song yet; Instagram and TikTok didn't exist; and the iPhone 2G—considered by most the granddaddy of smartphones—was less than two years old.

It was also the year a young boy from Iowa saw the ocean for the first time. And a few more things.

August, 2009

Malibu, California

They sat on the bus bench slurping ice cream cones, three sets of eyes glued to the store across the street.

A seagull squawked from a nearby tree. A guy on a mountain bike pedaled past and smiled. Every few minutes a car cruised by, braking at the stop sign before continuing.

Just another lazy summer day in Malibu.

Everything perfectly normal.

If they just knew what they were looking for.

The store's front door opened. A mother and daughter walked out and headed for the parking lot. The top of a stuffed toy animal stuck out from the little girl's shopping bag. Diana thought it was a giraffe. Jeffrey guessed a snake. Margaret said nothing.

The mom and girl got in their car and drove off. A few stores down, the clock in the window of a mini-market displayed the time: 3:15 p.m.

Jeffrey and Margaret decided to take pictures, maybe they'd be useful later. Tossing what was left of their cones in a trash can, they walked down opposite sides of the street snapping phone shots—the toy store, the parking lot next door, the ice cream shop on the corner, street views up and down the block.

Diana, meanwhile, stayed on the bench sucking liquefied ice cream through the hole she'd made in the bottom of her cone. By the time her friends re-joined her, the market's window clock read 3:28.

Then 3:38.

"Well, Zero Hour is long gone," Margaret noted. "Now what?"

Jeffrey shrugged. "Let's wait a little longer."

So they did, passing the time with jokes and small talk.

When the bird in the tree let loose with three ear-splitting shrieks Jeffrey flinched, prompting snickers from the girls. The boy from the boonies clearly wasn't used to screaming seagulls.

3

Then more of nothing. An occasional passing car, a pair of bicyclists, a few customers in and out of the market.

Sudden motion to their left snapped all three heads in that direction—a small dog streaking full speed down the middle of the street directly toward them as a young girl chased after it frantically screaming its name.

The rest came in a wild blur.

A car turned left at the corner directly into the dog's path. The terrified animal froze. The car slammed on its brakes, careened right, jumped the curb, and plowed through the fire hydrant they'd just been standing by, screeching to a stop inches from the toy store's front door as a giant water plume from the broken hydrant exploded into the sky, drenching everything in sight.

And then it was over.

Before anyone could breathe.

Calm to chaos to cascading waterworks in the blink of an eye.

The mini-mart clock read 3:48.

Right time.

The toy store sign showed 2247 Pearl.

Right place.

Both straight from the text.

The one they got ninety minutes ago.

Part I

California Dreaming

"Every adventure requires a first step."

The Cheshire Cat
Alice in Wonderland
Lewis Carroll, 1865

Chapter 1

Saturday Night, Two Days Earlier
Des Moines, Iowa

Jeffrey

Your Simple Guide to Using Your New Phone. Ha! Whoever came up with that title had one twisted sense of humor.

I'd been sprawled on my bed for what seemed like days now, reading the owner's manual for my new phone, trying to get my only three contacts—my mom's, my dad's, our landline—into my Contacts Manager.

Easy, right? Three lousy numbers.

Not.

Easier would be learning to fly with my hands duck-taped to my butt.

As you may have guessed, this was my first mobile device. An early birthday present from my mom for my trip. I know, sounds weird—almost thirteen, first phone, twenty-first century. Well, you'd probably understand if you knew me better. For now, though, I needed to get this add-to-contacts function working.

I re-read the page for the millionth time, then carefully tapped each phone number before clicking Save.

Please wait...

The little circle spun, and spun, then...

Sorry, invalid command. Please try again.

Arrgh!

I tossed the stupid manual over by my suitcase. I'd take it with me on my trip. Maybe by some miracle it'd make more sense later. I fell back on my bed and stared up at the ceiling, wondering what was more pathetic: spending half the night trying to add three contacts to my phone, or only having three to add.

But more about my phone later...

I was all packed and ready for my big end-of-summer trip. With school starting in nine days, this was my last chance for some real action in the otherwise boring life of Jeffrey James. And this time I had high hopes because my lifelong dream was finally coming true. *I was going to California!*

Me, who'd never been west of the Iowa state line.

Me, who'd never seen the ocean before (I kid you not).

Though considering where I lived—Des Moines, Iowa, practically the bullseye of America—never seeing the ocean shouldn't be all that surprising. The nearest one was a thousand miles east, and the next nearest almost twice that far west.

Even the nearest "non-ocean" with anything close to a beach, Lake Michigan, was five hours away. And I'd been there once, to Lake Michigan, and, yes, it was pretty big, for a lake. But even if you couldn't see all the way across it, you still knew *Michigan* was on the other side. Not exactly my fantasy destination—no offense, Michigan.

Soon though, I'd be splashing around in the biggest of them all: The Glorious Pacific! *Thousands* of miles wide, with all kinds of exotic places on the other side.

Jeopardy! Alert: The Pacific Ocean is the largest body of water in the world, covering nearly one-third of the Earth's surface and holding more than half its total water supply.

Sorry about that. The *Jeopardy!*-Jedi strikes again. Sometimes it's hard to control.

Anyway, I was on my way to visit my cousin in LA. Yep, Los Angeles, California. The City of Angels. Home to all the calendar photos hanging in my room. Surfers surfing, bodies baking, sunsets blazing. For the past two months that's all I could think about. White sand, pounding waves, palm trees galore.

Well, except for last night when I dreamed I was sitting in the front row of *Jeopardy!*, filmed (of course) in *Los Angeles, California.*

In case you missed it, I'm Jeffrey James. Yeah, the boy with two first names—as if I hadn't been teased about that since forever, even though that's totally my parents' fault.

Also as mentioned, I'm almost thirteen—three weeks shy of entering the Wonderful World of Teendom.

So why was this *Jeopardy!*-crazed, phone-challenged kid from Middle America so pumped about turning the big One-Three, visiting a cousin he'd never met, and traveling to a far-off state to dip his toes in saltwater?

Well, let's just say these first twelve-point-nine years of pre-teen life hadn't exactly been a fun-fest. True, there was that trip to Lake Michigan. Also, the day my dad taught me to ride a bike and we rode around for hours. But other than that, fun for me has basically come from books.

Pathetic, I know. But true.

Oh, and while on the subject of reading, I read somewhere that the Pacific Ocean was so big you could fit *two-thousand-eight-hundred* Lake Michigans inside it. You heard right. Twenty-eight hundred giant lakes, each about the size of West Virginia (I checked), into one humongous ocean.

Now that's big. And a perfect example of the things you learn from reading.

Also, a great way to prep for the "Lakes and Oceans" category on *Jeopardy!*

Hey Alex, let's make it a true Daily Double!

Boy, I really needed this vacation.

Chapter 2

Burbank, California

M argaret watched the lighted numbers on her nightstand clock click to 10:31 p.m.—the earliest she'd been to bed all summer.

Usually, when school was out she never hit the pillow before midnight. But tomorrow she and her mom were picking up her cousin at the airport, and though they were close in age (she was six months older), they'd never actually met, just exchanged a few birthday greetings by phone. Which meant it was going to be weird, and Margaret figured the best way to prep for weird was at least getting a decent night's sleep.

Jeffrey's parents—Uncle Eddie and Aunt Karen (her mom's sister)—were getting divorced and shipping him out for this last week of summer vacation. They were calling it his early birthday present but Margaret knew better. Nothing says "birthday present" like getting shoved off for a week in Burbank with distant relatives so you'll forget your parents are splitting up and throwing you to the wolves.

Making matters worse, Margaret wasn't what you'd call a people person. More of a *no*-people person. Something she totally blamed on her first name which she'd hated since birth. Because when you start life hating what everyone calls you, it's only a matter of time before you start hating everyone who calls you that.

In fact, until she was six she couldn't even *say* her own name, at least not so you'd recognize it. It always came out more like *Naagit*, which actually sounded a whole lot better than Margaret anyway.

And the "standard" nicknames weren't any better. Margie? Maggie? Margo? *Seriously?* Picking one of those was like having to pick which eye to poke out.

Then right before school ended, some idiot in her algebra class started calling her Maggots. Great. Another one to flush down the toilet. Her best hope was that, with high school starting soon, the name-calling might stop. Though probably not. As a lifelong Margaret, she knew firsthand classmates rarely stopped being mean because they got older. They just got sneakier—less in your face, more behind your back.

All of which summed up why Margaret was a loner, always had been, always would be, and proud of it. Ever since her dad died when she was four it had been just her and her mom. Which was fine, mostly, though sometimes a tad boring, adding yet another reason she hoped Jeffrey wasn't too weird.

Quirky, she could handle.

Freakishly creepy, not so much.

Unfortunately, he already had three strikes against him—a tweener, she'd never met, from Iowa—so she wasn't holding her breath.

Though at least she'd have company for a while.

Sometimes even loners needed that.

Chapter 3

Sunday

Jeffrey

The girl sitting next to me was hot.

Not sweaty hot. *Wow* hot. If anyone was sweating, it was me —because of the Dream Girl sitting next to me.

She was already on the plane when I boarded, and I could tell she was from California. Probably on her way home from somewhere. Nothing specific, she just had that breezy California look. Reminded me a little of that actress who played Storm in the X-Men movies— Halle something. A younger, softer version. Caramel skin, perfect cheekbones, electric eyes, killer smile. You get the picture.

I had the window seat, so when she leaned in to watch us taxi down the runway, she was so close I could feel her breath on my left ear. Of course I pretended not to notice, kept staring out my window. Not that I minded, staring out my window, since this was my first plane ride and there was plenty to see (though the best view was sitting right next to me).

I figured she was slightly older than me, not by much, and definitely not a big deal. I was also pretty sure she was alone because when the older guy in the aisle seat next to her tried to make conversation, she shushed him and he shut right up. I didn't think a friend or relative would take attitude like that without saying something.

When we stopped taxiing, I leaned back against my seat to cleverly watch her out of the corner of my eye. She was playing with her phone.

"You'll have to turn that off now, young lady," the flight attendant warned, hovering over our row. I decided that was a good thing. If she couldn't use her phone maybe she'd give me a shot. Could happen.

Once we were airborne, I grabbed the travel magazine from the front seat pouch and began flipping through it—too fast to look real but I couldn't help it. I also leaned back again, hoping to repeat my little corner-of-the-eye trick. Only this time it didn't work because she was leaning back too.

So I kept page-flipping.

It happened on page fifty-four, a colorful double-page ad for Hawaii.

"Speed-reader, uh?"

Omigod. She was talking to me.

Naturally I froze, afraid to look up, eyes riveted to the happy luau scene in my magazine. Until I heard a vaguely familiar voice mutter, "Not really."

Very slick, Jeffrey.

I closed my magazine, tucking it slowly back in the pouch to buy myself time to think of something more clever to say. Luckily, she came to the rescue before I bombed out again.

"Sorry, didn't mean to intrude. You just seemed a little… tense." She nodded to the magazine in the pouch. "You were really workin' those pages, and I couldn't help wondering if it was the take-off… or me?"

Whoa. Did not see that coming.

"Truthfully?" I asked, again buying time.

"No lie to me," she grinned. "What, you think I missed that corner-of-the-eye thing?"

So much for clever.

I shrugged. "Then I guess maybe a little of both."

I'd read somewhere that honesty was a good way to connect with girls—that and puppies—so this was me doing my best honesty.

"A little of both?" she repeated.

"Well, this *is* my first plane ride."

Her eyebrows shot up, which was fun to watch.

"Wow," she whispered. She chewed on her lower lip. "So what about the 'both' part?"

Uh oh. Too Much Honesty.

"Okay, well yeah, probably a little bit you, too… but in a good way." I felt my face flush. "Sorry. I'm not exactly Mr. Smooth, in case you couldn't tell."

She giggled at that. But not a mean giggle. A cute little adorable giggle.

"Not Mr. Smooth, eh? Well, I'll take that as a good thing." She stuck out her hand. "I'm Diana."

I looked down like I wasn't sure what it was.

"Don't worry, I won't bite."

Ouch. I reached out and shook it, then immediately launched into my default babble mode.

"Nice-to-meet-you-I'm-Jeffrey-James-and-you're-the-first-Diana-I've-ever-known-I-mean-met-in-person-are-you-from-California?"

All that blasted out in one garbled, cringy breath—while still pumping her hand, which I instantly stopped doing as soon as I realized I was still doing it, before adding, "I'm from Iowa."

Yeah, I really said that.

But, again, she just smiled. Adorably.

"Well, it's nice to meet you too, 'Jeffrey James from Iowa.' And, yes, I am from California, born and raised. By the way, I love your name. Cute and catchy, unlike mine."

I gave her a look. "What's wrong with Diana?"

She rolled her eyes. "Mom was a big Diana Ross fan. You know, The Supremes? Back in the Ice Age?" She chuckled. "She apparently got that from *her* mother. Anyway, who wants to be named after an ancient pop star? How'd you like walking around as Elvis?"

I shrugged. "No worse than having two first names that start with the same letter."

She snickered. "That's what makes it so cute."

"Yeah, me and Billy Bob," I mumbled, prompting another little giggle.

"Plus, Diana's too boring."

My eyes widened. "*Boring?* Are you kidding? What about Princess Di? Or that Roman Moon Goddess?" I paused. "Or Wonder

Woman?"

She gawked at me like I'd popped a second head.

"*Wonder Woman?*"

I nodded. "Yeah. Guess what her real name was, or is? I'm not sure whether superheroes are past or present. Anyway, when she's not Wonder Woman-ing?"

"I'm gonna take a wild stab and say Diana?"

"Bingo! Diana of Themyscira."

She wrinkled her forehead so I repeated it in syllables.

"Thuh-MEZ-ki-ra—where Wonder Woman and her sister Amazons are from. Also called Paradise Island."

She jerked back. "Whoa, moon goddesses and superheroes? You must read a lot." She thought for a moment. "But wasn't Wonder Woman white?"

"Hey, superheroes can be any color they want. Think Black Panther, Storm, Lion Man."

"*Lion Man?*"

I nodded again. "Pretty sure he was around even before your prehistoric Supremes." I paused to let my vast comic book knowledge sink in. "Surely you don't think all caped crusaders come in one flavor?"

Which earned me an actual Laugh-Out-Loud. The Nerd from Iowa made Wonder Woman laugh.

The Love Gods were smiling down on me.

My fantasy flight ended way too soon. Still, by the time we landed I'd learned a lot about the new love of my life.

She was fourteen and returning to California from New York where her mom lived. Her parents were divorced (the one thing we almost had in common), and she and her dad lived in Brentwood (a ritzy town by Beverly Hills I'd read about during my pre-trip research). I think she also mentioned her father was a lawyer, but I'm not sure. Once those heart-stopping eyes lasered in on me, my concentration kinda crumbled.

When she told me all this stuff, she never seemed to be bragging. More like it was all silly and boring. But it was while we were taxiing to the terminal that things really got wacky, because that's when she suggested we *trade phone numbers.*

I swear.

And while still recovering from that, I think she said something about calling if I needed a tour guide, though—between those laser eyes and the plane's air pressure—I may have hallucinated that last part.

But I nodded anyway, like I got such offers all the time. Why not play along, right? Even though I knew she was either joking or being polite and that as soon as we got off the plane, that would be it. *Bye, have a nice life.*

I mean, come on. The Moon Goddess from Brentwood offering the Babbling Idiot from Nowhere a tour of LA? What could possibly be wrong with that picture?

We walked off the plane together. I'd never experienced anything like that, walking off the plane—walking anywhere—with someone like Diana by my side. Now I know how Thor feels when he blasts through enemy walls. *Jeffrey James, Master of the Universe.*

As we entered the main terminal, she started waving to a man obviously waiting for her. About my mom's age and very California-Cool. Dark wavy hair, movie-star tan, faded jeans, untucked cream-colored shirt, loafers with no socks—and the whitest teeth ever. Piano-keys white.

"Who's that?" I asked.

"Ty. My driver. Actually, kinda my substitute dad, since my real one—bless his little heart—travels on business a lot." Waving to Mr. Cool, she added, "He lives on the property."

Her driver. Substitute dad. Lives on the property.

Welcome to California.

As she walked toward him, she glanced back and gave me one of those California half-smiles. So I fired one back, my best Midwestern hey-I-do-this-all-the-time-and-you're-not-breaking-my-heart smirk, though I don't think it worked.

Scanning the terminal for my own driver, I spotted a girl about my age standing next to, I was pretty sure, my Aunt Susan. At least they were both looking at me and the woman was waving and smiling. Not so much the girl who looked like she might've eaten something bad and was trying not to puke.

Offering a small wave back, I took one last look at my Dream Girl as she and her Crest-whitened substitute dad faded into the sunset (actually, down the escalator), then walked over to my new substitute family.

And the strangest/best week of my life.

Chapter 4

The first hint that something was up with Jeffrey's new phone happened in the airport parking lot.

As they neared Aunt Susan's car, Jeffrey's pocket buzzed. Pulling out his new device, he saw the missed-text icon. Hoping it was Diana telling him how much she already missed him, he tapped it. But instead of a text, the screen displayed a single character: Ø

After climbing into the back seat, he showed it to his cousin. "Any idea what this means?"

Margaret looked, then shook her head. "Just re-boot it."

When he did, the symbol was gone, so he put his phone away, buckled up, and let the moment pass.

To a kid from Iowa, the drive from the airport to Aunt Susan's was like a fifty-minute carnival ride. The LA freeway system was a non-stop maze of twists, turns, skylines, graffiti, endless billboards, and more cars than he'd ever seen at one time—making polite conversation with his hosts nearly impossible.

Once they finally got off the freeway, Aunt Susan drove into a cozy neighborhood of single-family homes. Pulling into their driveway, Jeffrey noticed potted plants on the porch and a large tree in the front yard. He commented the tree looked perfect for climbing.

"It's a California Pepper Tree," Margaret advised. "Got another one out back." She almost smiled. "And this street is Pepper Street."

Jeffrey shook his head. "Only in LA."

"Burbank, actually."

"What's the difference?"

Which brought up the whole LA Thing—Margaret explaining how what outsiders called "LA" was really a giant patchwork of eighty-eight separate cities, with two hundred more "semi-cities" (places with their own names, acting like cities), all lumped together as "Los Angeles."

"Some of them—like Burbank and Beverly Hills—aren't even part of LA," she told him. "At least not the actual city; they've got their own mayors and fire departments and such. While others—like Hollywood and Westwood—*are* part of LA, but pretend they're not by using local names instead."

It was all way too confusing for a boy who grew up in one town with one name. Des Moines, *period.* Not a pretend city, or a city in a city, or a city with a name it really wasn't.

Still, this was great *Jeopardy!* data. Eighty-eight cities, two hundred fake cities. Hollywood was LA, Burbank wasn't.

"How do you know all those details?" Jeffrey asked.

"Did a report last year in my Social Studies class. My one big A of the year."

She got out. Jeffrey grabbed his backpack and suitcase and followed her up to the porch. Aunt Susan unlocked the front door and went inside, but Margaret told him to leave his things there and led him around a side gate to the backyard.

It was bigger than he expected. A concrete patch about the size of a volleyball court took up the center, surrounded by plants and shrubbery, with a basketball hoop and backboard at the far end. But what really caught his eye was the little house off to the side shaded by their other pepper tree. A *real* house, not a playhouse or dollhouse. With shingled roof, glass windows, even a welcome mat.

Margaret led him to its front door, pulled out a key, unlocked it, and stepped inside. Motioning around the room, she announced, "Welcome to Margaretville."

Jeffrey walked through the doorway into a fully furnished bedroom/living room combo—complete with couch, carpets, bed, armchair, coffee table, desk, dresser, mini-fridge in the corner, and cute little bathroom.

"You live here?" he asked.

Margaret nodded.

He stared at her. "By yourself?"

She nodded again. "We call it the guesthouse, but I'm its only guest."

Jeffrey was speechless. His thirteen-year-old cousin lived in her own house!

After locking up, Margaret led him through the back door of the main house and down a hallway to his bedroom for the week. About the same size as his room back home, there was a bed and nightstand on one side, a desk and dresser on the other, and a window facing the backyard.

He walked to the open window and looked out. In the distance, huge blue-gray mountains encircled the neighborhood. It was why they called this part of LA—okay, Burbank—"the Valley." Gazing off at the massive hills, he thought of all the awesome places just beyond: Hollywood, the entertainment capital of the world; Beverly Hills, home to the rich and famous; and his new favorite, Brentwood, the land of Diana.

But mostly he imagined the one thing that truly made California *California*, mere miles from where he now stood: The Mighty Pacific.

He could hardly wait.

His day had begun a world away. In a flat, landlocked place best known as the Hog Capital of America. Fast-forward a few hours, and here he now stood looking out over the City of Angels, where shining beaches, magic mountains, and perfect weather made dreams come true.

He sucked in a breath of warm California air and sighed.

From pigs to paradise faster than that trip to Lake Michigan.

Chapter 5

M argaret was pleasantly surprised. Her cousin wasn't freakishly creepy. Actually, he was much easier to talk to than she expected. Usually, she had trouble with kids her age. Okay, with kids *any* age. But once she and Jeffrey got talking, she realized how much they had in common.

He grew up an only child, now lived with only his mom, and admitted being a little uncomfortable around most people (though after seeing him with that babe at the airport, that last one could be changing).

All of which perfectly described Margaret: no siblings, just she and her mom, and when it came to making nice with others, well, that's why loners were called loners.

After dinner, Margaret kept Jeffrey company in his new bedroom while he unpacked. As he transferred a pile of T-shirts from his suitcase to the dresser, she walked to the desk where he'd stacked four books he'd brought. Picking up the top one, she began thumbing through it.

"You gonna read all these?"

He shut the top drawer and looked over.

"Probably not. Just habit, I guess. In case I got bored." He nodded toward the open window. "Which I'm pretty sure ain't gonna happen." Then he noticed the book she was holding—*The Wizard of Oz*. "Well, except for that one. That's my all-time fave, probably read it a dozen times."

"Then why bring it?"

"It's my block-buster."

"Huh?"

"Writer's block. When I'm stuck and need a push."

She still looked confused.

"You know, when you're staring at a blank page, trying to write something, but your head's totally empty?"

"Sounds like me in Algebra."

He grinned. "I brought it in case I do some writing, maybe a travel journal or something." He grabbed a load of socks and the phone handbook he'd brought and dropped them into the second drawer. "Whenever I need a little writing push, I whip it out, skim a few pages, and, poof, my mind starts chuggin' again. I think Baum was a genius."

She gave him another blank look.

"L. Frank Baum—the guy who wrote it. *The Wizard of Oz*. Well, actually, its real title was *The* Wonderful *Wizard of Oz* but they shortened it for the movie. Anyway, it always reminds me of why I love writing. I mean, flying monkeys? melting witches? magic slippers? Written more than a century ago? Before movies and cars and Xboxes?" He shook his head. "Still blows my mind."

Margaret flipped through the pages, stopping at a color drawing of the four main characters—Dorothy, the Scarecrow, the Tin Man, and Lion—strolling down the Yellow Brick Road. She thought back to the first time she saw the movie. Sweet memories. Christmas Eve, she was three or four, snuggled safely between her mom and dad on the couch. Everything perfect. A long, happy time ago.

Snapping back to the present, she noticed a blue bookmark a few pages past the Yellow Brick Road picture and pulled it out. Jeffrey's name and the year were printed across the top. She held it up. "What's this?"

Glancing up briefly, he returned to unpacking. "Nothing," he mumbled.

"Well, 'nothing's' got your name on it," she teased.

"It's for reading... books."

"Really? How many?"

He shrugged. "Thirty-one."

Her eyes darted from the bookmark to him. "In one year? Thirty-one actual books? Are you kidding me? I doubt I've read that many my whole life. What are you, some kinda speed-reader?"

He smiled. "Second time I've heard that today."

She shook her head, slid the bookmark back, and returned the book to the stack. "Heck, the only things I've ever won are those fake tattoos my dentist gives out after cleaning my teeth."

Jeffrey snickered, dumping the few remaining items he'd packed onto the bed and zipping up his suitcase. "Well, you can read any of those you want. I could even leave them and you could mail them back later. Well, except for *Oz*."

He walked to the window and peered out. "Truth is, when you live in Iowa, have no friends, and hate video games, you either die of boredom or read a lot."

"Well, join the crowd," Margaret said, "at least the no-friends part. Well, people ones anyway."

He turned. "What's that mean?"

"I volunteer at an animal shelter. So my buds are the four-legged kind, which I actually prefer. They don't call you names and are always glad to see you. Well, the dogs anyway. Not so much the cats. Well, some of them even."

"Hey, I like that. Working at an animal shelter. But why no friends? I mean, you live in California. How could you not have friends?"

She gave him a look. "Seriously?" She pointed to herself with both index fingers. "Just lookee here."

Jeffrey raised his eyebrows.

She raised hers back. "What, you think I'm joking? Hey, guess what the super-cool chicks around here do for fun? You know, ones like—I hate to say it—but like that hottie you were drooling over at the airport?"

She didn't wait for an answer. "They trash girls like me. Then add a lame name like Margaret and, voila, welcome to *my* world—The No-Friends Club, Burbank Chapter."

She blew out a breath. "You really think because I live in California I can't be miserable like you in Corn Country?"

Jeffrey chuckled. "Corn Country?" He wagged his head. "Well, I don't think your name's lame, and I never said I'm miserable. Bored? Okay. But not miserable. And you shouldn't be either." He squinted at her, head to foot. "You seem relatively normal to me." He broke into a grin. "But, hey, what's a drooling dweeb from Corn Country know?"

Turning to hide her smile, Margaret started down the hallway for the kitchen. Jeffrey followed, talking the whole way.

"And I'm sure Diana wouldn't make fun of you either. I mean, she was okay with Corn Man, right? So why not his poor pathetic cousin?"

Margaret's hidden smile widened.

The boy did grow on you.

In the kitchen, Margaret boiled water for two hot chocolates while Jeffrey sat at the table and called his mom. Tried to anyway. His first attempt was a wrong number. Getting through on his second try, Karen sounded exhausted. Besides the two-hour time difference, she reminded him about their neighbor's birthday party she'd hosted that night. So he kept the conversation short: nice flight, safe at Margaret's, ate dinner, great weather.

After he hung up, Margaret brought two steaming mugs to the table. While waiting for them to cool, she surprised him by suggesting they organize their next day's schedule. Of course, once he mentioned never seeing the ocean, it was a no-brainer.

"Santa Monica here we come!" Margaret chanted. She said it was her go-to beach, on a bus route she used regularly, then got him really fired up by providing juicy details of their trip:

In the morning, they'd catch the bus around the corner and take it out of the Valley into Hollywood (she told him "the Valley" meant the *San Fernando* Valley, but Jeffrey already knew that). In Hollywood, they'd get off at Hollywood and Vine—one block past the Capital Records Building (that place shaped like a stack of old vinyl records seen in practically every Hollywood photo)—and walk down the boulevard to the Kodak Theatre.

"*The Kodak Theatre*," Jeffrey whispered. Even dorks from Des Moines knew of that place—all the big-time events televised from there. Movie awards, concerts, *American Idol*.

From there, a second bus would take them all the way down Santa Monica Boulevard, along the last mile of historic Route 66, to Ocean Avenue.

"And that's it! Walking distance from there to the big blue

ocean!"

She rose from the table and collected their empty mugs. "It may not be the fastest route, but it's definitely more fun than the freeway or train." She finally grinned. "And those Midwestern toes will touch beach sand by noon."

Sweet.

Chapter 6

Monday

Jeffrey

My first OMG moment was on the plane, obviously: The Girl of My Dreams *talks* to me.

As was my second: The Girl of My Dreams *trades phone numbers* with me.

But neither prepared me for OMG Number Three.

It happened early Monday morning. The excitement of waking up in California and my upcoming beach trip had already pushed those earlier airplane highs off to the side. Aunt Susan was cooking pancakes before leaving for work, Margaret and I were sipping grapefruit juice at the kitchen table, and my new mobile device was sitting on my placemat minding its own business.

Until a sudden buzz startled me.

My phone was ringing!

I assumed it was my mom since she was the only one I'd called with it. But when I read the screen, juice almost shot out my nose.

Diana.

My cousin must've thought I was having a heart attack. Eyes bulging, face beet red, staring down at the display with that half-shocked/half-glazed look the guy in the movie gets when he realizes he's just been shot. Margaret read the name upside-down, did a quick eye roll, then got up to help her mom at the stove.

For what seemed like forever I couldn't move, just kept watching my phone vibrate. By the third buzz, even Aunt Susan had turned to look. Finally, before the fourth buzz stopped I'd regained enough muscle control to tap the answer key. Raising it slowly to my ear as if it might electrocute me, I listened without speaking.

Somehow sensing I was there, this bouncy, hyper voice chimed in. "Hey, Jeffrey James from Omaha. Guess who?!"

Which only paralyzed me more.

The perky voice continued, "Yep, it's that crazy chick from California you thought was gone forever. Well, surprise!" She paused. "Hello? Earth to Jeffrey James? Cat got your tongue?"

To which I finally managed a feeble, "Hi Diana…"

At the stove, Margaret and Aunt Susan were all smiles.

"So this is how they teach you to talk to ladies in Indiana?" Diana asked.

"Iowa," I croaked back.

"Well… are you ready?"

"Huh?"

"For your tour."

This could *not* be happening.

"You were serious?"

"Serious as Wonder Woman's Wonder Suit. Which, by the way, is one seriously sick suit. I just found it online."

I had no response to that, but apparently didn't need one since she kept going, slower this time, like she was hypnotizing me, which she kinda was.

"Now repeat after me," she droned softly. "Yesterday was not a dream…" (pause) "that Brentwood Brat was real…" (pause) "totally sitting next to me on that plane…"

And so it went. Diana talking, me occasionally forming words. Not many and not well. When I was finally able to make a complete sentence about Margaret and me planning a trip to Santa Monica, Diana had a better idea.

"How 'bout Zuma? Up by Malibu? Where the uber-cool hang. Satisfaction guaranteed."

Malibu. Another name I'd heard my whole life. In songs, movies, books. My favorite wall calendar even had a Malibu sunset on the cover. All these famous places suddenly coming to life.

Hollywood. Santa Monica. Malibu.

"Zuma?" I repeated, glancing up at Margaret who shrugged,

then nodded. "How do we get there? We're taking the bus."

"No worries. I'll pick you guys up."

"Wait. Didn't you say you're fourteen?"

"Roger that, JJ. But surely you remember my trusty sidekick Ty?" Before I could answer, she added, "Until the Great State of California sees fit to grant me a learner's permit—in exactly sixteen months, I might add—I must sadly rely on Ty to handle all vehicular operations."

Like she was talking to a four-year-old, which felt about right.

I looked up at my hosts and mouthed: *She. Has. A. Driver.* Earning me another eye roll from Margaret, who then turned to her mother with a can-we-go? look.

Aunt Susan scrunched her mouth, looked at me, thought some more, and finally nodded. At the same time, Diana prompted, "Address, please?" as if she could see what was happening.

I motioned for Margaret to write it on a napkin and read it back to Diana. "Need directions?" I added like an idiot.

"What? No GPS in Indio? See ya at noon. Ciao."

"Iowa..." I repeated to the empty phone line.

* * *

Trusty Ty arrived right on time. While he waited outside, I met Diana at the door. Leading her into the kitchen, I made the short intros with my cousin.

Since we'd already put swimsuits on under our clothes, there wasn't much to pack. As a smiling Diana watched from the kitchen table, Margaret and I loaded two cloth bags—towels, sunblock, an extra top for her and a T-shirt for me in one; snacks and water bottles in the other. Then, after one final check of doors, windows, and lights, Diana led us out to the car.

Okay, to be fair, calling what greeted us in the driveway a "car" would be like calling the sun warm, or Diana cute.

Understatement of the century.

It wasn't flashy like those long stretchy things celebrities get out of before heading down the red carpet. In fact, what hit me first was how old it looked. But a good old. Not like my parents old, more like my *grandparents* old. Maybe even *their* parents old. Yet not really looking old.

I know none of that made sense. But you'd understand if you saw what was parked in Margaret's driveway. It made me think of watching old black-and-white war movies with my dad late at night on weekends. There'd always be some big-shot German general getting chauffeured around in a super-cool automotive masterpiece way too classy for normal folks.

Well, one of those masterpieces was sitting there in front of me.

The exterior was gray, but not garbage-can gray—more of a glowing silver, like a spotlight was shining down on it from the heavens. The hood was long and creased into three sections, and the sides had wide fenders curving around gleaming whitewall tires big enough for a small kid to sleep in. The headlights were shaped like mini-torpedoes, framing a chrome grille so bright it made my eyes water. And inside the grille, a dozen thin brass-colored rods were lined up vertically like a mouthful of gold teeth snarling back at me.

The final touch was the hood ornament. A Greek god of some kind—Mars, Mercury, Jay-Z—arched forward like a ballet dancer, guarding two big black letters—*RR*—etched below his feet.

Which even the Corn Man knew meant Rolls Royce.

But clearly not your standard version (if that's even a thing). No, this was definitely your one-of-a-kind, drop-the-mic model.

And there, smiling behind the wheel with teeth brighter than those giant whitewalls, sat Ty. In a chauffeur's cap.

After patiently waiting while we gawked a while longer, he got out, did a cute little half-bow, tipped his hat, and opened the rear door. Stepping inside, my first reaction was the same as on the plane ride with Diana, and at the breakfast table when my phone buzzed.

This cannot be happening.

Diana sat between us, giving Margaret and me our own window seats, and once Ty shut our door, a pleasant scent filled the air. Fine leather with a hint of lemon. Fresh, clean, expensive.

I couldn't stop breathing it in.

Buckling my seat belt (added later, I'm sure, since I doubt passenger safety was a big concern in those war-movie days), I noticed one of Margaret's neighbors glaring at us from her porch across the street. Probably miffed seeing her teenage neighbor and friends getting chauffeured in a ride worth more than some houses.

But I just glared back, until she finally turned away. Nothing boosts your confidence and glare-back abilities better than sitting in a chauffeur-driven vintage classic.

Once Ty got settled behind the wheel, Diana did the honors.

"Jeffrey, Margaret, meet Ty."

"Ty?" Margaret repeated.

Looking up through the rearview mirror, he replied, "Yes, ma'am. T-Y, as in *thank you, thank you very much.*" Spoken in a pretty decent Elvis Presley twang.

"It's short for Tyler," Diana explained as he started the engine. It growled to life like a tiger, quickly softening to a low purr. Seconds later, he eased the dream machine out the driveway, slipped into Drive, and launched us down Pepper Street.

When that same neighbor looked over again, I grinned this time—so caught up in the moment I almost started singing *We're Off To See The Wizard.*

Chapter 7

Jeffrey

We took local streets instead of the freeway, no doubt so Diana's new friends could enjoy the full feel of limo life at a leisurely pace. Cruising along Victory Boulevard, a comfortable commercial-residential mix slicing through the Valley, it didn't take long for me to start babbling again.

"You drive around like this a lot?"

Diana nodded. "Since Dad's gone on lawyer stuff so much, it's mostly me and Ty. We do have a part-time maid…" (of course they did) "…but Ty does all the driving and we take lots of road trips. Right, Ty?"

"Yes, Miss Diana," he said in a corny "servant" voice.

Diana whispered, "He doesn't really talk like that. He's playing. He's an actor."

I had no idea what that meant.

After a while, we turned onto a busier street called Laurel Canyon that eventually narrowed into a windy road out of the Valley.

Once we finally straightened out again, Diana asked if we'd like to stop for lunch. Margaret suggested a place nearby called In-N-Out, a few blocks from where her mom worked in West Hollywood. And soon I was devouring the finest burger of my life (a Double-Double with Cheese), with an equally drool-worthy chocolate shake and fries.

With stomachs happily stuffed, we were soon back on the road. At a red light on Santa Monica Boulevard, Diana informed me we'd be turning onto Pacific Coast Highway in a few miles.

"But don't call it that," she warned, "unless you want everyone to know you're from Ohio."

"Iowa," I corrected.

Ignoring me again, she winked. "Around here it's just

'PCH'—and never 'the' PCH."

My cousin smiled at that.

Inching our way in heavy traffic, I soon learned that being "a few miles" from PCH wasn't as close as it sounded. Not on a weekday, in the summer, on Santa Monica Boulevard, at lunchtime. Though doing it in a chauffeur-driven, leather-seats-like-butter, snarling Double-R—while sitting next to the Girl of Your Dreams—does ease the pain a bit.

And sure enough, a thousand stop lights and forty-five not-so-horrible minutes later, we hit the California coast.

Ah, the Pacific Coast Highway—I mean, PCH—what can I say? Whatever you call it, words don't do it justice.

After driving through the brown, summer-dried underbrush of Laurel Canyon, merging onto PCH was like Dorothy dropping out of black-and-white Kansas into full-color Oz.

High-energy beach life zipped by my window in a parade of motion and colors. Rugged cliffs on one side, fluffy sand dunes and oceanfront homes on the other. Surfers darting through traffic with boards tucked under their arms. Volleyball nets scattered among blankets and beach umbrellas. Cars topped with surf racks crammed into every conceivable parking space. And palm trees everywhere.

But of course the true showstopper was impossible to miss, stealing the glory from everything else: The Pacific Ocean! Right before my eyes! My first live view of it.

And it was everything I'd imagined and more. An endless blanket of deep blue filling every space in all directions clear to the sky. It's hard to describe, seeing it like that for the first time. The closest I can come is one of my mom's favorites: *Gobsmacked.*

Struggling to roll down my window (my first ride without power buttons), I caught Diana grinning at me. When I figured it out and lowered the glass (the crank goes clockwise), a blast of hot ocean air hit me like a flame-thrower. Actually made me dizzy. But a good dizzy, like being smothered in a warm cloud.

I'm not sure how hot salty air blasting in your face like that can make you woozy, breathless, and excited all at the same time. But if you've ever cruised PCH on a perfect summer day with the windows down, you know.

Several miles up, we closed in on an old yellow pickup motoring along with two surfboards stacked in back. As we passed it, its rear bumper sticker came into focus, four words printed across a bright orange sunset.

All Good, No Worries.

I chuckled to myself. If California had a state motto, that should be it. Exactly describing my feelings right then: hot ocean air tickling my face, great vibes and great people around me, winding up the California coast in our silver chariot.

If we were in a movie, that's when the camera would've zoomed out for a birds-eye shot of us skirting up the sparkling shoreline as the hard-driving surf music kicks in.

All Good, No Worries, indeed.

Chapter 8

After passing too many beaches to count—Sorrento, Will Rogers, Topanga, Las Tunas—they finally came to a sign welcoming them to Malibu. Minutes later, Ty flipped on his left blinker and slowed to a stop in the center lane. Across the highway, a large wooden plaque read Zuma Beach County Park.

Once traffic cleared, they turned into a roped-off lot surrounded by a snack bar, white sand, and glittering ocean. As Ty pulled into a parking space and cut the engine, Margaret dramatically gestured out her window.

"Ah, the brightness and glory of the Emerald City."

Jeffrey stared at her. He'd heard that before. No, he'd *read* that before. Then it clicked. "Hey, that's from my book! I thought you never read it."

"Page eighty-eight," Margaret said, exiting the limo.

Jeffrey got out the other side and ran around to her.

"Say what?"

She gazed out at the ocean. "Fourth paragraph."

Diana was now standing next to Jeffrey, listening.

Margaret turned to them. "You're right. I've never read it, *The Wizard of Oz*." Her eyes twinkled. "But there is one little skill I do have—well, besides shooting hoops which I'm also pretty good at." She paused, waiting for them to ask.

Jeffrey obliged. "And?"

"Okay, so last year my history teacher had this nickname for me he'd use when no one was around. He called me Mega-Mind."

Diana stared at her. "Why?"

"I remember things."

"Like, what, a photographic memory?"

"Sort of. I've never been officially tested, but I've done the research. It's called H-SAM. Highly Superior Autobiographical Memory." She snickered. "But don't worry, it doesn't mean I'm 'superior.' Ha, if only. Just different. There's also a scientific name, but it sounds more like a fatal disease so I stick with H-SAM. Anyway, whenever I see or hear or read something, it gets burned into my brain." She shrugged. "Like, forever."

Diana's eyes widened. "*Shut Up!*"

Margaret grinned. "Like I said, it's got nothing to do with intelligence. My brain just doesn't delete stuff. Once it's there, it stays, permanently. I'm not sure exactly where, or how, but with a little effort I can always find it."

She shook her head. "Which, to be honest, can get downright annoying. I mean, think of all the stupid things you *don't* need to remember. Like the day you started kindergarten…"

Her eyes darted back and forth as she collected her thoughts. "Seven years, eleven months, seventeen days ago. September 4, 2001, a Tuesday, because that Monday was a holiday, Labor Day." Her lips tightened. "And I'm like, who cares?"

Diana and Jeffrey were too stunned to speak.

"Or how about that In-N-Out we ate at? Do you really need to remember that the out-of-order sign on the bathroom door had the 'r' missing? Is that really worth knowing in, say, ten or twenty years?" She flipped her head back and forth. "Well… *I'll* know it then.

"But it's great for history tests. Dates, names, places. See it once and done. No sweat." She chuckled. "Unfortunately, not so much for algebra, since that's not really a memory thing."

She looked at Jeffrey. "Anyway, last night when I was flipping through your *Oz* book, that Emerald City line was the fourth paragraph on page eighty-eight."

Diana was shaking her head in awe. "That is so sick. Can you show me how to do it?"

Margaret smiled. "'Fraid not. I've got no idea how it works."

While they peppered her with more questions, Ty, who'd been listening from the far side of the limo, retrieved their bags and set them down beside them. That instantly ended the conversation as each girl grabbed a bag and took off, leaving Jeffrey standing there alone.

Ty called out that he'd be back in a few hours, offered Jeffrey a sympathetic smile, got back in the Rolls, and drove off.

Reaching down for the remaining bag, Jeffrey hesitated. He looked around. If ever there was a moment worth preserving, this was it. Digging out his phone, he snapped three shots in different directions: the girls silhouetted against the waves, the snack bar surrounded by creamy white sand, and the Zuma Beach sign with the coast highway behind it.

Satisfied, he dropped his phone and flip-flops into his bag and raced off after the girls. Seconds later, his feet sunk into beach sand for the first time in his life... and everything seemed to stop. Standing there, momentarily frozen in place, he took it all in: the baking sun, the cloudless sky, the girls splashing in the water, seagulls squawking, waves crashing, hot sand between his toes.

Pinch me, Toto, we're not in Iowa anymore.

*   *   *

The first thing Jeffrey did when he hit the water was lick his fingers. Silly as it sounds, if you've never splashed in saltwater, that first taste is pretty wild.

After playing in the waves for a while (mostly the girls showing him how to dive under them to avoid getting pancaked), Diana casually asked if they'd like to see her special place.

Which surprised even Diana, since she'd never asked anyone that before.

Without hesitation, both cousins nodded. Why not? Diana certainly hadn't disappointed them so far, and it sounded innocent enough. Of course, most fateful decisions sneak up on you like that.

Diana led them up the shoreline, past sunbathers and wave-riders, to a more isolated stretch of beach. Along the way, they kept asking where she was taking them, but all she'd say was they'd find out soon enough.

Eventually, they came to a large rock formation blocking their path. About eight feet high, it rose from the water, crossed the wet sand in front of them, and extended onto the beach before tapering off. The only way to pass it, short of a long detour over hot sand, was to climb it or wade into the ocean and swim around it.

Without a word, Diana began trekking up the damp rock face, carefully choosing the cracks with the best traction. Mimicking her steps, Jeffrey and Margaret followed in single file.

At the top, the rock formation leveled out to a flat slab, perfect for taking in the stunning 360-degree view of ocean, coastline, beach, and highway.

"Wow," Jeffrey said softly, slowly spinning around.

Diana walked to the platform's northern edge and nodded downward. "That's where we're going."

Below them lay an untouched strip of sand completely separated from the rest of the beach. An offshoot from the rock formation they stood on curved around it like a backward C, forming a hidden oasis with a very private ocean view.

Before anyone could comment, Diana began climbing down. "Careful," she cautioned, "this side's a lot steeper."

A few feet from the bottom she pointed to a shaded area off to the right where the rock wall met the sand. "That's it," she said.

But all Jeffrey and Margaret could see was a dark shadow against the rocks. Holding her hand up for them to wait, Diana paused until a small wave rolled back out. Then, clutching her bag, she jumped. A few seconds later the others followed.

Once at sand level, the fuzzy shadow Diana had pointed to sharpened into a black archway. A cave opening.

Diana's special place.

As she started toward it, Jeffrey looked out to sea.

"You sure the waves won't flood us in there?"

"Positive. They barely make it in," she called back, disappearing inside.

Jeffrey looked at Margaret, who gave him an I'll-go-if-you'll-go shrug, before they followed their new friend into the darkness.

Chapter 9

Jeffrey

My first sensation was the temperature drop. Cool, but not cold. And the air. Fresh, crisp, salty.

Once my eyes adjusted, enough light filtered in to see things better. The space inside was pretty big, high enough to stand without bumping my head, and wide and deep enough for a small car to fit. A thin film of water covered most of the ground and, as tiny waves trickled in, little sparkles of sunlight danced along the walls and ceiling like an old-school disco ball.

Even cooler, though, was how the inside was shaped. It wasn't a round dome like the caves in old Flintstones cartoons. Instead, the back wall went straight up three feet, then took a sharp *outward* turn before sloping to the top. This made the bottom section jut out like a big stone couch, flat enough to sit on and high enough to dangle your feet without touching the ground.

"Very nice," I whispered.

As Diana spread her towel across the "cave couch," I noticed the candles lined up against the back wall. Three of them, the fat kind you put on coffee tables. Diana saw me looking.

"I bring new ones every few months," she said. "They last a long time." She set her bag behind her towel and hopped up, positioning herself cross-legged on the ledge facing the cave opening. "They're unscented," she continued, "because—" she inhaled deeply, "—nothing can compete with this."

She was right. If you could bottle that crisp cave scent, you'd make millions.

We unfolded our towels on both sides of her, stashed our bags, and climbed up. Then we just sat there and quietly gazed out to sea, the cave opening framing the view like a live-action ocean painting.

Diana finally broke the silence.

"As you can see, this place is pretty invisible. In all my times here, I've never run into anyone. I'm sure others come, but they never disturb anything. My candles are always here and there's never any trash."

When she stopped talking, we returned to our private little worlds, the peaceful scene sweeping us away—the trickling tide, the ocean colors, the salty air, the distant rumble of breaking waves.

After a while Diana reached back and scooted the candles in closer. Fetching a lighter from her bag, she lit each one before sliding them back against the wall. Instantly, the cave took on a warm glow, like being in our own secret clubhouse—which I guess we kinda were.

"I come here a lot," she said. "A couple times a month at least, more in the summer. Been doing it for years." She flashed a crooked smile. "The benefits of having your own driver, and California weather."

She took in another deep breath, exhaling slowly. "Some people chill with music, or take long baths, or sit in the forest and meditate." She motioned around. "This is *my* medicine."

I perked up. "Oh darn. What time is it?"

Diana chuckled. "Don't worry, we've got plenty of time before we need to get back."

"No, not that. I promised my mom I'd call when she got off work. She's done at four, so two our time."

I checked my phone. 2:05.

"Perfect," I mumbled, keying in Mom's number.

Diana shook her head. "Forget it."

"What?" I glanced at my screen. "Oh, 'no service.'"

"Phones don't work here," she explained, "and don't bother trying outside either. There's no signal until about halfway back. This whole area sticks out from the rest of the coastline."

Of course, me being me, I tried anyway—clicking keys then listening—but nothing happened. I set my phone down. "Guess I'll try later."

Margaret pulled snacks and water bottles from one of the bags and passed them around. Soon we'd lost track of time again, munching beef jerky, sipping water, staring out to sea.

Until my phone blinked on.

I looked down, confused. "I thought you said…" Picking it up, I squinted at the screen. "How can a message get through if there's no service?"

Diana was shaking her head. "No way. My phone's never worked here and I've had three different phone plans. Signals don't get through. Nothing in, nothing out."

Yet there it was on my screen, a single line of text.

2 2 4 7 p e a r l ! 3

Diana held out her hand. "Lemme see."

I handed it to her and she recited the line out loud.

"Two, two, four, seven, pearl, exclamation point, three."

She stared at it. Suddenly her face brightened. "Hey, there's a Pearl Street in Malibu." She turned to me. "You sure you don't know anyone around here?"

I shook my head.

"Who else has your number?" asked Margaret.

I nodded to Diana. "Her and my mom. Just got the phone two days ago, right before this trip."

Margaret pulled her own phone out of her bag, clicked it on, shook her head. "No bars, no service."

Diana handed my phone back. "Let's check it out!"

"Check what out?"

"The address! I mean, it looks like one, right? Up to the exclamation point."

She hopped off the ledge. "C'mon, it'll be an adventure." Retrieving her T-shirt and shorts from her bag, she tugged them on over her bathing suit. As she began rolling up her towel, she nodded to the candles. "Blow those out, please."

Exchanging glances with Margaret, I did as instructed, then we slipped on our clothes and followed Diana out.

At the top of the rock formation we stopped to catch our

breath. Margaret asked Diana, "What about the last part of the text, after the address, if that's what it is? The 'exclamation point, three'?"

Diana thought about it. "A time maybe?" She shrugged. "Like the exclamation point's some kinda separator—address on one side, time on the other?"

Sounded pretty flimsy to me, but I guess anything's possible when nothing makes sense.

Diana pulled out her phone. "It's 2:15. So if that three *is* a time, we've got forty-five minutes till blast-off."

She put her phone away and started down the rocks, calling out, "I'll call Ty when we get bars."

Halfway back, Diana got through to Ty. Checking my own phone, I noticed the mystery text was gone—which was weird—but at least we had a Mega-Mind to remember such things. And with three bars now showing, I called my mom while the girls walked ahead.

Once Mom heard where I was, she got really excited, bombarding me with beach questions and advice (which beach? with whom? use sunblock, drink water, do the stingray shuffle). Then she updated me on the party she'd hosted the night before for her best friend (and neighbor) Ellie. By then we'd reached the parking lot, so after promising to send each other pictures, I signed off.

Waiting for Ty by the snack bar, Margaret helped me send my three Zuma shots to Mom. We also discussed what to tell Ty about the text, ultimately deciding not to mention it at all. At least not yet.

It wasn't that Diana didn't trust him. We just didn't want to look like complete idiots when our big adventure fizzled out. Which, despite Diana's enthusiasm, I'm sure we all thought would happen. Because with all the millions of texts flying through cyberspace every day, an innocent technical glitch made more sense than anything else.

So when Ty arrived, Diana told him a teensy white lie: that she'd found the Pearl Street address on *her* phone, couldn't remember whose it was, and wanted to check it out on our way home.

A mile down the highway, my phone dinged with two new photos from Mom, of her and Ellie at their party. When I showed them to the girls, Diana commented, "Wow, folks in Oklahoma look remarkably human."

"Iowa," I muttered back, pocketing my phone and never imagining those shots would come up again.

Chapter 10

P earl Street was Malibu's version of a business district. Three palm-tree-lined streets with local shops on both sides.

Cruising down the twenty-two-hundred block, they discovered that 2247 was in fact a real address. One store from the corner on the far side of the street. The sign above it read Toy Town of Malibu—a normal-looking toy and hobby shop with two display windows framing the front entrance. In one window, model trains looped around a figure-eight track. In the other, game boxes were stacked in front of an elaborate Lego landscape.

After pausing at the stop sign, Ty continued to the next block and pulled over. Looking up at Diana through his mirror, he asked, "You sure about that address?"

They all turned around for another look out the back window. The store was sandwiched between a small parking lot on one side and an ice cream parlor—The Malibu Creamery—on the corner.

Which gave Diana an idea.

"Guess I got the address wrong," she announced. "But how 'bout some ice cream before we leave?"

Ty set the parking brake. "You guys go, I'm good."

They scooted out and Diana walked up to Ty's window. "Don't worry about us. Take a break. We'll get some ice cream, walk around, do a little window-shopping."

He nodded. "Be back in an hour. Call if you need me."

After he drove off, they crossed the street, strode past the ice cream shop, and entered Toy Town of Malibu.

*   *   *

The bell on the door jingled. Glancing around, Jeffrey's face lit up. As a lover of games, gadgets, and any kind of make-it-yourself kit, he could spend hours in a place like this if he weren't on a mission. They counted four other customers: a lady and little girl picking through a shelf of stuffed animals and two boys in the corner playing with model rockets. Behind the counter, a clerk sat on a stool —early twenties, bedhead hair, blotchy cheeks, a handful of chin whiskers, sketchy hygiene.

The guy looked up, didn't speak or smile, then returned to his beat-up paperback book.

After exchanging glances, the three headed down different aisles and began browsing. But all they saw was exactly what you'd expect to see in a cool toy store: games, dolls, model cars, toy trains, hobby kits, and every kind of ball imaginable.

What they didn't find was why this address had popped up on Jeffrey's phone. No big flashing sign announcing *Hey, Here's Your Clue!* So ten minutes later they walked out as clueless as when they'd walked in.

Gathering around the fire hydrant at the curb, Diana spoke first. "Well?"

Jeffrey gave her a look. "Well, what?"

"Anything suspicious?"

Margaret started laughing. "Yeah. My Beach Barbie was missing one of her sandals." She tilted her head. "Not exactly our finest Sherlock moment, I'd say."

"So now what?" asked Jeffrey.

Diana turned toward the corner. "Ice cream, anyone?"

*　　　*　　　*

By the time Jeffrey picked out his French vanilla/strawberry/chocolate mint cone, the girls had long since picked out theirs, paid, and left. Gingerly balancing his towering three-scooper, he crossed the street and joined them on the bus bench.

After several licks, he noticed they were still eyeballing the toy store. "So we're conducting surveillance now?" he asked.

Wiping her chin with her napkin, Diana shrugged. "Nothing better to do."

Jeffrey nodded, despite having no clue what they were

43

surveilling—because when you're on an ice cream stakeout in Malibu on a gorgeous summer day, who cares? So for the next forty minutes, they slurped cones, eyed the store, joked around, took pictures, soaked up the sun.

Until the clock in the mini-mart window struck 3:48, and their perfect afternoon shattered into eight seconds of heart-stopping chaos.

The dog. The girl. The car.

Screeching brakes. Exploding hydrant. Raging water.

Nightmare on Pearl Street.

Chapter 11

Jeffrey

First you freeze. Something that sudden, that scary, that violent, totally paralyzes you.

Deer-in-headlights times ten.

Then that first wave of ice-cold hydrant water hit us, and, dropping our cones, we shot off the bench like rockets—Diana and I rushing to the car, Margaret racing after the drenched dog.

Through sheets of cascading water, the inside of the car was barely visible, though I was pretty sure a lady was behind the wheel. Then I saw her head move. Good sign. I managed to get the driver's door open, and saw no blood—also good. The woman, clearly dazed, showed no obvious injuries.

As she struggled with her deflated airbag, I pushed it aside and gently held the seat belt off her chest while Diana unbuckled it. A crowd began to form. Someone opened the passenger door, turned off the ignition, and set the parking brake. I quietly asked the woman if she'd rather stay where she was or get out. She nodded, which I took to mean she wanted out.

With each of us holding an elbow, Diana and I guided her out, nudging her along until we cleared the hydrant downpour and got her seated in a plastic chair in front of the mini-mart. A clerk brought out a roll of paper towels that we used to help dry her off as sirens sounded in the distance.

When the lady finally spoke, her first question was about the dog. Margaret, who'd since joined us, assured her that the dog was fine. Soaked and scared but otherwise unharmed and safe with its grateful owner.

Minutes later a fire truck arrived. Then the police. We moved away to make room for two paramedics who began checking the lady's eyes and blood pressure. By then, the gushing water had formed a small river down the gutter, threatening to jump the curb and flood the shops.

Stepping back for the first time, I surveyed the area. It looked like a TV news scene after a hurricane. But even more chilling was thinking about what had brought us here in the first place.

An address and time in a text.

One that suddenly didn't seem so random.

For the next half hour, we gave statements to two police officers while Ty, who'd returned soon after the crash, stood behind us listening. By the time we finished, a city water crew had shut off the hydrant, the lady's car had been towed, and the flooded gutter was down to a trickle. Several shopkeepers stood outside their stores sweeping puddles.

Refusing further medical treatment, the lady was now sitting in the passenger seat of a police car talking on her cell phone, looking frazzled and damp but otherwise okay.

Since the police blocked off both ends of the street, Ty had parked two blocks away. Following him back to the Rolls, we shuffled along like The Walking Dead—adrenaline spent, minds and bodies shot.

Back at the limo, we retrieved our beach towels and dried off as best we could. On the drive home, Ty found a classical station on the radio to fill the silence since no one felt like talking.

*   *   *

Ty left the engine running in Margaret's driveway while Diana walked us to the front door. On the porch, we renewed our pledge to keep quiet about the phone text, at least until we figured out what was going on.

Inside, we headed for separate bathrooms—down the hall for me, the guesthouse for Margaret. I stood under the hot shower a long time, trying to wash away the day's stress with the fire hydrant grime. And once I dried off, brushed my hair, and changed into fresh clothes, I almost felt human again.

When Margaret came in from the guesthouse, I was already at

the kitchen table describing our crazy afternoon to Aunt Susan. Most of it anyway. As promised, I left out the text.

Leaning back against the counter, Aunt Susan listened intently, not saying a word, though her bulging eyes said enough. But after assuring her everyone was okay—the lady driver, the dog, the three of us—her eyes unbulged, slightly.

At the end of our story, my cousin motioned toward the backyard. "How 'bout some hoops before dinner."

She grabbed a basketball from the closet and headed for the back door. Following her out, I glanced back at my aunt. She'd resumed her dinner prep, chopping onions at the counter. But her glazed expression spoke volumes. Probably counting her blessings— that her precious daughter and favorite nephew were out back shooting baskets, and not splattered across some Malibu storefront.

JOSH EBER

Part II

Trouble In Paradise

"We could certainly use a detective."

Nancy Drew Mysteries, Book 5
Carolyn Keene, 1931

Chapter 12

Diana had her cave, Jeffrey his books, and Margaret had basketball.

Which, like so many other things, she traced to growing up an only child. Because contrary to popular belief, life without siblings was no picnic. All that stuff about single kids getting spoiled by their parents and leading charmed lives made Margaret laugh.

And one of the hardest parts was the whole going-out-to-play thing. Kids with siblings never had to worry about that. They had built-in playmates twenty-four/seven. They could go out and have fun anytime. Then once outside, loud brothers and sisters playing together usually attracted other kids from the neighborhood, and soon everyone was having a grand old time.

Not so for the only child. And definitely not so for Margaret. For years, going out to play meant either doing it alone or walking over to the kids playing across the street and standing there like a doofus while they decided whether to be cool or not.

Until she discovered basketball—thanks to her mom and their next-door neighbor, Ruth.

For as far back as Margaret could remember, the two women had shared a fanatic obsession for the LA Lakers. "Avid fans" didn't begin to describe it. Rarely missing a televised game, they'd take turns watching at each other's homes and going absolutely berserk in the process. Cheering, booing, yelling at the announcer, throwing popcorn at the screen. All of which provided the perfect escape for a lonely kid who hated going out to play by herself.

And before long, Margaret was right there with the grown-ups —cheering, booing, even memorizing player positions, rankings, and records.

Then one Christmas her mom and Ruth surprised her with a basketball and backboard, which the women set up by the guesthouse. And from that moment on, Margaret and basketball were inseparable.

No longer did the lonely kid on the block need or care about neighborhood playmates. Every possible minute she was out back practicing. For hours. Free throws, jump shots, layups, dribbling.

She even learned to mimic the TV announcer's voice whenever she scored, turning her make-believe games into thrilling "national" events.

It was therefore no surprise that, after such a tense day in Malibu, Margaret was out back shooting hoops. Unfortunately, the mismatch with her cousin was obvious, and awkward.

At first, they took shots in silence, Margaret effortlessly making all of hers, Jeffrey making none of his. Soon, however, Jeffrey lost interest, his mind still stuck on the crash and that text.

Following an especially cringe-worthy dribble to the basket, Jeffrey turned to his cousin. "You know what they always say in every detective novel ever written?"

Margaret grabbed the rebound. "The butler did it?"

He snickered. "No. That they don't believe in coincidences."

Margaret didn't respond. Setting up her next shot off to the side where the backboard was useless, she arced in a perfect nothing-but-net.

Jeffrey watched in amazement, then walked to the lawn chair by the guesthouse and sat. After watching her sink two more, he yelled out, "You really think that crash was a coincidence?"

Holding the ball, Margaret turned to him. "Why? Because it happened in front of that toy store?" She bounced the ball twice. "Hey, accidents happen. All the time. Especially car crashes in LA." She bounced the ball again. "That text was probably spam. Some jumbled ad for the toy store blasted out to the masses."

"Jumbled spam? You're really going with that?"

She shrugged. "Or maybe some coded message for someone else, that you got by mistake."

"Still wouldn't explain *when* it happened."

"You mean at 3:48?"

He gave her a how'd-you-know-that? look.

She smiled. "The clock in the mini-mart window."

"Ah." He nodded. "See?"

51

JOSH EBER

"See what?"

"The 'three' at the end of that text, and the crash happening at three-something."

Margaret shook her head. "Doesn't prove a thing." She began spinning the ball on the tip of her index finger, slapping its side to keep it spinning. "Plus, it was wrong."

Jeffrey watched her ball-balancing act, mesmerized. Finally, he forced himself to look away. "Wrong, how?"

"The timing."

"Huh?"

She let the ball drop, trapping it with her foot. "Happening at 3:48 means it was forty-eight minutes wrong."

"But still the third hour."

She shrugged. "Or maybe you're trying to fit things where they don't fit to match this big mystery Diana's got you believing."

"Maybe."

She picked up the ball and headed for the house. "C'mon. I'm starved." Jeffrey got up and followed. As she held the back door open for him, she said, "You don't really think some random phone message *predicted* all that, do you?"

It didn't sound like she expected him to answer, so he didn't.

*   *   *

After a terrific "California dinner"—baked salmon, steamed artichokes, avocado salad—they returned to the guesthouse. Margaret curled up in her armchair, head back, eyes closed; Jeffrey sprawled out on the floor, hands laced behind his head, staring up at the ceiling. In the background, soft music drifted from Margaret's bookshelf speaker.

As the third song ended, Jeffrey cleared his throat and, still gazing upward, said, "You know there's only one way to find out."

Margaret's eyes stayed shut. "Yep."

Jeffrey kept staring up at nothing. "Back to the cave."

"Yep."

Jeffrey slowly turned to her, resting his head in his hand.

52

"When?"

Margaret's eyes fluttered open. "Tomorrow?"

He looked at her for a few beats before rolling back over to refocus on the ceiling. "Let's see what Diana thinks."

Three minutes later, Jeffrey's phone rang.

It was Diana. She'd been thinking the same thing. She'd pick them up at nine.

Chapter 13

Tuesday

B y 9:30, they were cruising west on the 101 freeway. Not that great for sightseeing, but much faster to Zuma.

For a while, nobody talked. Ty had his favorite jazz station playing, Diana swaying to the music, Margaret staring out her window. Everyone mellow but Jeffrey, who was deep in thought over something that had kept him up most of the night.

But not the accident or the text.

Diana.

Sure, it was partly the normal boy thing: Brentwood Babe dazzles Des Moines Dweeb. But it was more than that. By the time they hit the Malibu Canyon exit, he couldn't hold it in anymore.

He turned to Diana. "Can I ask you something? And promise not to take it wrong?"

She lifted her head and looked at him, those hypnotic eyes pulling him in like a magnet. "You've got my undivided attention."

He paused, thinking how to put it, finally just spitting it out.

"You know that expression 'when something seems too good to be true...'?"

"It usually is?"

He nodded. "Yeah. Well, that's kinda how all this feels." He gestured around the limo.

Diana creased her forehead. "I'm not following."

"Well..." he shrugged, "I guess I just don't get it."

That got Margaret's attention. She turned from her window.

"Don't get what?" asked Diana.

"Why you're doing all this. I mean, don't get me wrong. I'm lovin' it. Who wouldn't? It's the most fun ever." He sighed. "But... it's like, you just met me, and you know Margaret even less. And a girl like you... doing all this for someone like me... and my cousin..."

Now even Ty was looking up at them through his mirror.

A long silence followed.

"A girl like what?" Diana said finally.

"Huh?"

She leaned forward, smiled at Ty through the mirror, then closed the privacy glass separating them from the driver's section. Leaning back, she turned to Jeffrey and cocked her head. "You said 'a girl like you.' I asked what you meant."

Surprised by the question, he took a moment to answer.

"Well, definitely nothing bad. You're... I've just never met anyone like you before. I mean, you could be hanging out with anyone."

Embarrassed, he looked down. "I guess I'm not used to someone like you being so nice to someone like me."

Taking in a long breath, he blew it out. "Look, on the plane I figured you were being polite, and that would be it. But now, you're like... really really nice, and it's... sort of overwhelming."

More dead silence. Until Diana finally whispered, "You mean, not being Mr. Smooth and all?"

Which instantly broke the tension. Jeffrey couldn't help but smile. But Diana wasn't done.

"Maybe you shouldn't always worry about 'getting it.' Maybe there's nothing to get." When he didn't respond, she asked, "Are you havin' fun?"

"Duh."

"Enjoying yourself?"

He nodded.

"Well, me too. End of story."

Turning away, she stared straight ahead. "Oh, and thanks for the compliment. I think." Her lips tightened into traces of a smile. "The 'never-meeting-anyone-like-you' part."

Another long moment passed before she slowly turned to him again. "Besides, don't you agree that yesterday was pretty awesome? I mean, obviously not the crashed-car-almost-squished-dog part. But, you know. Helping that lady? Rescuing that poor little dog? We made a great team, right? And look what we're doing now. Hot on the trail of a pretty cool mystery…"

Jeffrey shrugged a nod.

She rolled her eyes. "Alright… and because you're so darn cute, Mr. Not-So-Smooth Jeffrey James, you get the long answer too."

She sighed. "Yesterday morning, when I thought about calling you, I was actually thinking some of the same things you mentioned. How different we were and all. But then I thought about our plane ride and decided maybe we're more alike than you think."

This time *Jeffrey's* eyebrows rose.

She continued.

"Okay, and I'm going to be totally honest here…" She mumbled to herself, "I can't believe I'm telling you this," then took a deep breath. "The truth is, I've spent most of my life being told I'm pretty. Well, first it was 'cute.' Then 'pretty.' And more recently," she made a face, "when guys think I can't hear them—'hot.' God, I hate that word. Anyway, you get the picture."

Jeffrey nodded, making a mental note to permanently delete the word from his vocabulary.

But she still wasn't done.

"I'm not trying to be any of that! I don't *want* to be any of that! I mean, I'm only fourteen. But some of my dad's friends sometimes seem to forget that. Men, women, doesn't matter. The way they look at me? Not the way you're supposed to look at a fourteen-year-old, if you follow. And it's not my fault. I'm not doing anything wrong. I don't wear flashy clothes. I don't try looking older than I am. I'm just being fourteen."

She nodded toward Ty up front. "That's why he's always been my rock, protecting me from a lot of that crap. Of course, he can't help with the morons at school, but I can handle them. When you're born and raised in Brentwood, you get used to it."

She stopped. "I guess that doesn't mean much to someone from—"

"—Iowa," Jeffrey finished.

"Yeah, there. Anyway, ninety-nine percent of Brentwood teens are brats. It's in their DNA. Rich Parents Syndrome. Yeah, I know, mine are too. But most of those idiots actually think that means something. That it makes them special. That they're owed it. The boys try acting all super-cool and grown-up, when they're really the opposite. And the girls are all going nuts over their seven-hundred-dollar kicks from Neiman's. Like any of that matters."

She looked from Jeffrey to Margaret. "Bottom line is, even in the short time I've known you two, I'm way more comfortable with you than with them."

Suddenly she stopped talking, the abrupt silence hanging in the air. But at least Jeffrey knew enough to keep his mouth shut this time—just appreciate that this beautiful person chose *him* to share all this with.

He was one lucky guy.

With no clue what Neiman's was.

Or seven-hundred-dollar kicks.

But Diana had more.

"At least I know I'm not special just because my family has money. And I don't want people treating me by how I look. I mean, at the ripe old age of fourteen I'm already sick of it all."

She locked eyes with Jeffrey. "Remember on the plane, when you talked about not having many friends?"

"Any," he corrected. "Well, until now I guess."

Margaret smiled.

But Diana remained serious.

"Well, that really hit home, because…" she paused, her gaze dropping, "…neither do I." The corners of her mouth curled into a tiny smile. "Well, until now I guess."

With that, she leaned forward, slid the privacy window open, sat back, and stared straight ahead like nothing happened.

A few beats later she whispered, "Maybe I should just move to Idaho."

"Iowa," Jeffrey whispered back.

"Or there," she said, that tiny smile returning.

Chapter 14

A fter Ty dropped them off in the Zuma parking lot, they weaved around blankets, surfboards, and sun-worshipers toward the water. Tagging behind, Jeffrey couldn't stop curling and uncurling his toes, savoring that indescribable sensation of hot sand mixing with the cool layer below.

When they reached the tide line and turned north, motion to Jeffrey's left caught his eye. A group of large birds were gliding low over the waves in the same direction they were going. Jeffrey counted nine of them. With long beaks and huge wing spans, they seemed to float in the air, wings spread wide without flapping, somehow keeping the same distance from each other in a precise pattern.

"Check it out," he yelled. "A perfect V."

The girls looked.

"Pelicans," Margaret called out.

"California Brown Pelicans," Diana added.

The flock continued up the shore, wings frozen in place. Suddenly the leader pumped twice, made a slight shift in direction, then resumed his glide. An instant later, the others followed, flapping twice before correcting course.

What a sight.

California Brown Pelicans.

Jeffrey wondered if that meant they only flew in California. How'd they know where the border was? More likely, Californians just loved slapping their name on everything. California Pelicans. California Pepper Trees. California Redwoods. Driving through the Valley, they'd passed a California Pizza sign. Even the vultures here were California Condors.

He couldn't think of anything like that back home. Somehow, "Iowa Ice Cream" just didn't cut it.

Once the birds melted into the horizon, he looked around for the girls. They were standing on top of the rock platform, all smiles, watching him birdwatch. Flashing them a sheepish grin, he picked up his pace.

On to the Bat Cave.

*   *   *

They sat on the rock ledge like before, cross-legged, candles flickering, cave walls aglow. After confirming the cave's dead zone (no bars on any of their phones), they drifted into easy conversation.

Jeffrey enlightened them on Iowa's claim to fame as the Hog Capital of America—"seven times more pigs than people." Diana talked about her mother's charity work in New York. And Margaret had a question for Diana.

"Hey, why's Ty look familiar?"

Diana smiled. "Maybe you've seen him on TV, a commercial or something."

"Huh?"

"There's a lot more to Ty than you think. He likes it that way, keeping things private."

"He does commercials?"

"More than that. Like, the Rolls? It's his."

Jeffrey's eyes bulged. "What?"

"He owns it."

"No way."

Diana chuckled. "He's not really my *driver* driver, like an employee. He just likes cruising around like that. He's got plenty of money and owns a bunch of cool cars he keeps at our place since we've got a big garage. He's one of my dad's oldest friends. They started law school together, but Ty switched to film school, then got rich with Internet stuff. But he never lost the acting bug, or his thing for cars."

Jeffrey whistled. "That Rolls must be worth a fortune."

Diana nodded. "I think he likes playing chauffeur because it's a great way to drive his precious cars around while staying invisible. He says people 'don't see' limo drivers. It probably also sparks his acting juices, studying other people without them noticing."

She pulled a banana out of her bag and began peeling. "What's really cool is that he's totally fine with people assuming he's 'just the driver.' Far as I'm concerned, that makes him the perfect role model. *Do what makes you happy, to heck with what others think.*"

She grinned. "I'll say one thing. He's the least stressed person I know." She took a few bites of banana.

"Anyway, sometimes he goes out on auditions. Just for kicks, like playing chauffeur. He doesn't need the work, doesn't need to drive me around, doesn't need to live on our property. It's just fun and easy, and Ty's big on 'fun and easy.' Though his house at our place *is* pretty chill."

She finished her banana, dropping the peel in her bag. "So you might've seen him in a commercial or TV show, though he never mentions it."

Margaret blurted out, "Does he have a girlfriend?"—quickly regretting how wrong that sounded. She was actually thinking of her mother. They were about the same age, plus the man was handsome, super-nice, and definitely getting more interesting by the minute.

Diana gave her a funny look. "Whoa, girl. A little young for him, don't ya think?"

Margaret blushed. "Not for me, silly." But that's all she said.

From there, the subject somehow turned to names. Both girls agreed that Jeffrey's sounded like a superhero's secret identity. Clark Kent. Peter Parker. Jeffrey James. Which of course got Margaret talking about how much she hated *her* name.

"Sounds fine to me," Diana told her, "much less boring than mine. Still, if it really bugs you, I'll be glad to help."

"How?"

"Come up with a new one. Maybe not totally official, but at least something *we* could call you."

"Hey, go for it."

So Jeffrey and Diana began throwing out names, some silly, some interesting. Until Diana suddenly grew quiet, her eyes locking in on Margaret.

"What?" Margaret asked.

But Diana just kept staring. Then, finally, in a low spooky

voice, as if revealing the Secret of the Universe, she whispered, "*M...*"

Followed by her eyebrow thing.

Margaret waited for more, but Diana just repeated it in that same creepy tone. "*M...*"

"What? Like Dorothy's Auntie Em?" Margaret asked.

Diana shook her head. "No, just the single letter. Be bold, girl. How many names are one letter?" She glanced at Jeffrey for support. He was already nodding. Of course he was. If Diana asked him to cram snails up his nose, he'd just ask how many.

Margaret tipped her head back to consider it.

It did sound kind of exotic.

M.

Like the mystery woman in a foreign movie. Plus Diana was right, she'd never heard of anyone with that name, or with just one letter. Meaning, she'd be one-of-a-kind, which sealed the deal.

And so... on a special summer day in a secret cave at Zuma Beach, California, the Girl-Formerly-Known-As-Margaret was unofficially rebranded "M." The three celebrated the occasion with a round of chocolate-covered pretzels.

Forty seconds later, Jeffrey's phone lit up.

Lifting it slowly, he brought it close to his face. In the flickering cave light, the display made him glow like a cartoon monster. The girls waited for him to say something but he just kept staring at it.

Finally he sighed and handed it to Diana. "M" scooted in closer for a better look.

This time there were no streets or letters, only numbers, lots of them, on both sides of an exclamation point.

3 2 3 6 5 0 2 6 8 8 ! 1 2

The girls studied it. Finally, M blew out a breath and shrugged. Diana shook her head and handed the phone back to Jeffrey. Gazing at the screen, he quietly began counting. A moment later he looked up. "Ten on the left and two on the right."

Diana wrinkled her nose. "What?"

"Ten numbers on the left side of the exclamation point, and two on the right. Any thoughts?"

M answered quickly. "A phone number's got ten numbers."

Diana looked at the text. "And if the beginning's an area code, it's here in LA since 3-2-3's local."

M agreed. "Yeah, my mom's Hollywood work number starts that way."

Jeffrey nodded. "Okay. So what about the 'one, two' at the end? A time again? The twelfth hour?"

Diana hopped off the ledge. "Only one way to find out. Let's go!"

"Where?"

"Back in cell range to call."

Ten minutes later, when they all had bars showing, they stopped to make their call. Since the new text had disappeared again from Jeffrey's phone, M keyed the ten numbers into her own phone from memory. Tapping the Call button, she clicked to speaker. After four rings, a young, too-perky, pre-recorded male voice answered.

Hey, thanks for calling Sam's Sports! Southern California's One-Stop Sports Shop! Located in the heart of Hollywood—on Sunset at the 101—we are Everything Sports! Unfortunately, our associates are currently busy handling other sports lovers right now, so please hold that thought and we'll be right with you. Or leave your number and...

M pressed the End button.

Diana perked up. "Hey, I know that store. One of my dad's clients owns a building down the street on Gower." She whipped out her phone and speed-dialed Ty, winking at Jeffrey. "And wait till you see this place."

Ty was nine blocks away finishing breakfast. When he picked them up, Diana innocently asked if he'd take Sunset Boulevard part of the way home.

"I know it's slower, but I'd love to show our tourist here more of LA," she explained, not mentioning the "One-Stop Sports Shop" also on Sunset.

Chapter 15

Although it passes through the Santa Monica Mountains, the western half of Sunset Boulevard is not your typical mountain pass. Gracefully s-curving its way from the coast to West Hollywood, it slices through a handful of upscale, village-themed communities, offering sixteen memorable miles of prime Southern California real estate.

Enough to keep Jeffrey glued to his window as they passed places he recognized but never dreamed of driving through. *Pacific Palisades, Brentwood, Westwood, Beverly Hills.*

Then, just when he thought the sightseeing was over, they hit the Sunset Strip—and instant visual overload.

Billboards the size of office buildings bombarded them from all sides: movies, clothes, television shows, rock stars. Wherever Jeffrey looked, it was larger than life. It reminded him of watching TV on New Year's Eve, the ball dropping in Times Square. Only instead of the massive New York crowds, the Strip had massive lines of cars.

In fact, hardly anyone was walking on Sunset—or anywhere in LA, for that matter. As far as Jeffrey could tell, the only reason sidewalks existed here was to separate the buildings from the roads.

When a small road sign finally welcomed them to Hollywood, the s-curves of Sunset straightened out to a relatively normal four-lane business street. While waiting for a red light at Sunset and Vine, Diana nudged Jeffrey, pointing out his window.

"Worth a shot?" she asked.

And there it was, perched near the top of the hills separating Hollywood from the Valley, shimmering in the sunlight. The iconic Hollywood sign!

Like everyone else on the planet, Jeffrey had seen it a thousand times, but never in real life. Zooming in with his phone, he snapped three epic shots.

Several streets past Vine, Jeffrey began noticing huge block-long, walled-off, single-story buildings with guarded gates.

"Movie studios," Ty explained. "Once upon a time, long before Amazon and Netflix, these places ruled the entertainment world. Paramount, RKO, Columbia, Warner Brothers." He pointed to an enormous fenced-in white structure that looked like a remodeled Civil War plantation. A sign above it read Sunset Bronson Studios.

"That was the original Warner Brothers, where they made the first 'talkie'—the first time actors spoke in a movie. Called 'The Jazz Singer,' released in 1927. Before that, movies were silent. No voices, just background music."

He caught Jeffrey's eye in the mirror. "So now you can tell your peeps back home that you saw the actual birthplace of the modern movie."

Jeffrey was loving it. For a *Jeopardy!* freak, this stuff was golden. A guided tour of the Entertainment Capital of the World, narrated by a real Hollywood actor.

At the next block, Diana asked Ty to pull over. Jeffrey looked around to see why. Then he saw it, across the street. A very large, very blue building.

Sam's Sports.

It didn't take a genius to see why Diana remembered the place. Even across four lanes of traffic, no one could miss, or forget, Sam's Sports. It stuck out like a giant sore thumb. A giant *blue* sore thumb.

"Holy Cow," Jeffrey snickered. "You could see this place from the Space Station."

The girls chuckled. But it was true. Except for the glass doors and windows, every inch was blue. *Blindingly* bright blue.

Walls, roof, window frames, awning, even the concrete blocks in the parking lot and the A/C unit peeking up from the roof. Like one of those jets that sprays red stuff on forest fires had dumped a million gallons of day-glow blue on the building, then re-loaded and repeated a few dozen more times.

The place sat just yards from the freeway off-ramp, set back from the street with a dozen or so parking spaces in front. In the center of the parking lot, rising high enough to surely be visible for miles down the freeway, a giant pole supported an enormous sign announcing in big blue letters *Sam's Sports!*

And in case you weren't sure what "Sports" meant, the exclamation point at the end was shaped like a bat over a ball.

Clever.

Ty cut the engine and turned around. "And why exactly are we here?"

Thinking fast, Diana said, "I mentioned this place to Jeffrey earlier and thought he might like a few shots to remind him how crazy Hollywood is."

Jeffrey played along. "Yes, this blueness must be documented," he said, digging out his phone.

Opening his door, Ty gave them one of those ah-you-silly-kids headshakes adults give silly kids. "Well, I'm grabbing some water bottles from the trunk," he said, exiting the car.

Jeffrey also got out and, walking around from the traffic-side to the curb, propped his phone against the limo roof and snapped two long shots of Sam's across the busy boulevard. When he returned to the back seat, the girls were still watching the blue building as Ty continued rummaging in the trunk.

"So now what?" Jeffrey asked, stashing his phone away.

"Well, I don't think we missed anything," Diana said. "Everything looks normal, well, except for the blue. No car crashes. No exploding hydrants." She squinted. "Pretty quiet inside too, from what I can see."

M checked the time. 1:02. "Plus, the twelfth hour's officially over," she noted.

Ty returned to the front seat with four water bottles. Handing three to his passengers, he cracked open the fourth and took a long swig. After wiping his mouth with the back of his hand, he noticed everyone still focused on the store.

"You want me to go in there with you?" he asked.

But they were all thinking the same thing. Why bother? With no idea what to look for, it'd be a repeat of yesterday at the toy store. Three blind mice. Plus, if something major *was* going on inside, they'd likely know about it, either through the windows or by someone rushing out.

Diana answered for them. "Nah, that's okay. I think we're ready to head back to the Valley and drop these two off."

Ty started the engine and merged back into traffic. Glancing at the store one last time through his side mirror, he muttered, "I've driven by that place a thousand times. Something's different."

Chapter 16

Wednesday

After a surprisingly good night's sleep, M was up by eight. Brushing her teeth, she stared into her bathroom mirror, mentally counting all the things she'd gotten wrong these past few days.

Her cousin a loser? Wrong.

A boring final week of summer vacation? Wrong.

But the biggest surprise was Diana. Seeing her that first time at the airport, the girl looked too perfect. The kind of calm, confident beauty M would instantly hate if they met under different circumstances. Especially after watching the way her cousin gave her those ga-ga eyes when she walked off.

The way *all* guys acted when girls like Diana walked off.

M had spent her whole life despising girls like that, and the pathetic boys who fell for them. They were the ones who called her names. They were the ones who got everything without working for it. They were the ones who didn't care about grades, or sports, or being nice. Because they didn't have to. They still got all the boys, all the attention, all the fun, no matter how silly or stupid or mean they were.

But Diana?

Boy, did she ever get that one wrong.

First, Diana inviting her to the beach before even meeting her? Who does that?

Then, how genuinely nice she was?

But especially how she treated Jeffrey. Or for that matter, that she even called him in the first place. Not that there was anything wrong with her cousin. Oddly enough, M actually liked him. He was fun, witty, easy to talk to. Even kinda cute, in a geeky, cousiny way.

But let's face it, a babe-magnet he wasn't. And definitely not the type you'd expect someone like Diana to call, let alone hang with.

In M's world, she and Jeffrey would normally be on someone like Diana's *least*-likely-to-hang-with list.

Yet here they all were, having the time of their lives.

Then Diana coming up with M's new name? How cool was that?

So, yeah, Diana was a huge surprise. But the clincher was that little speech she gave on the way to Zuma yesterday. Never in a million years would M have imagined someone like Diana having the same kinds of feelings M had (the outsider part, not the beauty-queen stuff).

She washed off her toothbrush, rinsed out her mouth, and took another long look in the mirror. Was she really any better than all those girls she grew up hating? Hadn't she first judged Diana by the way she looked? Before even giving her a chance?

Maybe it was time to re-think that whole judging-a-book-by-its-cover stuff. Or always expecting the worst in people.

Maybe this whole Jeffrey-Diana adventure was about more than just having fun.

Then again, maybe she should quit staring in the mirror and grab some breakfast.

*　　　*　　　*

Entering the main house, she found Jeffrey at the kitchen table halfway through a bowl of Cheerios. A second bowl, spoon, and napkin sat across from him on a placemat next to the cereal box. Since her mother had already left for work, Jeffrey must've done that.

"Good morning," she said, walking to the fridge for the milk.

"Hey," Jeffrey grunted through a mouthful of oats.

As she poured herself a bowl, Jeffrey's phone buzzed. From his expression, M could tell it was Diana. She watched as he mostly listened, occasionally smiled, said "okay" a few times and "I think so, but I'll check," before hanging up.

Setting his phone down, he looked across the table. "She says she wants to take us 'someplace different' today."

M waited for more but Jeffrey just shrugged. "That's all she'd say. Oh, and to wear sneakers, not flip-flops, whatever that means. Said she'd be here in an hour."

"So what was the 'but I'll check' part?"

His mouth slowly curled into a grin.

"Oh yeah, almost forgot. She also invited us to spend the night. Said to bring overnight stuff and swimsuits."

M tried not to act too excited, but a sleepover at Diana's? How could you not? Any fourteen-year-old with her own limo driver surely lived somewhere worth seeing.

She speed-dialed her mom to get permission. Susan's only condition was to get Diana's address, phone number, and "that driver's" name and number.

Jeffrey called Diana back and got the required information, which M then relayed to her mom. Minutes later, after apparently deciding no serial killers were lurking at Diana's, Susan phoned back with official sleepover approval.

Mission accomplished, both of them returned to their Cheerios, pretending not to be as thrilled as they were.

Jeffrey finished his cereal first. But instead of getting up, he stayed at the table and stared awkwardly at M as she continued eating. Finally, she stopped mid-mouthful and gave him a whats-up? look.

He scratched his forehead. "Can I ask you something?"

Uh-oh. Last time he asked that it turned into that heavy limo conversation with Diana. Reluctantly, M nodded.

"Promise not to laugh?"

She shrugged, returning to her cereal.

Jeffrey cleared his throat. "So what's Neiman's?"

M snapped her mouth shut before Cheerios shot out. Then, after managing to swallow without choking, she burst out laughing before quickly apologizing. "Sorry, kinda took me by surprise there."

"What's so funny?"

"No, it's… never mind." Choosing to treat it as a teachable moment, she put her spoon down and for the next five minutes patiently educated her adorably clueless cousin on Life in the Fast Lane, Brentwood-style.

The malls, the brands, what's hot, what's not—and of course Neiman-Marcus, where the ridiculously rich shopped till they dropped, then got up and shopped some more.

"And seven-hundred-dollar kicks?" asked Jeffrey.

"Sneakers."

His jaw fell open.

"They make seven-hundred-dollar sneakers?"

M snickered. "Oh, you have no idea."

Chapter 17

Jeffrey

We cruised through a different part of the Valley this time, though Diana still wouldn't tell us where we were going.

At a stop light, she leaned forward and slid open the privacy glass. "Hey Ty, why don't you give our friends here the four-one-one on this fine motorcar." She turned to me and winked, apparently knowing what was coming.

"My pleasure," he replied, tipping his hat through the mirror as the light turned green. "Ladies and gent, may I present the incomparable 1948 Rolls Royce Silver Wraith. That's W-R-A-I-T-H, rhymes with eighth, the Scottish word for spirit or ghost."

So began the fascinating history of his spectacular ride, spoken with the love and affection of a father describing the birth of his child. We learned about the imported rosewood from Madagascar, the Italian Corinthian leather, and how the vehicle was originally customized for the personal use of the chairman of the Rolls Royce Company in England.

Never once did he mention he owned the thing.

When he finished, Diana thanked him before closing the privacy pane. Leaning back, she tucked some loose strands of hair behind her ear. "Look, before we get there, I wanted to apologize."

"For what?" I asked.

"For sending us on those wild goose chases."

M turned. "What're you talking about?"

"You know. First, to the toy store, then to Sam's. That's why I'm taking you where we're going now. Well, one of the reasons. I figured it was a good way to put all that silliness behind us."

"How do you know they were wild goose chases?" M asked.

"Well, after yesterday's dud at Sam's, it seems pretty obvious that the toy store thing must've been a fluke too. Just another LA car crash." She slowly shook her head. "And there I was, trying to turn a couple of cell phone glitches into some grand adventure."

M shrugged. "We don't know that for sure."

I looked at my cousin, surprised by her sudden change of heart. Shooting baskets the other day she'd argued the opposite.

I turned to Diana. "I agree with M. I mean, think about that first text. How everything happened exactly when and where it said it would, location and hour."

M nodded. "And both texts popping up in your dead-zone cave, where you said signals were impossible? Yeah, once is maybe a phone glitch. But two days in a row? Only in your cave, and only on Jeffrey's phone?" She shook her head. "Something's not right there."

I smiled. The girls had totally flipped positions—Diana now the doubter, M a solid maybe. But before we could discuss it further, Ty pulled into what looked like a block-long strip mall. Except strip malls don't have horses out front.

*   *   *

Riverside Riding Stables was a sprawling, single-story complex on the edge of Griffith Park (one of the largest city parks in the country, Google later informed me, donated by a guy with a name even sillier than mine: Griffith J. Griffith).

Diana said she took riding classes there on Saturdays, but switched days for us. She described the place as a horse-lover's dream, with monthly horse shows, riding lessons, equestrian supplies, horse rentals, and scenic trails that snaked through the adjoining Santa Monica Mountains.

After letting us off in the parking lot, Ty drove off to do whatever he did when he left us. On our way to the entrance, my cousin and I confessed we'd never been on a horse before. But Diana assured us there was nothing to it. Except for maybe the "English saddles" we'd be riding.

"They take a little getting used to," she said, explaining that, unlike the more common "Western" version, English ones didn't have saddle horns. "That's the big round knob sticking up in front that you always see movie cowboys holding with one hand while flipping the reins with the other. English saddles don't have 'em."

I wasn't sure what that meant, but it didn't sound serious.

Entering the building, we were greeted by a cheerful lady manning a desk near the front. After a brief conversation with Diana, whom the lady clearly knew, and a quick phone call to someone in another part of the building, we were directed down a narrow pathway that twisted through the complex. Made of dirt and straw, it reminded me of the Yellow Brick Road. Only instead of corn fields and scarecrows, this one was lined with horse stalls, storage areas, a few offices, and lots of hay bales.

As we passed a small shop displaying saddles and other horse gear in the window, Diana stopped.

"You guys go on. I'll meet you over there." She waved to two men in cowboy shirts at the far end of the building, holding the reins to three really big horses. One of the men waved back. "Gotta do something first," she said, disappearing into the shop before we could object.

So we continued down the Yellow Dirt Road. When we got to the end, the two guys somehow managed to get us up on our saddles (with a small step ladder and much patience). That's when I discovered what "no saddle horn" meant. Because, with nothing to hold onto but two thin leather straps, the only thing keeping you upright—on a very large, very tall, semi-wild animal—was your *balance*.

Definitely not the smartest way to design a saddle. Like building a motorcycle without handlebars.

Once we got relatively steady in our saddles, the men gave us a way-too-quick horseback-riding lesson: where to put your feet, how to hold the reins, kick to start, pull to stop.

By then, Diana had returned with a small paper bag. Walking over to my horse, she dug something shiny out and handed it up to me. A thin silver bracelet with a horseshoe charm in the center. "Here, put this on," she said, before walking over to M's horse and handing her an identical one.

"What's this for?" M asked.

"It's a lucky horseshoe, silly." Pulling out a third one, she fastened it around her own wrist, crumpled the bag, handed it to one of the stable guys, and quickly mounted her horse—with no help or step ladder.

"Three matching lucky bracelets," she announced, patting her horse's neck. "To watch over us while we ride."

Then, with a flick of the reins and click of her tongue, she led her horse out toward the riding corral, yelling back, "Or consider them member keys for our new secret club."

"What club?" I called out, as the stable hands led our horses through the same archway behind Diana.

"The one we started yesterday in the cave," she yelled back.

My cousin and I looked at each other, trying not to smile. But for two kids who'd never been members of anything, it wasn't easy.

*   *   *

My horse's name was Spits.

Which should've been a clue.

Note to self: When your horse is named Spits, ask why.

Though it didn't take long to find out.

Whenever I jostled the reins to try directing Spits this way or that, he'd show his displeasure by snorting loudly, tossing his head back, and letting loose with a nasty glob of spit.

And clearly Spits had been practicing. Each shot flew in a perfect backward arc, nailing me dead-center every time. Mostly on the front of my shirt, except once in my hair and another by my right nostril. Fun times.

Naturally, M and Diana found this hilarious. Even our riding instructor had trouble not snickering. But I refused to let Spits defeat me. I was beginning to have too much fun to let him rain on my parade. Ha!

Fortunately, the liquid bombs eventually tapered off and, halfway through our session, stopped completely. Spits and I had bonded. Sadly though, all good things must end (as I learned on my plane ride). And before I knew it, I was bidding farewell to dear Spits, offering him a carrot the instructor gave me ("keep your palm flat so he doesn't accidentally bite off a finger").

As I watched the horses being led off, what amazed me most —well, besides not falling off my English saddle and dying—was how much fun I'd had after initially being scared to death. Had to be a deep lesson there somewhere.

In fact, the only real casualty, besides a soggy shirt, was my rear-end. I must've missed the part about how to keep your butt from smacking the saddle a hundred times a minute when your horse trots. Apparently my cousin missed it too, because as Diana power-walked to the parking lot, M and I hobbled along like a pair of barefoot ninety-year-olds tip-toeing through broken glass.

Then something odd happened. Off to the right, a stable employee was washing down a horse with a hose and brush. The hose was attached to one of those old-fashioned water pumps, the kind with a long handle you'd normally push up and down, though I think this one was for show. Above the handle, hanging from a wire wrapped around the top, a handwritten sign read "For Horses Only." My first thought, naturally, was a stupid joke—that horses couldn't read. But before I could embarrass myself by wisecracking that, M stopped dead in her tracks.

I looked over. She was frozen in place, eyes fixed on the girl grooming her horse. Or maybe she was staring at the pump, or the sign, or just spacing out. I couldn't really tell. But whatever it was, it was weird, like someone had pressed her Pause button.

Seconds later, she blinked twice and resumed walking as if nothing happened. When I caught up with her, the intense look on her face convinced me not to ask questions. Then once outside, I saw Diana and Ty leaning against the limo, giggling at us shuffling along like two butt-aching old geezers, and forgot all about it.

Chapter 18

Every out-of-towner deserves a trip down Ventura Boulevard. At least some of it anyway, since the whole route can take hours.

Listed in the record books as the longest continuous strip of businesses in the world, it stretches east to west across most of the Valley, passing through a bunch of those semi-cities along the way. Studio City, Van Nuys, Sherman Oaks, Encino, Tarzana, Woodland Hills—eighteen miles of non-stop, wall-to-wall storefronts.

Bars, food, furniture, clothing, office buildings, liquor stores, every chain ever franchised, motels, restaurants, cafes, convenience stores. You name it, Ventura Boulevard has it times fifty.

The plan had been to show the young out-of-towner a short stretch of it—through Van Nuys—on their way to Diana's. But Jeffrey had other ideas. Two blocks into the tour, his eyelids started drooping. Spits had done him in. So before he passed out, Diana asked if anyone was hungry.

Up to then, M hadn't said a word. Since leaving the stables she'd apparently been stuck on whatever had set her off back by that water pump. But as soon as Diana mentioned eating, she perked up.

"Hey, maybe we could find a place up by that store in Malibu," she suggested.

Diana gave her a look. Malibu was thirty miles *past* Brentwood, a sixty-mile round-trip detour. Not to mention, *they were cruising Ventura Boulevard*—home to half the eateries on the planet.

"Why?" Diana asked.

M blinked rapidly. "I'm not sure. Something at the stables got my brain ticking. I think about Monday's crash, but I can't jog it loose." She shrugged. "I thought maybe going back there might help."

Diana thought for a moment. She really hadn't planned much for the rest of the day. And maybe M's mad memory skills would finally lead them somewhere. She leaned forward and opened the privacy pane.

"Hey, Ty. You think we could take a little detour before heading home? Maybe stop by that ice cream shop in Malibu?"

Instead of answering, Ty abruptly pulled into an empty parking place in front of a Starbucks. The three exchanged glances, not sure what was going on. Shifting into Park, he turned around, slowly scanning each face. "Okay guys, what's up?"

Busted. They should've known they couldn't keep things from him for long. But first, they needed to discuss it in private.

"Could you give us a minute?" Diana asked. He nodded. She motioned for M to open her door and the three got out. Huddling back by the limo trunk, Diana spoke first.

"I can't lie anymore. I trust him completely. Besides, I'm sure he'd be helpful. He's smart and has way more experience than all of us combined."

Jeffrey agreed. "Personally, I'm fine with that. Plus, let's face it—no Ty, no wheels."

M smiled. "I'm sure you can guess my answer."

They returned to the limo.

Once M closed the door, Ty said, "Well?"

"Okay," Diana replied. "But first, please understand that the only reason we didn't mention this before," she glanced at her partners-in-crime, "was so you wouldn't think we were nuts."

That said, she poured out the whole story: the two anonymous texts popping up on Jeffrey's new phone—a number almost no one knew; how the first one included the toy store address and the second had listed the phone number for Sam's; how both appeared in Diana's cave—a cell dead zone; and how they'd used the ending number in each text as the hour to visit that location.

"And before you say it," Diana continued, "we already know. We're probably making a mountain out of a molehill. I mean, yeah, the first text sent us to that Malibu store right before that crash, which totally freaked us. But then nothing happened yesterday at Sam's."

When she stopped talking, Ty remained quiet, his eyes drifting out the window. "And why do you want to go back to Malibu now?" he asked.

M took that one. "Something about Monday's crash keeps

nagging me, but I'm not sure what. I thought going back there might help me think of it."

Nodding slowly, his next words took everyone by surprise. "You guys ever hear of Nancy Drew?"

The Iowa book-lover's face lit up. "Sure! *Nancy Drew Mysteries.* Not as old as my *Oz* books, but pretty close."

"Wasn't she a movie or something?" Diana guessed.

Ty smiled. "Maybe, but Jeffrey's right. Way back, not long after those first talking movies hit the screen, a new book series came out that turned Nancy Drew into America's favorite teenage detective." He flashed his too-white smile. "Whose biggest fan just happened to be my grandmother! And when she eventually ran out of bookshelves and passed her collection on to my mom, guess who grew up with Nancy Drew books all over the house?"

Jeffrey laughed.

Ty nodded. "Yep. Ol' Nancy basically taught me to read. Heck, by the time I was nine, I wanted to *marry* that girl. But mostly it sparked my passion for mysteries, and my childhood dream of someday doing what Nancy did.

"Even as I got older and reality hit—when it finally sunk in I'd never be a real detective—I still hoped someday I'd at least get to play one as an actor." He grinned. "But, hey, this is *way* better!"

He spun around, checked the side mirror, and pulled back onto the boulevard. No one spoke, unsure if his story was over.

At the next intersection, he turned right, glanced up in the mirror, and pressed on. "Yeah, maybe it's a molehill, but maybe it's not. And since you can't fly if you don't try, I say we let our resident Mega-Mind loose and see what happens!"

Swerving onto the 101, he floored it and, pointing forward, shouted, "So onward, fellow detectives! Time to crack this case wide open and make ol' Nancy Drew proud!"

With a broad smile, Diana turned to her friends. "Now *that's* what I'm talking about!" she hooted.

Chapter 19

The one good thing about obliterating a fire hydrant? Clean streets!

They'd made good time on the freeway and through Malibu Canyon, and were now cruising down a spotless Pearl Street. No skid marks, no accident debris, no candy wrappers, no dirty curbs. A shiny new fire hydrant sparkled in front of the toy store. A far cry from the dirty, wet war zone they'd left two days ago.

Ty parked on the next block, one space up from where he'd parked on Monday. Exiting the limo, they noticed a young couple strolling down the sidewalk holding hands. As the pair got closer, they gazed at the Rolls, then broke into wide grins. That seemed to be the typical reaction people had when seeing Ty's ride for the first time. Unlike most limos, especially those long snobby ones that attracted more sneers than smiles, the sight of a 1948 one-of-a-kind RR Silver Wraith apparently puts everyone in a jolly good mood.

Smiling back at the couple, they crossed the street. At the corner, Ty asked M, "Any idea what you're looking for?"

She tightened her mouth. "Still working on that."

As they neared the toy store, M stopped suddenly, her eyes locked on the newly installed hydrant with that same intensity Jeffrey had seen at the stables. They watched her, saying nothing.

Nearly a minute passed. Finally M blinked several times, looked up and down the street, then refocused on the hydrant. "Something's different," she mumbled to herself. "I mean, besides it being new, obviously."

She walked a few paces and turned, re-checking the hydrant from her new angle. When that didn't seem to help, she looked up at Ty. "Remember yesterday when we left Sam's? You said something about things looking different but you weren't sure what?"

He nodded.

"Same vibe I'm getting."

A few beats later she turned toward the ice cream shop. "C'mon. Maybe a good brain-freeze'll jump-start the Mega-Mind."

*   *   *

They sat on the same bus bench as before, across from the toy store, the girls on each end, Ty and Jeffrey wedged in the middle. Ty held a sundae cup, the others slurped cones. After buying their ice cream, M had suggested sitting there for a while so she could "take in the scene."

After several minutes of quiet consumption, Diana leaned forward to check on M on the far side of the bench. Cradling her cone in both hands, her eyes were closed and her head tipped back, apparently lost in her memory zone again. Diana nudged Ty to look, who nudged Jeffrey.

As they all watched her, M started to speak, slowly, eyes still shut, as if narrating a dream. "Okay... right before the crash, after that mother and daughter drove off, there was only one car left in the lot." Her eyes blinked open and she pointed with her cone to the toy store parking lot. "A blue VW, in that second space there."

The others exchanged glances. If this was that same movie, the spooky music would start now.

Closing her eyes again, M paused for several seconds before starting up again. "A crumpled juice box was on the window ledge a few feet from the door, on the right." Her eyes popped back open and she pointed to the spot.

More time passed, more ice cream consumed.

Finally M stood, looked both ways for traffic, and walked into the street. She stopped halfway, eyes riveted to the hydrant. She remained that way, statue-like in the middle of the street, long enough for the others to start worrying. Fortunately, no cars drove by.

Then, as Diana was about to call out, M turned, walked back to the bus bench, sat, and quietly began licking her cone.

Seconds later she shot up off the bench, sending Jeffrey's cone flying. Pointing across the street, she shrieked, "That's it!"

"Holy Moly!" Jeffrey moaned. "Thanks for the heart attack."

Leaning down to wipe up what was left of his cone with his napkin, he asked, "What's it?"

"On the hydrant!" M shouted.

She turned back around to see three worried faces staring at the crazy person. Taking in a breath, she exhaled slowly. "Okay, sorry. Didn't mean to lose it." She shook her head at the ice cream mess Jeffrey was cleaning up. "Sorry about that, too. But now I remember what was different, between the old hydrant and this new one. Something was on it. Hanging from the top."

Glancing up and down the street again, she started back across, motioning for the others to follow. "C'mon, let's see if that same clerk's working today."

*   *   *

Before they went in, Ty convinced them they'd have better luck without him and walked back to the limo to wait. "Three innocent kids asking questions beats a creepy old dude acting nosy" was how he'd put it.

Dumping what was left of their cones (and Jeffrey's slimy mess) in a trash can, they followed M into the store. The same clerk was behind the same counter in the same chair in the same position. Probably reading the same book. The only difference this time was there weren't any customers.

Approaching the counter, M took the lead.

"Excuse me."

The guy slowly raised his head.

"Remember us from the other day?"

No recognition, no expression, no response.

M continued. "We were here on Monday? Right before that awful accident out front?"

"Congratulations," he sneered.

Lovely attitude. Why'd they let jerks work in toy stores?

But M kept at it. "Can I ask you a question?"

He looked at Diana, then Jeffrey, then back at Diana—a little too long on Diana. Creepy. Finally, he turned back to M. "What?" He closed his book around his finger to keep his place.

"That fire hydrant out front?" M prompted.

"Yeah?"

"Not the new one there now, the one that got smashed. Did you notice anything unusual about it? Before the accident, obviously."

"Unusual?" He scanned them suspiciously. "About a fire hydrant?" His lips curled into a nasty smile. "Yeah, it laid golden eggs."

So much for innocent kids asking innocent questions.

Dropping her polite act, M switched to bad-cop, shooting him a killer stink-eye. Diana and Jeffrey did the same which, amazingly, seemed to help.

"Like what?" he asked, his tone slightly less obnoxious.

"I'm trying to remember what's different about it from the one out there now." She offered a hunch. "Maybe something on top?"

He smirked. "Bird crap is all."

Switching back to nice, M said, "Look, we're just curious, okay, and could really use your help. For a school project." Maybe he was too dumb to realize school was out. Then Diana flashed him one of her stop-the-universe smiles, and the storm clouds instantly parted.

"You mean the leak?" he asked, his tone nearly human.

M's eyes widened. "The leak?"

His gaze moved slowly from Diana back to M. "You know, drip, drip, like a sieve? For a good month before the crash. Totally messed up the sidewalk."

M grinned at her team. Progress. Finally.

He wasn't done.

"Yoda... that's what I call my boss, not to his face, but anyway, he had me sweepin' outside every morning so it wouldn't puddle and reek. And I'm like—hello?—pay me minimum wage and have me do the *city's* job now? Why don't I repave the street while I'm at it?"

He grabbed a crumpled sales receipt off the counter, bookmarked his place in his book, and set it down.

"Couple weeks of that and I finally called the city myself." He shook his head. "Ever deal with the city of Malibu?" He snickered.

"You'd have better luck finding Nemo." Seeing their reaction, he shrugged. "Yeah, even I was a kid once." He tilted his chair back, now fully into his story. "Anyway, two guys show up with clipboards and do this three-second lookie-loo. Then, poof, they're gone." He chuckled. "Takes me longer to pop a zit."

Eew.

"Then a few days later they're back again and I get all warm and fuzzy thinking it's finally gonna get fixed. No more sweepin' curbs. But nope, they're out there bending down, pretending to take notes, then—poof—they're gone again. So I'm like, hey, sign me up for that gig. Big Malibu bucks for doing nothing?" He fake-sighed. "Except then I wouldn't have Yoda to bad-mouth anymore."

They waited for more but the guy just shrugged. "That's all, folks."

Jeffrey spoke for the first time. "You mean it kept leaking?"

The clerk looked at him like he'd just been beamed down from space. "What part of 'that's all, folks' don't you get, Sporto?" He turned back to M. "Nothing happened. Nada. Diddly squat. Had to keep sweepin'. By last week, twice a day. So, yeah, Ol' Lucy Leadfoot did me a real solid launchin' that sucker into outer space."

Suddenly his expression changed. "Hey, what kinda school project happens in the summer?" The three turned for the door.

"Yeah, right," he yelled after them. "A school project on fire hydrants? Hey, here's a title for ya: 'See Spot Pee." He laughed at his lame joke.

At the exit, Diana turned back toward the creep and, flashing another blazing smile, spoke for the first time. "Hey Sporto, have Yoda check out our Yelp review tomorrow. He's gonna love it." As her smile dissolved into a devilish sneer, she spun around and walked out the door.

Jeffrey decided she was even hotter trash-talking like that. Lucky for him he only *thought* that forbidden word.

Chapter 20

Jeffrey

B y the time we returned to the limo, my cousin had reverted to her silent space-cadet mode again, so Diana and I briefed Ty on the clerk's story.

I wasn't sure why M had turned trance-like, but it seemed best to leave her alone. Not that it mattered, since something else was about to jolt her back to reality without any help from me.

Diana's house.

Even a quick glimpse of the place was like a power-blast of ice water. One minute, my cousin was totally zoned out, unsure what planet she was on; the next, Ty turned into their driveway and her eyeballs nearly exploded.

Despite the high walls and double gates obscuring the view, it was obvious we were entering a whole new world.

Ty pushed a button on his key fob and the Pearly Gates slowly parted. I could almost hear the trumpets begin to play. We continued up a long pathway through a park-like setting of trees, flower gardens, and shrubbery manicured into geometric shapes. The first structure I noticed was out M's window, a one-story building at the end of a side road, and I admit, I was a little disappointed. Diana's house wasn't nearly as big as I expected.

Then the six driveways—three on each side leading up to six separate archways—came into view and I realized this wasn't their house, it was their *garage.*

Two really cool cars—one black, the other dark red—sat in two of the driveways. A third one, bright yellow with black trim—parked on the cobblestone strip that encircled the structure—looked more like a spaceship. This had to be part of Ty's auto collection, the one Diana described in the cave.

As we drove on, I looked out my side of the limo and got my

first view of the main house. Either that, or we'd arrived at the Dark Knight's castle.

Too dazed to speak, my eyes popped and my jaw dropped—like Wile E. Coyote in those Roadrunner cartoons right before he gets pulverized by a heavy flying object.

I may have also stopped breathing.

Leaning back to capture the full size of the place through the limo window, I counted three separate roof lines, four balconies (that I could see), and a bunch more archways, all perfectly blending into one breathtaking mini-palace. Okay, scratch the "mini."

Glancing at my cousin, her expression confirmed she saw what I saw. Mouth open, eyes wide, eyebrows arched so high her forehead was gone.

Ty pulled up in front of a dozen shallow steps leading to the mansion's front entrance. As we got out, he retrieved our overnight bags, gave us a quick "Catch you guys later," and took off. Diana started up the steps but my cousin and I just stood there, temporarily paralyzed, gaping at the magical sight before us like two kids facing their first dragon.

After sufficient gawk-time, we picked up our bags and climbed the steps to join our hostess, who was patiently waiting in front of two massive doors with brass knockers that looked like the ones Dorothy used when she visited the Wizard.

Offering us a warm smile, she turned and, with a hand on each doorknob, pushed through the double doors like a princess entering her castle. No key, but who needs one with palace gates? Or maybe an invisible light beam scanned her eyeballs.

Once inside, the double doors closed automatically, so slowly you could barely see them move. We followed Diana across an entryway and up a staircase straight out of a movie, to a second-floor landing. While she continued down the hall, my cousin and I stayed at the banister to take in the view below.

I wasn't sure what we were looking down at. A living room? Study? Entertainment room? Whatever it was, it was big. Impressive artwork covered most of the walls, illuminated by tiny spotlights hidden in the ceiling. In the far corner, a gleaming white piano, even brighter than Ty's teeth, stood in front of panoramic windows that curved around the entire room, exposing their backyard (though calling it that was like calling the Rolls a car).

Out the left-facing windows, an enormous pool—the kind you see in travel posters—glistened in the sunlight. A small waterfall trickled into the deep end over actual boulders. Just past the pool deck, a manicured putting green—like a grassy miniature golf course without the kiddie stuff—covered an area about twice the size of Margaret's backyard.

Equally stunning was the view out the right-facing windows. Towering trees—oaks, palms, and others with bright purple flowers—rose above multi-colored garden blooms, with winding pathways snaking beyond my line of sight.

I noticed one of those paths, dotted with old-fashioned lamp posts, led to a spiffy-looking two-story house. If that was Ty's place, Diana was right. *Very* chill. A pair of chimneys poked up from the roof (a fireplace on each floor?), and two separate balconies jutted out from opposite ends of the second story, with an umbrellaed table and chairs in one, and a telescope and tripod in the other.

Yeah, I could live there.

A nudge from my cousin brought me back to Earth. I turned to see Diana waiting down the hall by another door. We caught up with her and followed her into her bedroom.

Since "big" is easily overused in a castle, let's just say her room could sleep a four-piece band with enough space left to toss around a Frisbee. But before we had time to drool, M spotted Diana's computer across the room—snapping her back to whatever she'd been thinking about on the drive over.

As she walked toward it, Diana motioned her to the desk chair, booted up the computer, entered a password, and stood back. M brought up Google Maps on the browser and typed in *2247 pearl malibu*. When the map appeared, she clicked Street View.

An image of the toy store and nearby shops appeared. She zoomed in on the same fire hydrant she'd been staring at an hour ago until it filled the screen. But it was too pixelated. Pausing for a moment, her face suddenly brightened.

"Our photos," she whispered.

Minutes later, with help from Diana and something called bluetooth, all seven phone shots we'd taken right before the crash were loaded and printed. Flipping through them, M stopped when she found one with the toy store positioned roughly the same as the onscreen Google image—the store head-on, the fire hydrant in the lower right.

She asked Diana if she had a magnifying glass. Diana pointed to a desk drawer. Retrieving it, M brought it within an inch of the paper photo, slowly moving it across the image. Occasionally she'd glance at the computer screen, zoom in and out, then return to the paper shot.

Another minute passed before she finally stopped over one section.

"There!" my cousin proudly announced.

Chapter 21

Handing Diana the photo and magnifier, M pointed to a spot near the top of the fire hydrant. "Look for yourself."

Diana examined it. But after a few seconds she looked up and shrugged. "Don't see anything." She handed the photo and magnifier to Jeffrey, who scoped the image for a while before also shaking his head.

Leaning over the photo, M traced a tiny line by the top of the hydrant with her fingertip. "See that little thingy running across the hydrant a couple inches below the top?"

She turned to the computer and pointed to the same spot on the fire hydrant in the Google Maps shot. "Compare that to this. It's a little blurry, but you can see that line's not in the Google shot." She clicked the box in the corner where it showed the date the image was taken. "Google took this shot two months ago. So whatever that is in our printed shot is new."

Jeffrey and Diana looked from paper phone shot to computer image, then back again. Though hard to see, there *was* a tiny difference. In the paper photo, a barely-visible thin line ran across the hydrant near the top, but not in the Google one.

"You sure that's not a scratch on the paper, or dirt on the lens?" Jeffrey asked.

"Positive." M ran her finger along the tiny line. "See how it bends there? A scratch or dirt wouldn't do that."

Diana took the magnifier and re-checked the image. Seconds later she nodded. "Okay, maybe that is something. A string or wire?"

"Exactly." M turned to Jeffrey. "Remember back at the stables when I spaced out on that water pump? I was focused on that 'For Horses Only' sign and now I know why. The wire holding it was wrapped around the top of the pump exactly like this wire on the hydrant before the crash."

Jeffrey shrugged. "No offense, but so what? Even if there was a wire, what's that got to do with the car crash or the phone text?"

M made a face. "I'm not sure. Something's still missing. Maybe whatever was hanging from the wire would tell us. If it was facing the store, we wouldn't have seen it from the bus bench, or when taking these pictures."

Then she remembered something. She brought up the search box and typed in *city of malibu.*

"What now?" asked Diana.

"That creep at the store said the city came out to check the hydrant leak, right? Maybe what was hanging there was theirs." She tapped the search button. "Let's find out."

After bouncing around the city's phone maze, M eventually got through to the right department. Street Maintenance. With her phone on speaker, she began pumping the clerk for information, impressing the others with her sharp questions. They quickly learned that a city law required "advance public notice" before major street work could begin. A sign had to be posted thirty days before starting the work, warning the public of the upcoming project.

M asked if that included replacing a fire hydrant. The clerk said she was pretty sure it did, so M asked if she could check if a certain hydrant had been tagged like that. The woman said those records weren't computerized but she could check the paper files later.

M gave the lady her email address and the hydrant's location.

"If you do find records for it, could you maybe attach a copy of the notice, or at least a sample of one?"

The clerk said she would.

*   *   *

With Diana's dad out of town on business, their maid off for the day, and no one in the mood to cook, Ty made a Rubio's run for dinner, returning with rice, beans, and a dozen fish tacos. After divvying them up on paper plates, Ty grabbed his, bid everyone goodnight, and headed out the back patio door toward his place.

The kids ate poolside, glued to the 120-inch flat-screen TV

that, with the touch of a button, slid up from the ground like a submarine periscope. They watched a summer rerun of a show called *Subject of Interest*—about this space-age computer that knows when people are in danger before they know it, so the heroes can swoop in and rescue them. This episode involved a young taxi driver unaware his next customer was some crazed weirdo.

After the show ended, Diana whipped up three Dr. Pepper floats and popped a giant bowl of popcorn. Taking their treats upstairs, they spent most of the next hour sitting on the floor around Diana's coffee table, listening to pop music on the radio and gabbing about anything other than crashes and texts.

Until the top of the hour when the local news came on.

It was the second news item.

A two-alarm fire the previous night in Hollywood.

Inside a commercial building on Sunset.

At a place called Sam's Sports.

"Called in by a passing motorist just before midnight, the fire was confined to an interior storage area. No injuries were reported as the building was unoccupied at the time. But the 101 off-ramp at Sunset was temporarily closed while clean-up crews cleared the area. Access was restored several hours later, so the morning commute was not impacted. A spokesperson for the business confirmed that, since the fire was limited to a back storeroom, the store would likely re-open in a day or two."

Diana turned off the radio.

For several minutes no one spoke.

Finally, Jeffrey repeated those critical words from the report.

"'Just before midnight'…"

"The twelfth hour," said Diana.

M let out a groan. "We completely blew it. How could we forget there's *two* 'twelfth hours' in a day? We automatically went with noon, never even considered midnight."

"Clearly our detective skills need some fine-tuning," Jeffrey observed.

They munched quietly, mentally weighing what it all meant. Something bad had happened. *Again.*

Where and when that second text said it would. *Again.*

Jeffrey said it first. "Two coincidences, back-to-back?"

Diana nodded. "Aren't coincidences."

After a kitchen run for soda refills, more popcorn, and a jar of peanuts, they re-huddled in Diana's room around the coffee table.

"Okay, what actual facts do we have?" Diana asked.

Jeffrey started. "Well, two events in two days—a car crash and a fire."

M followed. "With advance warnings of both on Jeffrey's phone."

Added Diana, "From anonymous texts we got in my no-text cave."

Jeffrey got up and walked to one of the full-length windows. Gazing up at the night sky, he said, "So let's talk about that last one first. How could we get those texts in the cave? I see three possibilities…"

"Something to do with my cave," replied Diana.

"Or Jeffrey's phone," M said.

Jeffrey turned around. "Or someone's messin' with us."

M made a face. "Huh?"

He shrugged. "Hey, I'm just covering all the bases here. Is there a way someone could mess with us like that?" Addressing Diana, he asked, "How sure are you that you can't send or receive texts in the cave?"

"Well, didn't we prove that? I mean, our phones showed no service both times we were there. You guys even tried calling out that first day, but couldn't."

"True. But that's out-going. What about in-coming?"

"All I know is, in all the times I've been there, I've never gotten a call or text."

"Maybe no one's called or texted you there."

She shrugged. "Fair enough."

"I'm not saying you're wrong, just asking. I'm no phone

expert, I've had mine exactly four days. So help me out here. What normally happens when someone tries to send you a text when you're out of phone range?"

He looked from one to the other. "Not just in the cave. Anywhere. I mean, is it saved and then comes through later when your bars are back? Or does it somehow get through anyway, like on a different frequency? Or does it permanently die?"

The girls looked at each other.

"Pretty sure it's the first one," answered M. "It gets saved for later. But what's the difference? I mean, who cares how they got through? The fact is, they did. So shouldn't we be focused on how these things could get predicted in the first place?"

"Sure. But if we at least knew how they got to us in the cave, maybe that'd narrow things down."

"How?"

"Well, if you *could* somehow send a text in there, it might rule out a random text glitch or phone issue."

Diana sighed. "Maybe."

Jeffrey thought for a moment. "How about this? The next time we go there, one of us stops halfway while still in signal range and waits for the others to get to the cave, then tries to send them a text—and we see what happens."

Leave it to the phone newbie to come up with the simplest plan.

M nodded. "Sounds good. Except you should be the one who goes to the cave, since it's your phone that's been doing the freaky stuff. Diana and I can wait and then message you."

A splash outside interrupted their discussion. Before anyone got spooked, Diana explained, "It's Ty, doing his moon drills." She and M joined Jeffrey at the window. "That's what he calls it. His nightly pool laps."

Sure enough, there was Ty, gliding along from one end of the pool to the other. The rising steam blurred the underwater lighting, giving the scene a misty, dream-like glow. Mesmerized by Ty's graceful rhythm, the three stood there watching him slice effortlessly through the water, ending each lap with a smooth flip-turn.

After several lengths, Diana said, "Hey, let's run this new stuff about Sam's by him, see what he thinks."

She and M began gathering their goodies from the coffee table as Jeffrey, still watching Ty out the window, called out.

"Wait!"

The girls looked over.

Turning toward them, an innocent grin slowly spread across his face.

"You think while you guys do that... I could maybe test out the pool?"

Diana burst out laughing.

No matter what, the boy was still on vacation.

Chapter 22

While Jeffrey changed, the girls carried two trays of fresh snacks and water bottles out to the patio. By then, Ty was drying off.

It was another sweet LA summer night. Warm breeze, twinkling stars, chirping crickets, the faint scent of jasmine in the air. Jeffrey arrived minutes later and launched himself into the deep end. After splashing around for a while, he turned over and, arms spread wide, floated on his back studying the stars.

Meanwhile, the girls updated Ty on the fire at Sam's and their uncertainty over what to do next. When Jeffrey finally got out, toweled off, and joined them, Ty asked, "Can you show me the texts?"

"Well, that's a problem. They disappear. With no record of them."

Ty thought about that. "Are the two that sent you to the Malibu store and Sam's the only weird ones you've gotten?"

"Except for one at the airport. But that was a single character —a slashed zero—not an actual line of text like the others. I probably pressed a wrong key, which cleared when I re-booted."

Ty nodded, grabbing a handful of popcorn. "Okay, so let's break down both messages. Each has two parts: the text itself and the actual event." He chewed for a while. "Since the texts vanish, I don't see much you can do with that. I suppose you could try getting phone records to see if that leads anywhere. But it probably won't."

Diana asked, "So what do we do?"

"First, I agree with what you said Jeffrey thought of. See if you can send texts into the cave. You probably can't, but it's still worth checking. But that's about all you can do as far as the texts go. Except maybe preserve any new ones that might come. Take screenshots from another phone, showing dates and times. That way you've got proof of when you got them and what they said." He shrugged. "In case that ever matters."

They all nodded.

"Which leaves the actual events. That's where you need to focus."

"How?"

He didn't hesitate. "Find a connection."

"To what?"

"Look at it this way: Both incidents—the crash and the fire—are either random or not. And if they're random, nothing should connect them. But if they're not, then—"

Jeffrey finished for him. "—there must be a link."

"Exactly. Something tying them together."

"Like what?" asked Diana. "What's a crash outside a toy store got to do with a fire in a sports place a half dozen towns away?"

Ty shrugged again. "No clue." He stood up, holding both ends of the towel around his neck. "But if you do find a link…"—he smirked at Jeffrey—"then you've got one seriously spooky phone there, buddy."

He turned and started back toward his house, softly humming the theme to that old *Twilight Zone* show.

Da-da-duh-da. Da-da-duh-da.

As he and his haunting jingle faded into the night, the air grew eerily quiet—even the crickets had stopped. The only sound was the creepy trickle of the waterfall spilling into the pool.

Jeffrey stood up, tightened the towel around his waist, and with a slight shiver, murmured, "I think I need a hot shower."

That reminded M of the fire hydrant, which sparked another thought. "And I need to check my email!" she said, hurrying off to the house.

*   *   *

Upstairs, Jeffrey headed for the bathroom, Diana collapsed on her bed, and M signed into her Gmail account on Diana's computer. She spotted the message right away—from mlacy@malibustreets.com, the subject line reading "Hydrant on Pearl."

"Alright!" she shouted. "Our clerk pulled through."

That got Diana up from the bed and Jeffrey back from the

bathroom. As they stood over her shoulder watching, M opened the message and read it out loud.

"*'A records check confirms that the fire hydrant in question was scheduled for replacement. As per Malibu City Code 131-6, it was tagged with a 30-day notice on August 5th, copy attached.'*"

Clicking the PDF attachment, the image sharpened into focus line-by-line.

NOTICE OF STREET MAINTENANCE

City of Malibu—Street Department

Location: __2247 Pearl (Hydrant)__

Please be advised that on or after 30 days from the date listed below the above-referenced street maintenance work will be performed. Refer all objections and comments to: Street Department Hotline, City of Malibu: 800-555-8778.

This notice shall remain affixed to said location for 30 days. Malibu Municipal Code No: 131-6.

Dated: __Aug. 5, 2009__   __JH Renaldo__

As they read it, Jeffrey's eyes kept bouncing back to the giant exclamation mark in the middle, which for some reason made him think of that other eye-catching one he'd seen recently—that vertical bat over the baseball at the end of that Sam's sign. Not eye-catching in the same way as this one, but still unusual.

Then he remembered something else: Each text had an exclamation mark, and those were weird too. Not how they looked, but where they were placed. Neither was at the end of the text, where exclamation marks belonged. Both were just mixed in with the other characters, defeating the whole purpose of an exclamation mark.

He'd never seen that before. In fact, he'd never seen exclamation marks like *any* of these before. No bat-and-ball ones, no big-bold-circled ones, and never stuck between random characters.

Could that be the link Ty was talking about? Unlikely, but still...

A weird exclamation mark on this hydrant notice.

A weird exclamation mark on the Sam's sign.

A weirdly-placed exclamation mark in each text.

Was it all some cosmic connection?

Or had he just swallowed too much pool water?

Chapter 23

Thursday

Jeffrey

I woke up Thursday morning feeling like a rock star.

Diana had assigned M and me separate guest rooms. *Big* ones. And when you wake up on your oversized, feather-filled pillows, to sunlight filtering in through silk curtains over floor-to-ceiling windows, in a bed the size of a small island, while gazing up at giant ceiling beams embedded with shiny brass studs... well, you're either dreaming, or just got crowned king.

As I lay there soaking it all up, my mind replayed the last few days of my vacation: back-to-back beach trips, a secret cave, horseback riding, a mansion with a waterfall and golf course, crazy text messages, moonlight swims, and miles and miles of limo-cruising. Oh, and a car crash, store fire, and Attack of the Killer Exclamation Marks.

A whirlwind California adventure in three days!

My week was flying by.

I reached for my phone to check the time. 7:10. Since arriving in LA, I'd been waking up early like this every morning, no alarms needed—probably afraid of missing a single California minute.

After allowing myself one final celebrity stretch, I got up and tried to make my bed, but it was too big so I just covered everything with the comforter. In my attached bathroom, I brushed my teeth, spent ten heavenly minutes under three rainwater shower heads that gently massaged me from all directions, then got dressed and went downstairs, figuring I'd snoop around before everyone got up.

Wrong. The girls were already at Diana's dining table, carrying on a lively conversation while devouring impressive forkfuls of whipped-cream-covered waffle pieces. True multi-taskers.

When Diana saw me, she gestured with her fork toward the kitchen. Following her direction, I discovered two steaming golden waffles—the size of dinner plates—sitting inside a massive chrome waffle-maker on top of the kitchen island, with a wide assortment of breakfast goodies scattered nearby: sliced strawberries, diced pineapple, four different syrups, a platter of bacon, a pitcher of orange juice, utensils, glasses, plates, napkins, and an industrial-sized can of Reddi-Wip.

Breakfast in Brentwood. Yeah, I could get used to this, too.

As I prepared my waffles, I glanced across the room—and nearly dropped my plate. Built into the wall between an enormous black refrigerator and a complicated-looking coffee-making thing was an actual *brick pizza oven*. I mean, seriously, unless you're Joe Domino or Papa John, who has a full-sized pizza oven in their kitchen?

Returning to the dining room with my pineapple/strawberry/whipped-cream masterpiece, I commented to Diana, "Your dad must love pizza."

"Came with the house," she explained between bites.

As I set my plate down, Diana's phone buzzed. She clicked it to speaker and Ty's voice came on. He skipped the greeting. "Hey, guess where I just was?" In the background, we heard traffic noise.

"I'm guessing you're not out back?" Diana slurred through a blob of whipped cream.

"Couldn't sleep," Ty answered. "But I'm heading back now. From Hollywood. Actually, from Sam's Sports."

"You're kidding. Why?"

"Well, after our little poolside chat last night, I decided to take a ride to clear my head, still thinking how something felt off with Sam's the other day. I knew the store wouldn't be open—this early and right after the fire—but figured no harm driving by, maybe something would click. Then I saw a guy hosing down the lot and pulled in."

We heard a horn honk. After a short pause, Ty continued.

"So I told the guy I was an old customer and asked when the store would re-open. Tomorrow, by the way. And after some car talk

—I'm in the Lambo so that's hard to avoid—I asked if there'd been any changes to the store lately. A shot in the dark. I said something looked different. And guess what?"

Diana rolled her eyes at us. "You're killing me here, Ty! *What?*"

"Okay, hold on…" We heard his engine rev, then, "All good now… Anyway, the guy was new, started a week ago, so couldn't really tell me much… at first."

"*Ty!*" Diana screeched.

"Okay, okay. Turns out it's the sign out front."

I smacked my knee. "I knew it."

"Hey, mornin' JJ."

"Hi, Ty."

"Different how?" Diana asked.

"It's new. They put it up Monday."

The day before the fire.

"Why?" Diana asked.

"Well, that's all he knew. He wasn't working there when they took the old one down."

Diana exhaled in frustration.

"But I gotta say," Ty continued, "I don't see much difference. Far as I can tell, it looks like the old one. Shinier, newer, maybe slightly bigger, yeah. I guess that's what made me think something looked different. But, other than that, it's pretty much how I remember the old one. Just the store name, nothing fancy. Anyway, I'll be home soon. Adios, amigos."

When he clicked off, I rose from the table. "C'mon. Let's take our own look."

Upstairs in Diana's room, I located the two photos of Sam's we'd printed the night before—the ones I'd taken when we parked across the street. Both showed the Sam's sign but like Ty said, it looked pretty basic. *Sam's Sports!* Nothing that would explain why the old one needed replacing.

Handing the photos to M, I hurried to the computer and moved the mouse to activate the screen. While the girls stood behind me I brought up Google Maps and typed in *sams sports hollywood.*

101

Clicking Street View, the screen filled with a shot of the store. I pointed to the date. "Okay, Google took this one five months ago."

M held one of the paper photos next to the screen and we instantly spotted the difference.

The exclamation point.

The paper photos showed the bat-and-ball thing at the end of Sam's Sports, but the older Google shot didn't.

"That's what I flashed on last night when we saw that fire hydrant notice! That big circled exclamation point in the middle reminded me of the stupid bat-and-ball mark on this Sam's sign."

"Why?" M asked.

I shrugged. "I guess 'cause they're both... weird. For exclamation marks. The one on the sign's not even a real exclamation mark. It's a bat and ball. And the one on the hydrant notice isn't normal either. It's a big circled thing that doesn't even end a sentence. Neither's a regular punctuation mark. And now we know the one at Sam's got put up right before the fire. Just like the hydrant notice right before the crash."

I did my own eyebrow thing.

"And here's something else. Think about both texts we got. Each one *also* had an exclamation mark, and those weren't normal either. Instead of being at the end of the text like they should be, they were just stuck between the other letters and numbers."

Diana chewed on her cheek. "Okay, either this is getting crazy, or you are."

I would've loved to discuss my mental state with her in greater detail but my growling stomach reminded me of more pressing issues. "To be continued," I said, rising from my chair and heading downstairs to finish my breakfast.

Turns out, whipped-cream waffles are just as good cold (especially with extra syrup)—and packed the perfect energy punch I needed for my next big idea.

Charts.

Chapter 24

S eated around the dining table, the girls watched Jeffrey draw his first diagram. Using the black marker and paper Diana had given him, he spoke as he drew.

"When I can't figure something out, I put it on paper." He numbered three lines. "Okay, we know three things for sure about each event. One, what each text listed—an address in one, a phone number in the other. Two, where each bad thing happened. And three, that a weird exclamation point was involved."

When he finished writing, he spun his drawing around.

```
                        Toy Store
  _____

                                   Where at Scene?

  1. Text Message (2247 pearl )  =  _____

  2. Event (car crash)   =           _____

  3. Exclamation Point   =           _____
```

"This one's obviously for the car crash." He tapped each numbered line as he continued. "Number one comes directly from the text, in this case, it was the store's address. Number two is exactly where the event occurred, in this case, the crash. And number three is where each weird exclamation point was found at the scene.

The girls were impressed. They had no idea where this was going, but the kid was a killer chart-maker.

He tapped the address on the first line. "Okay, where on the scene did we find this address?" He answered his own question. "Above the store's front door, right?" He wrote Store Entrance in the first blank.

He tapped the second blank. "The exact location of the car crash is easy since it destroyed that fire hydrant." He wrote Fire Hydrant in that blank.

"And now we know the weird exclamation point was also on the hydrant, on that hanging notice." He wrote Fire Hydrant in the third blank. Tilting his head back, he added check marks by the two matching entries before turning the chart around.

Toy Store		
	Where at Scene?	
1. Phone Clue (_2247 pearl_) =	**Store Entrance**	
2. Event (car crash) =	**Fire Hydrant**	✓
3. Exclamation Point =	**Fire Hydrant**	✓

He pointed to the check marks. "These last two—where the car crashed and where we found the weird exclamation point—both match." He tapped the top one. "But not this one. The store address was above the front door." He looked up. "Close, but no match."

After staring at his entries for a few seconds, he slid it aside and began drawing a second chart labeled Sam's, filling in the blanks without narration.

When he finished, he crinkled his lips.

"This one's worse."

He added question marks at the end of all three rows before turning it around.

```
                         Sam's
   _____

                                   Where at Scene?

   1. Text Message → 323 555 6869 = Front Show room ?

   2. Event (fire)           =      Back Store room ?

   3. Exclamation Point      =      Outside (on sign) ?
```

He tapped the first row. "Okay, the second text we got listed the store's phone number, which I'm guessing is on the phones in their showroom." He tapped the second row. "But according to that news report, the fire was in a back storeroom." He pointed to the third row. "And the weird exclamation point was on their sign outside."

He blew out a breath. "Zero matches. Showroom in front. Storeroom in back. Sign outside. All in or around the store, but not as exact as the fire hydrant matches."

Glancing from chart to chart, he frowned. "Two out of three matches for the toy store and none really for Sam's." He shrugged. "So much for charting it out." He pushed away both diagrams.

Diana said, "Not trying to be a pain here, and I love your charts, but remind us why we care if these things match?"

"Links! Like Ty said. If important parts of each incident somehow match, the texts aren't random."

Diana nodded. "Got it."

"So now what?" asked M.

The answer was obvious: back to the cave—for lots of

reasons. There was plenty of morning left; they still needed to do their text-to-cave experiment; and they might even get a new text offering more clues.

But mostly because this puzzle had already hooked them.

Chapter 25

Forty minutes after Diana somehow sweet-talked Ty into taking them back to Zuma, they were on the road again—swimsuits under their clothes, beach bags stowed in the trunk.

Jeffrey's third beach trip in four days!

When they hit PCH, Ty lowered the radio volume and made eye contact with M in his mirror. "You said you shoot hoops, right?"

"Yep," she beamed.

"That's my sport too. Did you see the court at the house?"

"No way."

"Behind the tennis courts."

Of course it was.

"So how 'bout some two-on-two sometime? I'll even take Diana," he joked.

"You're on," M shot back

Diana groaned. "Thanks, but I'd rather pour salt in my eyes."

Ty chuckled before he and M dove into a healthy round of basketball chatter—M describing what crazed Lakers fans she and her mom were, and Ty confessing he was too. But when the two started debating all-time best NBA players, Jeffrey and Diana—lost in what sounded more like Martian—just tuned them out.

In the Zuma parking lot, M got out first. Walking up to Ty's window, she held out her phone display. "That's my mom, on the right. From last year."

He took the phone and studied it. "She's very pretty."

"Thanks. Maybe you and Diana could come over sometime for dinner."

He grinned, handing it back. "Maybe so."

Sensing the others watching, she quickly stuffed her phone away and, offering a weak shrug, pretended she hadn't just tried setting Ty up with her mom.

After thanking Ty for taking them, they grabbed their bags and headed for the sand. On the way through the lot, they passed a parked car with a man sitting in the driver's seat eating a sandwich. The girls continued on but Jeffrey had to stop because a large white seagull was perched on the car's hood watching the guy eat.

It looked like a cartoon—man and bird three feet apart, separated by a windshield, staring each other down like a cowboy showdown. Guy chewing, gull glaring.

Jeffrey whipped out his phone and snapped two quick shots. They'd never believe this back home. You couldn't make this stuff up.

He caught up with the girls at the high-tide line. As they strolled north toward the cave, Diana told them late mornings were her favorite time at the beach. The Goldilocks Hours, she called it. Not too hot, not too cold—late enough for the marine layer to burn off, early enough for the sand not to be scorching hot yet.

Halfway to the cave, they all whipped out their phones.

"I've still got three bars," Diana said. She turned to Jeffrey. "We'll wait here. You go on." She checked her display. "It's 10:12. It should take you, what, fifteen minutes?"

Jeffrey nodded. "Tops."

"Okay, we'll text you from here at 10:30." As he headed out, she yelled, "Don't mess up my cave."

Jeffrey made it in twelve, his phone showing 10:24.

Spreading his towel across the rock ledge, he climbed up. It felt weird being in the cave alone, like he was invading Diana's privacy. Positioning his phone on his towel, he turned his attention to the tiny waves trickling in and out as the sunlight twinkled off them.

No wonder Diana loved this place. He hadn't felt this relaxed since, well, last time he was here. Smiling to himself, he watched a distant ship glide across the horizon, losing track of time.

Until his phone lit up.

The no-service icon flashed, quickly followed by a new text. This time no addresses or phone numbers, just a hodgepodge of characters. Diana must've punched in random keys.

S M L G T 1 4 ! 4

A short time later he heard the girls jump down from the rocks. When they entered, Diana eagerly looked at him.

"Well?"

"Got it!" He held up his screen.

The girls moved in closer to look, then exchanged glances.

"What?" he asked.

Diana frowned. "That's not what I sent."

She explained they'd sent two messages, seconds apart, each a single word. Text1. Text2. Nothing like the gibberish on his screen. Which meant either her texts got badly jumbled, or this wasn't hers.

M took a picture of it, preserving the date and time as Ty instructed. She pointed to the timestamp. "It was sent at 10:38, eight minutes after we sent ours."

Diana nodded. "By then we were three-quarters here, out of cell range."

Jeffrey considered that. "Well, at least that proves what we wanted to know: texts don't get through."

Diana shrugged. "At least not ours." She motioned to Jeffrey's screen. "Look, it's gone." She turned to M. "Let me see your screenshot again."

They passed it around but no one could make sense of it. Just a random jumble of characters. Still, they'd accomplished what they came for. They'd completed their text-to-cave test, and now had a fresh text to analyze (which even if not ringing any bells now, might later). So, with no reason to stay, they packed up and left.

Chapter 26

Ty picked them up an hour later, blaming the delay on a big lunch and "an important game" he had to finish watching at a nearby sports bar. So by the time they got back to Brentwood, everyone but Ty was starving. Apparently, fruity waffles don't last. Who knew?

That meant the first order of business was food, which Diana organized with a three-station assembly line at the kitchen counter, the trio pumping out three PB&J's in under three minutes—a likely world record.

Taking their paper plates upstairs, they gathered around M at the computer. On the way home, they'd recited their new text to Ty, but he couldn't make sense of it either, so a Google search seemed like a good place to start. Balancing her plate in her lap, M brought up the search box and typed in the text from memory—S M L G T 14 ! 4.

When that produced no usable results, she tried every variation they could think of, but still came up empty. Frustrated, she pushed the mouse aside and began working on her sandwich.

Diana and Jeffrey walked to the couch to work on theirs. When they all finished, Diana said, "Hey, how 'bout a tour out back? Maybe it'll recharge our batteries."

*　　*　　*

"Out back"—Diana's ridiculously modest term for the rear portion of the estate—seemed to go on forever. Only half-joking, Jeffrey asked where the electric golf carts were.

They walked past Ty's house, around the tennis and basketball courts, and eventually down a flower-lined path. Every so often, Diana would stop to identify different plant species for them.

Over a slight incline, they finally saw where she was taking them. A shimmering body of water, double the size of the tennis court, curved around a small grassy bluff.

Diana's Pond.

Guiding them to a slice of green near the water's edge, they sat on the plushest grass Jeffrey had ever felt. As a dozen or so ducks and geese glided by, Diana called some out by name. It was another "pinch me, Toto" moment for Jeffrey. Counting geese in a backyard pond in Brentwood, California.

After several blissful minutes sitting and staring, Jeffrey kicked off his shoes and stretched out, gazing up at a tiny cloud directly overhead. M finally broke the silence.

"Hey, how's Uncle Eddie doing?" She whispered to Diana that Eddie was Jeffrey's dad and that his parents were getting divorced.

"You do know I'm right here," Jeffrey reminded her, still focused on the cloud, "and can hear everything you're saying." After an awkward delay, he finally answered. "I dunno. We haven't talked lately."

"Why?"

"Why do you think? He moved out."

"Has he called you since then?"

Jeffrey sat up and looked across the pond, nodding slowly. "Yeah. But I haven't answered."

"Why not?"

He shrugged. "What's the point? He'll just feed me the same old parent lines. 'It's for the best.' 'It's complicated.' Blah-de-blah."

Diana wasn't sure whether to intrude. It certainly wasn't her business, but she did have feelings on the subject. Finally, she said softly, "Maybe you should try."

When Jeffrey looked at her, she smiled warmly. "I'll shut up if you want, but I do speak from experience." When he didn't object, she continued. "When my parents split up, I was furious. But then I started asking questions, to each one separately. I told them they owed me answers, that their actions hurt me as much as them, maybe more. That I had a right to be involved."

Plucking a few blades of grass, she blew them away. "Things changed after that. They began opening up, treating me like a person, and I started treating them differently too. I realized they were two good people struggling to do the best they could. But mostly I realized they both loved me no matter what." Her head tilted. "Just saying."

M stared at her. The girl was full of surprises, sharing such a touchingly intimate story. She turned to her cousin. "I agree. Maybe you should give him a chance. Tell him how you feel, instead of staying angry and bottling it all up. Uncle Eddie's a good guy, he'll get it."

Jeffrey didn't reply. Lying back on the grass, he laced his hands behind his head and refocused on the cloud. No one had ever talked to him the way the girls did. It actually felt good. Much better than always trying to handle things alone.

"Maybe," he said softly.

Things got quiet after that, each of them returning to their own little worlds. Almost like at the cave—except for the grass and trees and sky and ducks.

Ten minutes later, they walked back.

*　　　*　　　*

M stood at the window in Diana's room looking out at the grounds they'd just toured. Diana's trick had worked; she felt fully refreshed. On the couch, Jeffrey and Diana kept their distance, quietly discussing the differences between geese and ganders—giving M plenty of space to do her mental magic.

As M panned across the colorful view before her, something about the first five letters of that text—S M L G T—started nibbling at her brain. Despite finding nothing during her computer search, she'd seen those letters somewhere. Her gaze swept from Ty's house, past the flower fields, to the pool. The blinding sunlight reflecting off the surface of the water made her squint.

Which triggered something.

She closed her eyes and cleared her thoughts, imagining those five letters, nudging that just-out-of-reach memory closer. Hundreds of images began spinning in her head, like a Wheel of Fortune, fast at first, before gradually slowing down.

Until one finally snapped into place.

"The tower!" she gasped, rushing back to the computer. Diana and Jeffrey hurried over.

Opening a new browser window, she typed *santa monica beach* in the search box. When the results appeared, she clicked the Images option. The window filled with thumbnails—beach scenes from different angles, most showing the ocean shimmering in the sunlight much like the pool scene outside that had triggered her breakthrough.

Sometimes the strangest things sparked the Mega-Mind.

Scrolling down, she found the angle she wanted and clicked it. It was a wide shot of the beach—white sand, sparkling ocean, the Pier and Ferris wheel on the left.

But M was focused on the right side of the image, where a familiar wooden structure stood in the sand facing the water.

The lifeguard tower.

She turned to the others, her face beaming like a pirate uncovering treasure. Jeffrey and Diana exchanged baffled looks.

"Okaaaay…" Diana said slowly. "That's Santa Monica Beach. Got it. But—" She glanced at the other open browser window still displaying the five letters from the text. "Oh, I get it. You think those first two letters, the S M, mean 'Santa Monica.' But they could mean anything. Silver Marbles. Silly Meatballs."

"Sexy Mama," Jeffrey added, grinning like an idiot.

"Plus," Diana continued, "that ignores the rest of it—the other letters and the numbers on both sides of the exclamation point."

But M wasn't fazed. Diana had obviously missed it. So she adjusted the photo, bringing the rear of the lifeguard station front and center, then zoomed in. That's all it took. They both saw it. Stenciled in big black letters across the back of the tower:

S M L G T 9

"And that," M announced, "stands for 'Santa Monica Lifeguard Tower Number 9.' They're on every one. I've passed them a million times. *That's* why it seemed familiar."

She pointed to the nine at the end. "This one is obviously

Tower 9, so our text must mean Tower 14."

Diana stared at the picture, speechless, her friend's brain once again blowing her own brain.

A few beats later Jeffrey asked, "So does the four at the end mean the time again, the fourth hour?"

M shrugged. She thought back to the time-blooper they'd made with the Sam's text. "If it does, let's hope it's 'p.m.' so we don't have to sneak out tonight."

Jeffrey pointed to the time display at the bottom of the screen. "It's 3:04. So if it does mean four, we're running out of time."

"Don't worry," Diana said. "Santa Monica's close."

"Except we can't ask Ty again," Jeffrey said. "He just took us to Zuma."

But Diana called him anyway, using the excuse of updating him on M's new find, and her timing was perfect. Ty was walking out the door on his way to meet with his agent, whose Wilshire Boulevard office was a few blocks from the Pier.

Ten minutes later they were driving down San Vincente, M and Jeffrey's overnight bags stowed in the trunk for their eventual trip back to the Valley.

Jeffrey mentally notched up yet another beach trip—*four* now since Monday. Their second that day!

TGFT.

Thank God for Ty.

Chapter 27

Jeffrey

Ty dropped us off in front of a parking lot blocked by a "Lot Full" sign, promising to call in an hour with his ETA update.

After three trips to Zuma, I expected other beaches would be similar. Wrong again. Santa Monica was nothing like Zuma. Sure, both were awesome. But Santa Monica had bigger crowds, more sand, smaller waves, and even more things going on than at Zuma.

Besides the famous pier (according to Google, the first concrete one on the West Coast), it had a Ferris wheel, rides, shops, boardwalk, and an interesting blend of tourists and locals.

Since we still had time (Diana was right, it took sixteen minutes to get there), we hit the snack bar first—fries, cokes, and three giant pretzels—before heading off for Tower 14.

Threading through bodies and beach towels, we passed an old guy with a scraggly beard sitting cross-legged alone in the sand. He was barefoot but in street clothes, and staring blankly out to sea. What drew my attention was the towel spread out in front of him. On it, six large yellow onions were arranged in two neat rows. Next to them, a white paper plate with black-marker scrolling read: *Free Onions.*

I am not making this up.

The guy made no effort to offer them to anyone, just continued gazing off in the general direction of Hawaii. Naturally, I had to stop and stare. Another "only in LA" scene. Like the man-and-seagull show at Zuma.

Pulling out my phone, I snapped a shot to add to my you'll-never-believe-this collection.

I caught up with the girls not far from Tower 14. Directly in front of it, a six-foot-wide roped-off path—which I assumed was an emergency lane for the lifeguards—led down to the water. Nearby, a red rescue board stuck straight up in the sand like some exotic space cactus. A few feet away, two vehicles—a jeep and a four-wheeler—sat ready for action.

Planting ourselves a few yards south of the emergency lane, we set up our stuff with military precision. Towels. Food and drinks. Phones.

Once completed, I dropped to my towel to scope things out while the girls peeled off their street clothes, squeezed on sunscreen, and took their places next to me. Three warriors ready for action.

The only question was for what?

I suggested we employ the roving-eye technique: pan left, pan right, rinse and repeat. If you've ever seen one of those Felix-the-Cat wall clocks, with the eyeballs that click back and forth, you know the drill. Beach Surveillance 101.

Five minutes later my eye sockets ached so badly I needed a break. Grabbing my phone, I stood up and, circling the girls, captured shots in all directions—west to the water, east to the boardwalk, north and south along the sand.

Back at my towel, I realized I was the only male in sight with his shirt on. So as casually as possible I slipped it off. Unfortunately, it's hard being casual when your skin's almost the color of Ty's teeth. Thankfully, my companions were too busy eye-roving to notice.

After slathering on sun lotion, I resumed my beach patrol but immediately spotted the problem: way too much action. Everywhere. Families lounging under giant umbrellas. Toddlers building sand castles. Seagulls attacking leftovers by the trash cans. Three jocks tossing a football. A couple playing Frisbee. And more shiny-skinned California Girls than I'd ever seen.

And that was just the sand. The water was equally distracting. Body surfers, boogie boarders, kids on floats, and in a surfing-only zone—marked with flags in the sand—a dozen surfers sat on their boards patiently waiting for the next set.

Even the sky buzzed with activity. A biplane skimmed low over the water, towing a giant yellow sign announcing Happy Hour at a local club, while a news helicopter cruised in the opposite direction filming the crowd.

Suddenly a flash of red streaked by. A lifeguard in red trunks, sprinting full-speed down the emergency lane, snatching the rescue board mid-stride.

I tried to see where he was going, but only saw people playing in the waves. Then M yelled, "Look!" pointing past the swimmers to a fuzzy arm waving back and forth, barely visible over the choppy water.

We jumped up to join the crowd forming at the waterline. Hurdling over several small breakers, the lifeguard slid onto his board and began power-paddling toward the waving arm. Squinting into the sun, I glimpsed a head attached to the outstretched arm. Then a second head nearby. Two boys, one trying to help the other, both clearly in trouble.

A super loud buzzing exploded from somewhere on my left. Turning toward the noise, I saw a second lifeguard on a Jet Ski zooming around the Pier toward the struggling pair.

By the time the Jet Ski finally closed in, the lifeguard on the rescue board had scooped both boys onto his board. Handing his tow line up to the Jet Ski driver, who then secured it to an eye-hole in back, they all slowly motored toward shore, the first lifeguard swimming alongside the board to keep the kids from rolling off.

As they headed in, the jeep I'd seen parked earlier in the emergency lane skidded to a stop in the wet sand directly in front of us, forcing back the crowd. A third lifeguard jumped out, grabbed a walkie-talkie and binoculars, stood on the jeep's running board, and began tracking the Jet Ski and board. Once they got to waist-deep water, the jeep guy tossed his gear into his vehicle and waded out to meet them. Plucking the smaller kid from the board, he carried him to the sand while the original lifeguard helped the older one in.

Only then did I remember to breathe.

I'd lost all sense of time. The whole rescue might've taken ten minutes or ten seconds, I had no idea. It's impossible to describe the emotions racing through you when a life-and-death scene unfolds before you like that. Fear. Shock. Awe. All wrapped together.

Then something equally amazing happened. The crowd spontaneously began to clap, shooting chills down my spine. Total strangers celebrating two lives saved and the heroes who saved them.

No one thinks about what these lifeguards do every single day until you witness something like that.

As my heart rate began to slow, the applause died down and the crowd began to disburse. Back to blankets, boards, and fun in the sun.

Just another day at the beach.

Chapter 28

Returning to their beach site, the girls began to pack. They'd seen what they came for, time to go. As they shook the sand off their towels Jeffrey took another look around. Everything seemed pretty much back to normal, people resuming their pre-rescue activities. Yet something wasn't right.

"Hold on."

M continued stuffing her towel into her bag. "What?"

Jeffrey checked the time on his phone. 4:28.

"Let's stay a little longer."

They'd heard that line before.

"Why?" asked Diana. She motioned to the two boys still with the lifeguards. "We just confirmed our 'event of the day.' Which, if you're keeping track, makes three-for-three—three cave texts, three bad events."

Jeffrey looked around again. "I'm not so sure. Can't we relax for a while? It hasn't even been an hour. Ty won't be ready." He gave them a what's-the-harm? shrug.

Blowing out two exaggerated sighs, the girls re-spread their towels and dropped back down. Smiling at their dramatics, Jeffrey resumed his Felix-the-Cat surveillance as the now-familiar sounds of beach life kicked back in. Seagulls, kids, music, waves. A few minutes later the afternoon sea breeze started up and he happily put his shirt back on.

As the two rescued boys finally left the lifeguards, Jeffrey swiveled east in their direction, discovering a whole new scene worth watching: the boardwalk.

The Santa Monica Boardwalk, a ten-foot-wide stretch of cement separating Pacific Coast Highway from the beach, was crammed with every form of transportation but cars. Scooters, skateboarders, walkers, joggers, bikers, roller-bladers—all somehow sharing the same space without demolishing each other (despite many close calls).

Jeffrey even spotted a group of Segway riders—those two-wheeled motorized things he'd never actually seen in action before—zigzagging through the crowd. With their huge tires raising them a foot above everyone else, they looked like a pack of robotic ostriches weaving through the masses. He wondered how they stayed upright without falling forward, which probably explained the helmets.

Once he lost sight of them, his eyes drifted to the highway buzzing with traffic on the far side of the boardwalk. A half-block down, a light-controlled crosswalk stretched across the lanes to keep jaywalkers from becoming road-kill. Two groups of pedestrians stood on opposite sides waiting for the light to change. On the near side, heading away from the beach with their backs toward him, Jeffrey noticed a woman in a motorized wheelchair.

What caught his attention was the color of the lady's wheelchair. Red. *Really* bright red. Every inch of it. Seat cushions, spokes, armrests, even the hook in back holding her purse and shopping bag. The over-the-top color saturation reminded him of Sam's Sports. Blinding blue there, raging red here.

Only in LA.

When the traffic light turned, stopping the cars in both directions, the lady in the red wheelchair began motoring across with everyone else. That's when Jeffrey noticed a bearded guy in the other group, crossing from the far side toward the beach. He wasn't sure why the guy stood out, something just seemed off. And when both groups crossed paths in the middle, Jeffrey's hunch proved right.

As the Beard passed the lady's wheelchair, he casually slipped her purse off the back hook in one smooth motion, dropped it into the unzipped backpack at his side, and continued on without missing a beat.

He was so easy-peasy about it, no one in either group seemed to notice, including the wheelchair lady who kept rolling to the far side without a clue.

At first Jeffrey was too stunned to move. Like those first paralyzing seconds on the bus bench when the hydrant exploded. Had he really seen what he thought he'd seen? Surely someone would do something.

But no one did.

The thief continued across the street, turning left on the boardwalk, then casually looking around a few paces later to see if he'd attracted any attention. Satisfied he hadn't, he paused, zipped up his backpack, slung it over his shoulder, hopped the low boardwalk wall, and headed for the water. When he reached the wet sand, he turned south toward the Pier.

Just another guy enjoying a walk on the beach.

It all happened much faster than it sounds. A minute or two at most. Jeffrey swiveled around, locating the woman across the highway slowly fading away. Turning back toward the water, he watched the bearded guy stroll down the shore, not a care in the world.

That's when Jeffrey's inner Thor kicked in. Before he realized what he was doing, he shot up off his towel, eyes bouncing between thief and lady. "M, quick, I need you!" he yelled.

Startled, she jumped up. He pointed east. "See that lady in the wheelchair? Catch her! She just got robbed! I'll get the lifeguard. Take your phone, I'll call you."

M squinted, shielding her eyes with her hands, then without a word grabbed her phone and took off. No panic, no questions.

Spinning around, Jeffrey almost bumped into Diana who, hearing his frantic commands, was already up and ready. "Does your phone have a zoom?" he asked. Two quick nods. He pointed to the thief sauntering down the waterline. "See the guy with the backpack and beard? Keep your eyes on him. Get video if you can, but zoom from here. Do *not* go after him!"

He stepped back. Searching east again, he could barely make out the wheelchair lady, now a fuzzy red dot. Scanning the boardwalk for M, he found her at the traffic light, impatiently hopping up and down, ready to launch across the highway the second the light changed.

Sprinting the few yards to Tower 14, Jeffrey screamed up for help. The same lifeguard who'd driven the jeep during the rescue hopped down as Jeffrey—frantically pointing east, then south, then east again—babbled on about a robbery, a bearded guy, a lady in a wheelchair, a purse, and a backpack.

Luckily, lifeguards must take special classes to deal with crazy people because, before Jeffrey could finish, the guy was already on his four-wheeler racing after the Beard. Jeffrey rushed back to Diana, who was still tracking the thief with her phone. Standing beside her, they watched the lifeguard's ATV whine down the wet sand, red lights flashing. The commotion had drawn another crowd, everyone off their towels, glued to the action as if watching a movie.

Turning east, Jeffrey spotted M. She'd caught up with the lady and was kneeling beside her, talking. Waving to her, he grabbed his phone and punched in her number. She answered right away. Quickly, he laid out the facts—the purse theft and ongoing chase—which M relayed to the lady.

By the time he hung up, the two had turned around and were heading back to the beach. As he pocketed his phone, Diana nudged him.

The chase was over. The lifeguard had intercepted the guy just north of the Pier, and the conversation didn't look friendly—the lifeguard pointing to the backpack, the thief shaking his head.

When the lifeguard began speaking into his radio, the Beard abruptly looked eastward toward M and the lady, both now at the crosswalk waiting for the light. Jeffrey thought the guy might take off.

Until motion in the parking lot turned his head. Two police cars were pulling in, light bars flashing.

Game over, bro.

*　　　*　　　*

Forty-five minutes later, the cops had finished their questions, the bad guy had been taken away in a police car, and the beach had thinned out. A new crowd—in shirts, shorts, and sandals, carrying folded beach chairs and plastic cups—was now settling in for the nightly sunset ritual.

But all the three young detectives wanted to do was go home. Dragging themselves to the parking lot, Ty was waiting by the Rolls.

"I'm sensing a pattern here, guys. The Three Musketeers appear; cops and craziness follow." He opened the rear door for them.

"Yeah, we noticed," Diana huffed.

As they drove off, Jeffrey sighed. "I think we made the news. A lady and photographer asked questions and took pictures. How'd they get there so fast?"

Diana shrugged. "Maybe we'll be on TMZ."

On the way home, they described the whole scene to Ty. The brazen theft in the crosswalk, the guy caught red-handed with the lady's purse, the twelve hundred dollars in rent money still in her purse, the thief hauled away in handcuffs, and the spectacular teamwork involved: Diana tracking the guy, M catching the lady, Jeffrey quarterbacking it all.

Sylvia, the sweet little wheelchair lady, had even offered them a reward, but they'd refused. Being treated like heroes, even while pretending it was no big deal, was way better than money.

After they finished their story, Diana turned to Jeffrey. "How'd you know?"

"Huh?"

"That the text wasn't about those rescued kids?"

He rubbed the back of his neck. "Not sure. Just didn't feel right. It wasn't the same as the others. We could've stopped those—the car crash, the store fire—if we'd only figured things out in time. Maybe warned the dog owner, or the people at Sam's.

"But it was different with those kids. They would've been saved whether we got that text or not. Thanks to those awesome lifeguards." He shrugged. "Guess I was looking for something *we* could've stopped this time." He grinned. "And we sure found it."

Diana looked at him. "And you figured all that out in, like, seconds?" She shook her head. "Once again, Mr. James, I *am* impressed."

He tried not to smile, but his face turned the color of Sylvia's wheelchair.

*   *   *

123

That night at dinner the Santa Monica incident never came up because Susan kept asking about their sleepover. So instead of cops and criminals, they covered duck ponds, pizza ovens, and periscoping TVs. Which was fine. After the Malibu thing, Susan didn't need any more scary stories.

Later, back in the guesthouse, Diana called, suggesting they find something "fun but less stressful" to do before Jeffrey went home. "Like, how 'bout the observatory?"

She was of course referring to the Griffith Observatory, the world-famous astronomy center, not far from the Valley. M, who'd been listening on speakerphone, was up for it, but also offered another possibility. "Or the La Brea Tar Pits."

Jeffrey had never heard of that, so M gave him the quick lowdown. "Once upon a time when dinosaurs roamed LA, they'd get stuck in these giant pools of oil and die. So being LA, they just turned the whole thing into a museum."

She winked. "Trust me, it's creepy *and* cool. Big gooey dinosaur skeletons, your kinda place. But so's the observatory."

Since Jeffrey couldn't decide between outer space or dinosaur bones, the girls chose for him: both! The observatory in the morning, and the Tar Pits on Saturday.

Sadly, they never made it to the Tar Pits.

Chapter 29

Friday

The morning sun cast a pink glow across the kitchen table as M and Jeffrey munched Frosted Flakes. Much less exotic than yesterday's Brentwood breakfast, but who can resist Tony the Tiger?

Ten minutes earlier, Diana had called to say Ty was on board with the observatory—actually excited—and they were on their way.

With Aunt Susan already gone, the breakfast conversation quickly turned to yesterday's event at Santa Monica. Jeffrey was convinced it was connected to the other two incidents and that, despite his disappointing charts, they just had to find the magic link. M, however, wasn't so sure. After thinking more about it overnight, she'd begun questioning whether the Sylvia thing really had anything to do with that last text.

"It doesn't fit," she said through a mouthful of flakes. "Think about it. The text listed the tower number, not some purse-snatch in a PCH crosswalk. So even if it was another warning, wouldn't it be pointing us to that lifeguard station?"

Decent point.

She also questioned the timing.

"How can you be sure the bad stuff hadn't already happened before we got there? Or during the purse snatch? Or after?"

But Jeffrey had answers for that.

"Remember how everyone on the beach knew right away when those kids were getting rescued? Same for when the lifeguard chased down the bad guy. The whole beach watched both events. News travels fast there. So even if something bad happened *before* we got there, don't you think we would've heard about it?

"And if it happened *during* the Sylvia thing, we would've seen it, since we were all on high alert then. And if it happened *after,* it would've been past the 'fourth hour.'"

After more cereal-crunching, Jeffrey asked, "You notice any strange-looking exclamation points anywhere? Maybe on the tower or near it?" M shook her head. "Me neither. But we should look into that. Weird exclamation points are still the only thing even remotely connecting everything. I took pictures we can check later."

M finished her cereal, rinsed her bowl in the sink, then turned to Jeffrey. "I hate to say it, but it seems like our best play here is back to the cave. I know we keep doing that, but every time we do, we get another text—and more texts might lead to more clues."

Jeffrey nodded. "Let's bring it up at the observatory."

As if on cue, the doorbell rang. When M opened the door, she was surprised to see Ty standing by Diana instead of waiting in the limo. "Hey, thanks for taking us today," she told him, noticing a newspaper tucked under his arm.

"No problem. It'll be fun. Been ages since I've been there." He grinned. "Plus my calendar's pretty flexible."

M smirked. "Wanna trade lives for a while?"

In the kitchen, Ty walked to the table and unfolded his newspaper by Jeffrey's placemat. "Thought you guys'd like this."

M leaned in to read it. It was a thin neighborhood weekly called *The Brentwood Times*. Ty pointed near the bottom of the front page. "All hail our new heroes. Amazing how fast the hometown press finds 'news' when it involves a Brentwoodian."

Jeffrey looked up at Diana. *"Brentwoodian?"*

She shrugged. "Works for me."

The article was titled *With A Little Help From Her Friends— Local Teen Helps Catch Purse Thief*. Five paragraphs long, it described yesterday's big show at Santa Monica. How the three had saved sweet little Sylvia and her rent money, and helped the lifeguards get the bad guy. A statement followed from a Santa Monica Police Department spokesperson. The young heroes would be presented with Good Citizen Awards the following week (too bad Jeffrey would be back in Iowa). Next to the article was a photograph. The caption read:

Brentwood resident Diana Young, top left, with friends Margaret and Jeffrey, behind a grateful Sylvia Davis and lifeguard Albert Lee

Apparently, only adults and Brentwoodians rated last names in *The Brentwood Times.*

The picture showed the group smiling in front of Tower 14—Diana, Jeffrey, and M standing behind Sylvia in her red wheelchair with the lifeguard kneeling beside her. Albert and his fellow lifeguards had been nice enough to lug that heavy chair over the sand to the tower and back for the photos.

It was a great shot. The three of them in back, grinning ear to ear, arms wrapped around each other's shoulders, and cute little Sylvia in front cheerfully displayed her recovered purse while Albert the lifeguard looked on with that noble I-save-lives stare.

When they finished reading, Diana refolded the paper and handed it to M. "We can enjoy our media fame later. But right now we've got a date with the Universe, so stash this somewhere for our grandkids and we'll meet you outside."

*   *   *

The Griffith Observatory, the most visited observatory in the world (and, to Jeffrey's amazement, *free*), sits atop thousand-foot-high Mount Hollywood, overlooking the Greater LA Basin. And for two solid hours the foursome explored everything they could—from the five-ton, "most looked-through telescope on the planet," to the massive pendulum that tracked the Earth's rotation inch by inch.

Eventually though, they ran out of steam and retreated to the observatory's restaurant, aptly named The Cafe at the End of the Universe. For the next half hour, over coffee for Ty and grilled cheeses for the kids, they oohed and aahed about all the exhibits. When they were finally ready to leave, Jeffrey casually brought up returning to the cave. And to everyone's surprise, Ty agreed, confessing he'd been craving lobster bisque soup from his favorite cantina in Point Dume, two miles from Zuma.

So while the kids did their cave thing, he'd do his soup thing.

Chapter 30

The trip from the observatory to Zuma took fifty minutes. Record time for Friday in LA, though that had more to do with Ty's lobster-bisque craving than light traffic.

With no beach gear, they improvised—rolling up pant legs, plastic bags for shoes and socks, a blanket from the trunk for the cave. Diana even found some unused Hamburger Hamlet matches in the glove box for her candles.

But it wasn't until the Rolls drove off that Jeffrey realized what was missing.

The sun.

Back at the observatory, the weather had been perfect. Blue sky, no clouds, unlimited views. Nothing like the scene here today. Gray, misty, overcast. Words Jeffrey never associated with the beach.

But he knew what it was. The dreaded marine layer had arrived. That mysterious weather pattern which, until now, he'd only heard rumors of. It supposedly burned off by mid-morning, but not today, and from the looks of it, not anytime soon.

Not that it stopped the surfers. Just the opposite. There were twice as many as on previous days and the reason was obvious:

Surf's up, Dude! Gnarly waves!

Bigger, louder, and faster than anything Jeffrey had seen. Pounding the shore with such force they made the ground shake, spraying seawater everywhere. Mother Nature at her finest.

By the time they reached the rock formation, Jeffrey was soaked. When he got to the top, he paused to drip-dry and enjoy the view. Gazing out, he noticed a single pelican flying low over the water. It was the first time he'd seen one alone like that instead of in those impressive group formations. And for some reason, it looked sad. He wasn't sure why. Maybe it was the gray gloomy sky shading the scene. Or maybe it reminded him of how lonely things got back home.

A split second later the bird dropped like a rock into the water, popping back up with a fish in its beak. Jeffrey smiled. He'd completely misjudged that solo flight. It had nothing to do with being sad or lonely. It was about taking care of business.

Watching the bird fly off, a strange sensation washed over him: a pleasant one, like a weight lifting. As if all the negatives in his life were slowly slipping away—the loneliness, his parents' divorce, moving from the present to the past.

This week had given him a new sense of confidence. And now, standing over this endless ocean, it all became clear: that everything would be okay. Divorced or not, both his parents would survive and always be there to love and support him. Just as he too would survive—no, *thrive*—no matter the situation.

He smiled to himself, thinking of that diving bird. When things got rough, that's how he'd handle it—like that pelican— drawing strength from his flock to take care of business. Or like the locals here dealt with this marine-layer nonsense: Don't worry, stay focused, move on. Because eventually the sun always shines. Sometimes it just takes a little help from your friends to see it.

A rogue wave jolted him from his thoughts, crashing against the rocks, almost knocking him over. Sopping wet again, he looked around. He was alone. Then he heard the girls giggling below. Stepping carefully toward the slick edge, he began his descent.

Time to rejoin his flock.

*   *   *

Seated at their regular spots on the stone ledge, Diana lit the candles and Jeffrey positioned his phone face-up on the blanket. A few minutes passed before M asked Diana a question.

"Got any brothers or sisters?"

Diana gave her a where'd-that-come-from? look.

M shrugged. "Just curious. Obviously none at your house, but maybe at your mom's, or all grown up and gone?"

"Nope, only child."

"Wow. *None* of us has siblings? What're the odds?"

This, of course, led to a subject they all knew well: life as an only child. The myths of being pampered, envying classmates with siblings, the secret birthday wishes for a brother or sister.

"It's especially hard with no dad around," M admitted. "No one to shoot baskets with, stuff like that. I mean, Mom loves the Lakers and all, but it's not the same."

Jeffrey thought about M showing Ty her mom's picture and inviting him for dinner. Things were beginning to make sense.

Diana's face brightened. "Hey, that's it."

"What?"

"We need a name for our club, right?" She held up her wrist, reminding them of their new "club" bracelets. "So how 'bout 'The Only Child Club'?" She grinned. "If you think about it, it's actually *better* than siblings, since we got to pick each other."

M nodded. "Hey, I like that."

Jeffrey smiled. "Me too."

So, in the very spot where three days earlier The-Girl-Formerly-Known-As-Margaret received her new name, "The Only Child Club" was born. They marked the occasion with a round of high-fives.

This time, however, no texts interrupted their celebration. Jeffrey's phone never lit up, even after waiting another hour. The first time all week they'd struck out at the cave.

So they left.

*   *   *

Once back in the Rolls, M invited Diana to spend the night.

"Full disclosure, though," M warned, "no duck ponds or pizza ovens, and there's only my couch left to sleep on since Jeffrey's snagged the spare bedroom. But at least we've got plenty of overnight stuff—pajamas, an emergency pack of new toothbrushes—so we wouldn't need to stop at your place first."

Diana happily accepted, phoning her dad and getting permission. She also asked Ty if they could stop on the way for some sleepover goodies. A few blocks from the freeway, Ty spotted a 7-

Eleven on the ground floor of an office building and pulled in. As they drove down the ramp to the building's underground lot, Jeffrey joked it was the first 7-Eleven he'd ever been to with underground parking.

Ten minutes later they were back on the road, loaded up with party snacks, cruising the boulevard at a nice pace—until Ty hit the freeway and Friday Night Gridlock greeted them like a brick wall, turning the 101 into a five-lane parking lot.

While they inched along slower than walking, M asked Jeffrey if she could use his phone. "I should give Mom a heads-up about our new guest."

"Where's yours?" he asked, digging his out.

"Your dear sweet aunt has it. She needs one for work and steals mine whenever she forgets to charge hers."

As he held it out for her, a familiar number flashed on his screen. "Hey, my mom must've called while we were in 7-Eleven." He made a mental note to call her once they got to Burbank.

M took the phone, made a strange face at the display, then keyed in her number. Jeffrey wondered about that look, until a motorcycle roared by inches from his window and drowned out the thought.

Chapter 31

Friday Night

Ninety grueling minutes later, they turned into M's driveway. Susan was waiting on the porch, giving M her big chance to finally introduce her mom to Ty.

While the grown-ups chatted by the Rolls, the kids collected their snacks and overnight bags and went inside. Several minutes later, Susan came back in. The smile on her face suggested her introductory chat with Ty went well.

After welcoming Diana, Susan announced she'd made movie plans with neighbor Ruth. Promising to be home by midnight, she returned M's phone, set a pizza delivery menu on the counter with a twenty-dollar bill, recited the house rules—no visitors, lock doors, eat dinner—and left.

Grabbing the money and pizza menu, M led her friends out to the guesthouse.

The kitchen clock read 6:40 p.m.

Almost nine in Iowa.

*   *   *

It was another perfect summer evening in the Valley—mid-seventies, dusk slowly darkening the crimson-streaked sky, a gentle breeze blowing in through the guesthouse's open window. The three sat in comfortable silence, munching 7-Eleven goodies, sipping Slurpees, M's playlist streaming in the background. Diana was sprawled on the couch, M in her armchair, Jeffrey on the floor with his back against the wall.

At the end of the second song, Jeffrey broke the quiet.

"Can I just say something here?"

"I think you just did," M replied.

He continued, unfazed. "I realize our trip to the cave was a bust today, well, except for our new club name. But just because we didn't get a text shouldn't mean we stop investigating."

Crumpling her empty cookie bag, Diana tossed it at the trash can, missing by a foot. "We're not stopping," she said. "We're chillaxing."

Jeffrey got up, retrieved the crumpled bag, and dropped it in the basket. "Well, while you two chillax, I'm gonna take a look at the Santa Monica shots I took yesterday before things got crazy. Maybe we missed something." He turned to M. "Can you help me print them?"

M sighed, got up, bluetoothed Jeffrey's phone shots to her computer, and printed them out. He took the six photos to the couch, plopped down beside Diana, and spread them out on the coffee table. As he moved them around, Diana surprised him by leaning in and picking up two.

He looked at her. She shrugged. "They're the only ones showing the tower. And since its number was in our text, may as well start there." She leaned back and began studying them.

Jeffrey glanced across the room at M. Cradling her drink, her head was tilted back in the now familiar Mega-Mind-Trance position, her gaze focused on the ceiling.

"Wuzup, cuz?" he called out.

She didn't move. "Shhh. Give me a minute… Something I was gonna ask you… It'll come."

Jeffrey returned to his photos.

Minutes passed.

Setting down the two pictures she'd been studying, Diana rose from the couch and walked to M's computer.

Jeffrey looked up. "Think of something?"

"Not really. But if they've got that Brentwood news photo online, maybe I'll have better luck with it. It showed the tower behind us, and a digital version might be clearer."

Jeffrey nodded.

More minutes passed—Diana clicking links, Jeffrey checking photos, M spacing out.

Suddenly Diana yelled out.

"Whoa, guys. You really need to see this!"

They rushed over. The same photo they'd seen in the newspaper was on the screen in sharper detail. But Diana wasn't focused on the tower. She'd enlarged the section where Albert the lifeguard was kneeling beside Sylvia.

"Check it out. We couldn't see it in the newspaper version, but online here…" She zoomed in another notch. "Voila."

Jeffrey and M squinted. Albert's left hand was resting on the side rail of Sylvia's wheelchair. Yesterday when he'd chased down the thief, he'd been wearing his red windbreaker for sun protection, but had taken it off for the photos—exposing his arms.

And his tattoo.

On the inside of his left forearm, a few inches above his wrist. A circle about the size of a half-dollar.

With a dark blue exclamation point in the middle.

"Yes!" Jeffrey shouted. "I knew we'd find another one. That's three super weird exclamation marks in all three places we got warned about!"

He began pacing in a circle. "Okay, I know my charts didn't match up, but still… A weird exclamation mark on the fire hydrant. Another one on the Sam's sign. And now this one on Albert. Plus a weirdly-placed exclamation mark in each text." He turned to the girls. "All that can't be flukes."

But M wasn't listening. She'd remembered what had been bugging her. "Jeffrey!" she shouted, startling him. Her head tilted. "Four trips to the cave, but only three texts. Why?"

"Huh?"

"Every day we went there, we got a new text, except today." She paused. "Do me a favor. Check your log for missed calls today."

He took out his phone and looked.

No missed calls.

He showed it to her. Her eyes narrowed.

"What?" he asked.

"Where's that missed call from your mother?"

She waited a beat. "Remember? You mentioned she called while we were in 7-Eleven. I saw it too, when I borrowed your phone on the freeway. *That's* what's been bugging me."

He re-scrolled his missed call log. The one he'd seen on his phone today definitely wasn't there. It had vanished like the other three. And each of those had warned of bad things coming.

Vanishing text... his home number on it... where his mom was right then... bad things coming...

Clutching his phone, his thumbs flew over the keypad as he stabbed in the numbers.

Chapter 32

*M*om?"

Karen had answered on the third ring, immediately sensing something was wrong.

"Is everything okay, Jeffrey?"

He took in a controlled breath. He didn't want to frighten her.

"Yep. Everything's good. Just wanted to return your call and say hi before it got too late there."

"That's so sweet... even if I didn't call."

He frowned at the girls. "Oh. I just figured it was you. Someone called and I didn't get to it in time."

"Nope, not today. You sure everything's alright?"

His mom sounded fine, totally normal.

"Yeah, everything's great." He needed to keep things light. "I just never really got the chance to thank you for this trip. It's been truly amazing."

Both girls smiled at that.

"Oh Jeffrey, you're welcome. Such a nice way to end your summer vacation, huh? Hey, and while I've got you... Joe and Ellie rented a cabin at the lake this weekend to extend Ellie's birthday a little, and they invited me to join them. I just wanted to let you know. But I'll be back by Sunday night to get you at the airport."

She was referring to Lake Rathbun. Back when family life was "normal," Jeffrey and his parents would go there almost every summer. Two hours from Des Moines, it was the state's second-largest lake, with rental cottages, boats, and fishing.

"Sounds fun." What he was really thinking, though, was that the trip would keep her away from the house for a few days. After that text today, better safe than sorry.

"When're you guys leaving?"

"We're not sure. A storm's headed this way. The latest report said it's pounding Omaha right now."

Omaha was 150 miles west of Des Moines.

"Maybe you should leave tonight, ahead of it."

The sooner, the better, Jeffrey figured. Couldn't hurt.

"Well, I'm all packed, but last I heard we're set for tomorrow morning. I'll call you when we get there."

Jeffrey said goodnight and disconnected. Staring at his phone, he shook his head. He'd overreacted. His mother was fine. The week's crazy events were taking their toll on him. He needed to control his wild imagination.

He looked up at the girls and smiled. "Everything's cool. Let's order that pizza."

*   *   *

Once M phoned in their order—an extra large mushroom-pepperoni-pineapple—they picked up where they left off: Diana back on the couch playing with the photos, M in her armchair thinking about that missed call, Jeffrey at the window admiring the sky.

As the soft breeze soothed Jeffrey's face, he closed his eyes. There was something magical about summer nights here—more than the weather. The air felt alive with energy, the cozy soundtrack of the Valley wrapping up the day. A dog's lazy bark drifting in the distance. A mockingbird in the pepper tree chattering a final tune. The jingle of a nearby ice cream truck looping in the background. He could almost fall asleep standing there.

Across the room, M's eyes were also shut, but not to savor the vibes. A rapid-fire slide show was playing out behind her eyelids. As images zipped by, they began to lose speed, until the one she wanted finally slipped into place with an almost audible click.

Jeffrey's phone display.

Exactly as she'd seen it in the limo.

Her eyes popped open. "Okay, cuz, I got it."

He turned.

"When you saw that missed call today," she asked, "did you notice anything else?"

"Like what?" Then he remembered. Not the missed call, but

M's expression when *she'd* seen it. "You made a face."

She nodded. "Something was off. It wasn't a normal-looking missed-call number."

She got up from her chair, walked to the desk, opened a drawer, and dug out a pen and paper. Staring at the blank page for a few seconds, she jotted something down, paused, then closed her eyes.

Seconds later, she leaned over, scribbled some more, then repeated the process two more times. Pausing, thinking, writing.

Finally, she handed the paper to Jeffrey.

"*That's* what was on your display today."

- - - 5 5 5 0 1 0 4 ! 9 - 1 2

He studied it. Earlier in the limo, he'd only caught a glimpse, focusing on the seven numbers of his landline. But now he realized there was a lot more to it.

"What're those three dashes in front?" he asked.

"They're not dashes, they're placeholders. Three characters I couldn't remember. But they're obviously your area code since you already identified your landline after that. My thumb must've covered them when I took your phone."

Jeffrey nodded.

"But that's not why I made the face." She pointed to the five ending characters. "It was this part *after* your number. The 'exclamation point, nine, dash, twelve.'"

She looked up at him.

"Because missed calls don't end like that."

Chapter 33

S taring at what M had written, the format was all too familiar. *Phone number, exclamation point, more numbers.*

As she'd pointed out, it looked nothing like a missed call, and exactly like the texts they'd been getting. But if it was one of those, why hadn't it shown up in the cave like the others?

Still, everything else fit the pattern. Except for the *two* numbers at the end—9-12—instead of a single number like the others. Did that mean nine to midnight tonight? A three-hour range instead of a single hour? If so, which time zone? It was 7:30 here in LA, meaning it was already "nine to twelve" in Iowa.

But he'd just talked to his mom and she was fine.

Diana interrupted his thoughts.

"Hey, that first day we went to the beach? Didn't your mom send pictures? Your neighbor's birthday or something?"

Jeffrey nodded.

"In front of your house, right?"

He nodded again.

"Can I see them?"

"Now?"

She sighed. "Yes, Wonder Boy, now. Look, if what M saw on your phone today was really another warning, it's gotta be pointing to your house, right? Where that landline number is. So let's check any recent shots of your house. See if you notice anything."

When Jeffrey gave her a look, she shrugged. "Hey, stranger things have happened this week."

True that.

As he held up his phone to look for the pictures, it began to vibrate. Everyone froze.

He pressed the answer button, bringing it slowly to his ear.

The pizza guy was at the front door.

*   *   *

They were back in the guesthouse on M's couch, pigging out on pizza. Jeffrey sat in the middle, a pizza slice in one hand, scrolling through his mobile shots with the other. When he found the two photos his mom had sent, he held up his phone.

"Okay, this is on our porch. Ellie's on the right, my mom on the left. Joe, Ellie's husband, must've taken it."

The photo showed the two women standing by the front door hamming it up for the camera. Flashing goofy smiles, heads tilted, each holding a colored drink. But it was too close to see much of the house behind. So Jeffrey swiped to the second shot.

This one was better, taken from further back. The women were still on the porch but you could see more of the house behind and the yard in front.

Jeffrey studied it, but saw nothing unusual. Until something in the lower right corner caught his eye. Not his house, something in the foreground, by their front yard oak tree.

But it was out of focus, the camera too close. It could've been something in the tree, or maybe in front of it. Probably not important, but its unfamiliar shape piqued Jeffrey's curiosity.

He set his pizza down and pointed. "What's that?"

Diana shrugged.

M took the phone and stared. "Definitely not a branch. Different color, different shape." She continued examining it. "You think it's worth calling your mom back and asking?"

Wiping his hand on his pant leg (prompting a groan from Diana), he took the phone back and keyed in his mom's number. She answered on the first ring, all bubbly.

"Wow, son. Two calls in ten minutes. To what do I owe the pleasure?"

Faking a half-chuckle, he put her on speaker. "Just something I forgot to ask. Remember those pictures you sent, of Ellie's party?"

"Sure. Those silly ones on the porch. That was such a fun night. Sorry you missed it."

"Yeah, looks like you had a great time. Anyway, I was

curious about something on one of them, in the front yard. Maybe in the tree? Or in front of it? I can't tell, it's too blurry. But I don't recognize it."

"The tree out front?"

"Yeah."

The phone went silent as she thought about it.

"Not sure what you're talking about... Oh wait, I know." She laughed. "I swear I was going to tell you. Actually, I was about to order another one on Amazon before this lake trip came up."

"Slow down, Mom. What're you talking about?"

"Your tetherball. We had a minor mishap..."

"The tetherball out back?"

"Well, yeah, that's where it *was*. Before Ellie's birthday."

"Huh?"

"Ellie's daughter came by before the party to drop off a present, and she brought little Jacob along, Ellie's grandson. He's three already, if you can believe that. Anyway, you know how he loves spinning around on that tetherball, getting all dizzy then wobbling off. Well, while the grown-ups were yakking in the living room, next thing we know Jake's screaming bloody murder out back.

"Turns out he'd yanked the whole thing—rope and all—right off the pole and the poor guy was on the ground all tangled up. No serious damage though, just a skinned elbow. Nothing a little ice cream and Neosporin didn't fix."

She chuckled. "Well, except that your backyard pole is now... tetherball-less."

Jeffrey clicked back to the photo, and then he understood.

"Oh... so you hung it on the tree out front?" He gave the girls a puzzled look. "Why?"

"Yep. That's what you must see in that picture. Since the rope was still attached to the ball, Joe tied it to the branch out front so Jake could keep playing with it while we watched from the porch."

Jeffrey shook his head at the girls. "Okay. Well, thanks Mom. I guess that explains it. Have a great time at the lake." He hung up and sighed. Mystery solved. Another dead end.

Diana took his phone and squinted at the photo.

141

"What?" Jeffrey asked.

"You sure that's really a tetherball rope?"

He shrugged. "Well, you heard. They hung it there."

He looked again but it was too blurry to see much. Not that it mattered after his mom's explanation. Still, what could it hurt to transfer it to the computer for a better look? That's how Diana found Albert's tattoo.

"Could you put it on your laptop?" he asked M.

After she bluetoothed it, Jeffrey sat at the desk and began fiddling with the mouse while the girls stood behind him. "Got anything to sharpen it? PhotoShop or something?"

M pointed to an icon at the bottom of the screen.

He opened it and clicked the focus option. After some adjustments, the front yard tree looked more like an ink drawing than a photograph. But at least it was sharper. Zooming in two more clicks, Jeffrey gasped.

Diana saw it too. "I told you!" she shouted. "That does *not* look like a tetherball."

"No way..." Jeffrey whispered.

His brain knew what it was because his mom had just told him. But his eyes saw something else.

In this cartoonish ink drawing version of a tetherball hanging from a tree, with the weight of the ball pulling the rope straight and tight, the shape formed something they all instantly recognized.

A long white exclamation point.

Chapter 34

Jeffrey

The second I saw it, I freaked. Grabbing my phone, I called back Mom's cell. It went straight to voicemail.

Odd, since I'd just talked to her.

I tried our landline. After five rings Mom's recorded message came on.

I re-tried both numbers, but got the same result.

Then I tried Joe and Ellie next door, keying in their number from memory. But after six rings their answering machine picked up.

Shaking my head, I disconnected. "Should I call the police?"

M offered a doubtful look. "In Iowa?"

Diana was equally skeptical. "What're you gonna say? 'Hey, there's a tetherball hanging in my front yard, send in the SWAT team?'"

"I could mention the other things—the car crash, the fire at Sam's, what happened in Santa Monica."

M scoffed. "Yeah, right. 'Hey, a store in Hollywood put up a new sign and had a fire, and a guy at the beach tried to swipe a purse. *Now* send in SWAT.'"

They were right. Bad idea.

I tried Mom's cell and our landline again, but no one answered. I kept redialing but kept getting voicemail and message machine.

Maybe they left early for the lake. But why wouldn't she still answer her cell? And how could they leave so fast after my call?

Then I got an idea. I tapped in a number I also knew by heart. On the fourth ring I heard a click, some scratchy sounds, the phone dropping.

I waited.

Finally, after more noise—someone picking the phone up off

the floor—a sleepy male voice whispered, "Hello?"

"Uncle Charlie? It's Jeffrey."

My mom's older brother lived in Colfax, a two-traffic-light town twenty-five miles east of Des Moines. I heard my aunt's groggy voice in the background. Uncle Charlie said something to her, then came back on the line.

After apologizing for calling so late, I explained where I was and what was happening—that I couldn't get through to Mom after talking to her minutes earlier and was worried. I left out the tetherball-in-tree part.

He put me on hold and tried both of Mom's numbers. When that failed, he agreed to drive over and check, warning it might take a while because of the approaching storm. He promised to call when he got there and I reminded him where our spare key was hidden.

After hanging up, I checked the time. 8:25.

10:25 in Iowa.

I thought about those last two numbers in the text.

Nine to twelve.

Chapter 35

It was painful to watch. Jeffrey in full panic mode, waiting for Uncle Charlie to call back. Half-on, half-off the couch, legs bouncing on the balls of his feet, eyes darting from his phone to the girls, to the wall clock, then back to his phone again.

Every few minutes he'd call the same three numbers—Uncle Charlie's, his mom's cell, his landline. Keying in one, he'd jump up, pace with the phone to his ear, groan, then collapse back on the couch to key in the next. Each failed attempt deepening his gloom.

Yet he couldn't stop. Something was wrong. He felt it in his bones. Too many coincidences, too many unexplained connections. First, three disappearing texts pointing to places where bad stuff happened. Then, super weird exclamation marks at each location—on the fire hydrant, on the Sam's sign, on the lifeguard's arm.

And now, this new exclamation mark, the weirdest of all, hanging in front of his house on the same day this fourth text arrived with his *home number* on it. Which disappeared like the others.

All that couldn't be random.

But what could that tree-hanging mark be warning them about? Jeffrey's house? That tree? Their front yard? The rooms in his house where the phones with that number were?

And what did any of that have to do with his missing mother? *And why wasn't she answering his calls?*

Fifty-five gut-wrenching minutes later, Jeffrey's cell finally buzzed. It was Uncle Charlie, and the news wasn't good.

After rattling off the many reasons for his delay (strong winds, walnut-sized hail, a section of highway flooded, two road detours), and explaining why he missed Jeffrey's calls (he'd stuck his phone in the glove box to keep it from bouncing in the storm, the downpour drowning out the rings), Charlie finally reported his findings.

When no one answered his knocks, he'd used the hidden key, clearing each room like in the movies. But no one was there. No Karen. No notes. No nothing.

On the slightly positive side, he didn't find anything bad either. Jeffrey didn't ask for details, but he'd watched too many episodes of Dateline to know he meant blood or bodies.

In fact, Uncle Charlie said nothing seemed out of place. No dirty dishes, no messes, no keys or purses or cell phones left on the table signaling a sudden alien abduction. When Jeffrey wondered aloud if his mom might've left with the neighbors for the lake, Uncle Charlie snuffed out that idea. He'd already checked the garage and his mom's car was gone. Jeffrey knew if they'd gone to the lake, they would've taken Joe's SUV, not their Honda.

So where would his mother go this late on a Friday night? In a storm? *And why wasn't she answering her cell?*

He asked his uncle to check Ellie and Joe's place next door. As Charlie walked over, Jeffrey heard the wind howling in the background, his uncle knocking, followed by the doorbell ringing. When no one answered, Charlie checked the garage, but it was locked with no windows to look in.

Now Uncle Charlie was worried too. Despite reassuring Jeffrey that there had to be a reasonable explanation, he agreed it was time to call the police. Even if they couldn't file a missing person's report yet, the police could at least check for traffic accidents and stuff. Plus, the cops would pay more attention to a local adult brother than three freaked-out kids in California.

Promising to phone each other with any new developments, they hung up.

Chapter 36

*W*HERE ARE YOU?"

It was 1:25 a.m. in Iowa—more than two hours since his last contact with Charlie and Jeffrey was finally talking to his mom on the phone.

Well, not exactly talking. After spending the night fearing the worst, it was hard keeping his voice from breaking the sound barrier.

Karen had finally answered on what seemed like the thousandth try, sounding groggy but otherwise normal.

"Is everything okay?" she whispered back. "Why are you yelling?"

He lowered his voice, slightly.

"Sorry. But *where are you?*"

"At the lake," she replied, as if it were obvious. "Got in a while ago. We decided to take your advice and leave early. I must've conked out the second I hit the pillow.

"But I've been calling every ten seconds."

"I got up to use the bathroom and realized my phone was dead. I just plugged it in when you called." She paused, then spoke even softer. "Sorry for whispering, but we're sharing this bungalow and Ellie and Joe are in the other bed."

"But I called our landline too."

Karen considered this. "Well, all I can tell you is I took a shower right after we talked. Then Ellie and Joe came over and we decided to leave before the storm got any closer, and skedaddled. Probably a half hour after you called."

"But where's your car? You guys didn't take the Honda, did you?"

"No. Joe drove his SUV. Why?"

Jeffrey told her about Uncle Charlie's trip to the house and reporting her car gone.

"Oh my. I am so sorry for worrying you all. I better call Charles." She sighed. "The Honda's at the Langleys. Martha's car's in the shop so I let her borrow ours while I'm here."

Simple answers for so much worry. Those phone texts had turned Jeffrey into a crazed wreck.

"Anyway," Karen continued, "judging from the radio reports on the drive up, it's good we left when we did."

Jeffrey exhaled, giving the girls a weak thumbs-up. Listening to his mother's soft, calm voice helped slow his heart rate. Suddenly, all those crazy texts and weird exclamation marks seemed silly. He felt like an idiot.

He apologized again for calling so late, told his mom he loved her, and signed off.

After phoning his uncle to let him know all was fine, he collapsed on the couch. By then, the girls were prepping for bed: M in the bathroom, brushing her teeth; Diana in a new pair of LA Lakers pajamas, hovering over him with a blanket and pillow, waiting for him to vacate the couch.

Taking the hint, he grabbed his phone, commented "Nice pj's" to Diana, and headed for the door. Back in his room, he passed out with his clothes still on.

*   *   *

The call came at 7:30 that morning.

Lost in a coma-like sleep brought on by last night's meltdown, it took Jeffrey a half dozen rings to realize the buzzing was his phone.

The Langleys lived across from the Jameses. Early that morning, Mr. Langley had gone out to retrieve his newspaper, rushing back seconds later to report the shocking scene across the street. After peeking out the front window to make sure her husband hadn't lost his mind, Mrs. Langley had placed a frantic call to Jeffrey's mother at the lake.

Half of their front yard tree was gone.

The entire top—apparently torn off by the storm.

But that wasn't the worst of it. The force of the wind had sent it crashing through their roof, obliterating a five-foot-wide section of wall where Mrs. James' bedroom window used to be.

Yes, *that* tree. The one recently observed with a tetherball rope hanging from it.

By the time Jeffrey got the call, Ellie and Joe had already driven Jeffrey's mom back from the lake. She was staying with them while an emergency crew accessed the damage.

Weather reports estimated gale-force winds had pummeled the area shortly before midnight—right after Charlie left.

Within that "9-12" range in *both* time zones.

One block over, another smaller tree had also fallen, but with only minor damage reported to a backyard vegetable garden.

In fact, aside from overturned trash bins and scattered road debris, the neighborhood's only major casualty was Jeffrey's house, where his mother's unrecognizable bed now lay crushed beneath an eight-hundred-pound treetop.

It was a miracle no one had been sleeping there.

Part III

Home Sweet Home

"May the forces of evil become confused on the way to your house."

George Carlin

Chapter 37

Jeffrey

I left California that same afternoon, a day early from my planned Sunday departure (thus, no Tar Pits). Aunt Susan helped me change my flight, and when Ty came to pick up Diana and heard what happened to my house, he insisted on driving us to the airport.

We all piled into the limo—me, Diana, M, Aunt Susan—arriving at LAX with enough time for a farewell lunch at a restaurant called Gladstone's.

Jeopardy! Alert: There are ninety-seven food and beverage places at the LA airport. (I googled it in case there's ever an "Airport Dining" category.)

Before I walked to the security line, everyone took turns saying goodbye. I got a fist-bump and blinding-white smile from Ty. My cousin and Diana both gave me hugs—Diana's maybe a little longer and slightly less cousiny (though that might've been wishful thinking). My aunt squeezed me like my mom sometimes does and tousled my hair, which I hate (no offense, Aunt Susan).

Then, as I waited for my departure, alone for the first time since that morning phone call, so many thoughts began swirling in my head, I felt like I was in Dorothy's tornado.

*   *   *

We touched down in Des Moines a little after ten local time. Joe, Ellie, and Mom were waiting by the luggage carousel with yet more hugs, Mom offering an especially long one. Once back at Joe and Ellie's, Joe grabbed two flashlights and led me next door to check out my house.

The street lamp by the Langleys provided enough light without needing the flashlights. My first view of the front of our house was unreal. Yellow tape surrounded the entire area. The top of our tree had sliced straight through the roof and someone had already sawed off the rest of the trunk, leaving two big sections near the stump.

As we stepped up to the porch, I noticed that our screen door was gone. In its place, more yellow tape crisscrossed the door frame. Off to the side, several hard hats sat near the front window. Joe grabbed two and handed me one.

"Really?" I asked. He nodded so I put it on.

Tacked over our peephole was a notice. I read it with my flashlight. A warning from the City of Des Moines to enter "at your own risk" until a scheduled inspection the next day.

The front door was locked but Joe had Mom's key, so he pulled off the tape, unlocked the deadbolt, and we stepped inside. I tried the light switch by the door but it didn't work. Joe ran his flashlight around the room, stopping at two camping lanterns sitting on the floor five feet away. He walked over and lit both, instantly bathing the room in harsh bright light.

Junk was everywhere. Electric cords, chunks of drywall, splintered wood beams. Picking up one of the lanterns, Joe motioned me to follow. As we made our way through the debris toward my mom's bedroom, I pulled out my phone and started snapping pictures to send the girls.

When I peered into Mom's room, my knees almost buckled. As unreal as the outside view was, I still wasn't ready for it. A gaping hole ran from the roof down through what had once been her bedroom window. But far more chilling was the gigantic tree chunk now embedded in my mother's mangled mattress.

I flashed back to last night when I couldn't get through to her and had freaked out. I'd felt like such an idiot once I realized she'd been safe at the lake the whole time. But now, staring at that massive treetop across her mangled bed, I no longer felt like that idiot.

If I hadn't suggested they leave early for the lake...

I tried not to go there.

*   *   *

Amazingly, the city inspectors let us move back in the next day, officially declaring all but Mom's room "structurally sound" and the rest of the damage "cosmetic." A fancy way to say trashed-but-clean-up-able.

We called Dad that afternoon. He was at an insurance convention and offered to fly back to help. But Mom told him things were under control and to wait for his conference to end.

By Sunday night, the workers had removed the tree branches and debris, boarded up the front-wall gap with plywood, and covered the hole in the roof with a big blue tarp. We'd also set up the futon we kept in the closet for Mom to sleep on during reconstruction.

Not an ideal arrangement, and definitely not pretty, but better than staying at a hotel or someone's house.

Especially with school starting the next day.

Chapter 38

The beginning of any new school year is crazy enough. Multiply that by a hundred when you wake up each morning in a construction zone. So, needless to say, Jeffrey's first week was tough.

The workers basically had to rebuild a major part of the house in and around his mom's room. Roof, walls, window, floors. Which meant laborers everywhere, room-to-room yelling, radios blaring, saws grinding, nail guns pounding, scattered tools all over, and a bus-sized dumpster parked in the front yard.

Somehow though, by the second week, the noise and activity had faded into the background. Jeffrey's biology teacher called that human adaptation. Jeffrey even began using the workers' arrival time as his school alarm clock, since they always started at seven sharp. And with all of them gone by four, their nights became almost normal.

He'd also started discussing another trip to LA with his mom, maybe over winter break, and to his surprise, Karen was actually considering it. But for now, his focus was on the big day coming a week from Saturday. When Kid Jeffrey would make his grand leap into the realm of *Jeffrey James, Teenager*.

He was seriously considering T-shirts. Or business cards.

*   *   *

It was also during that second school week that M came to a surprising moment of truth: She actually missed her cousin. His silly humor, his nerdy questions, his child-like excitement over... everything.

Quite the change from the old Margaret. The lame-named grumpy loner waiting for a cousin she didn't need or want, praying he didn't bore her to death, while stink-eyeing the hot chick walking next to him.

Clearly, her Margaret-to-M transformation had changed more

than just her name. Since Diana and Jeffrey entered her life, her whole attitude was different. Not only did she now have a cousin worth knowing, but also a best friend a mere Rolls-Royce ride away.

Yet something still wasn't right, though she couldn't pinpoint what it was. Like that day in Santa Monica when those two boys got rescued and Jeffrey convinced her and Diana to stay longer, later calling it "a feeling" he'd had. She felt that now. Like a tiny bulb faintly blinking in her brain, trying to send her some kind of message.

At first, she'd chalked it up to mind-overload—her brain trying to slow down and return to normal after such an action-packed week. Or maybe a new school and school year were to blame.

But then last night happened. She'd been in her mom's room, chatting, and had casually glanced at the nightstand to check the time. And that's when that faintly blinking bulb in her brain started pounding like a jackhammer, sending her racing to her room to check those house photos Jeffrey took after the storm.

But it wasn't there.

So she called Diana.

*   *   *

Across town in Brentwood, something had also been bothering Diana. Not school or her two new friends. Hers was sleep-related. She called them her "storm dreams." Not exactly nightmares, but not exactly normal either.

They began the night Jeffrey sent those pictures of his beat-up house. She hadn't thought much of it at first. In school she'd learned that dreaming was the brain's way of exercising. Innocent stuff, no deep meaning. Yet these seemed different, especially the one last night that had literally jolted her awake and kept her up all night swiping through those phone shots of Jeffrey's place.

But she couldn't find it. And just as she was about to call M, her friend beat her to it.

Chapter 39

That Friday night, two nights after the girls began collaborating, Jeffrey's computer chimed. He'd been expecting the call. The girls had set it up during their lunch periods. He'd assumed it was his Happy-Day-Before-Your-Birthday call since tomorrow was the day.

But as the girls' faces appeared on the Skype screen, they didn't look like they were ready to sing him happy birthday. They were in Diana's room, probably another weekend sleepover, and something was obviously wrong. When he opened with his standard "Evening, ladies" line, all he got back were two forced smiles, like a pair of Walmart greeters trying to hide bad stomach aches.

M cleared her throat.

"Unfortunately," she began, "this isn't really a social call. Things have come up we really need to discuss."

M gave Diana a your-turn look, but Diana shook her head so M continued. "It's about those texts."

Jeffrey stopped her. "Wait." He held up his phone and smiled. "No need. Haven't gotten a single new one since I got back."

"Actually, it's not about *new* ones. For the last two days we've been back to working on the *old* ones…"

"But I thought we agreed to hold off on further sleuthing until my big LA comeback. Which might actually be over Christmas break. I mean, I know we didn't get all the answers we wanted, but can't we wait till then? Didn't we do enough for now? Rescuing Sylvia? Saving my mom?"

M shook her head. "We don't think this can wait. So hear us out, okay?" She took a swig from her water bottle.

"A couple nights ago I was in my mom's room talking, and when I checked the clock on the nightstand I noticed her landline."

"Okay."

"That's when it hit me that everyone who still owns a landline *always* has one in their bedroom. Especially moms—by their beds

—'in case of emergency.'" She made air quotes with her fingers.

"Okay," Jeffrey repeated.

"And I bet your mom does too."

"Sure. And that's important why?"

"Where is it?"

"Huh?"

"We've re-checked every photo you sent of your mom's destroyed bedroom and we can't find your landline."

Jeffrey thought about that. "I'm still not seeing your point."

Diana took over. "We expected to see it on her nightstand. But unless it got knocked over, it's not there."

"Well, that's probably what happened."

"Then why's the lamp still there? Seems like a lightweight lamp with a big shade would blow over easier than a bulky house phone. Yet the lamp's there, but no phone."

He shrugged. "Okay, if it'll make you happy, I'll ask my mom when we're done here. But what's this about?"

Ignoring his question, M asked another. "How many landlines total do you have at the house?"

"Well... the one in Mom's room, and another in the den. But will someone please tell me what the big deal is about our phones?"

"Look, it's probably nothing, so just do us a favor and check. Then call back and we'll talk more. But before you go, there's something else." She turned to Diana. "Tell him about your dreams."

Diana took a deep breath. "Okay, well ever since you sent us those storm pictures, I started having these strange dreams, about storms. Which I know isn't that weird considering what happened to your house. But it's what I'm doing in these dreams that's been freaking me out. I'm always searching for something I can't find, then waking up wondering what it was."

"Wait. Is this about our landline again?"

"No." She shifted in her seat. "Two nights ago, I finally figured out what I was looking for. And it jolted me awake and sent me scrambling for those house photos you sent. But it wasn't in your mom's room, or outside, or anywhere."

"What wasn't*?"*

"The tetherball!"

M nodded. "I looked too. It's definitely not there."

"I have no idea what either of you are talking about."

"The rope and ball that were hanging from that tree out front! The one we thought was a giant exclamation point. It's not in any of your pictures."

Jeffrey sighed. "Well, duh. That whole tree got blown away."

Diana shook her head. "No. Think about it. That rope was supposedly tied to the tree strong enough to hold up your neighbor's grandkid, right?"

Jeffrey nodded.

"So if you tie a knot that tight, don't you think it'd still be attached somewhere? Even if it got knocked down? Tangled up in some part of the tree? At least the rope? Maybe on that chunk in your mom's room, or out front on a branch somewhere? I mean, c'mon, both the ball and rope were white, right? Should be easy to spot."

Before Jeffrey could answer, M said, "Look, maybe it's important, maybe not. Just ask about it when you check on the bedroom phone, okay?"

"You're not going to tell me what's going on here?"

Diana shrugged. "Check first. Some of the shots you sent were pretty dark. Maybe we missed something. No sense getting worked up over nothing. Then call back, okay?"

*　　　*　　　*

After they disconnected, Jeffrey stared at the blank screen. Why would his mom's landline or that tetherball thing matter now?

He got up, walked down the hall, and peeked into his mother's room. Plywood sheets were stacked against one wall and his mom's bed was gone, but the nightstand was there—with the lamp sitting on it like the girls said. The only evidence it had survived the storm was a small dent on its shade. The workers must have picked it up off the floor.

So why wouldn't they pick up the phone too? M was right.

There'd definitely been a phone there. But the only things next to the lamp now were some long nails and a hammer.

He knelt down and scanned the floor. No phone. He searched for the wall jack the phone plugged into, surveying each wall still standing, and found it a few feet from the nightstand. But nothing was plugged in.

He walked out to the living room and found his mom watching a *Law and Order* rerun. She'd been nursing a cold all week, mostly from the couch, surrounded by pillows, Tylenol, and empty ginger ale cans. Hopefully, she'd be well enough for the road trip they'd planned for tomorrow.

After asking how she was feeling (much better), he brought up the bedroom phone. She explained that the week before his trip she'd moved it to the den when that one stopped working, because she used the one in the den more. She said she planned to buy a new one for the bedroom once the construction work was finished.

Then he asked about the tetherball.

And that's when he knew the girls were on to something, though he had no idea what.

Chapter 40

Back on Skype, Jeffrey told the girls why his mom's phone wasn't in her bedroom. Diana cut him off before he could finish. "And the tetherball?"

He sighed. "She threw it out."

Exchanging a quick glance with M, Diana asked for details. Jeffrey shrugged. "She got rid of it. Said it was too dangerous hanging from the tree like that out by the sidewalk."

He guessed the next question.

"When?" Diana asked.

"She's not sure. A day or so after Joe put it up."

"When would that be? In relation to the storm?"

"Joe hung it on the tree the day of Ellie's party, Sunday, after I left for the airport. The storm hit that following Friday, five days later. So it was gone a few days before the storm."

Jeffrey scratched his cheek. "I'm guessing that means something. And, from your expressions, not good. So let's hear it."

M hesitated. "Well, cuz, this obviously changes things."

"A lot," Diana added, reaching off-camera for a chart and handing it to M. "But I'll let the Mega-Mind explain."

"Okay," M began, keeping the chart flat on the table out of view. "But get comfortable, this might take a while." She cleared her throat again. "Since we'd both gone through those house photos multiple times, we already had a pretty good idea what you'd tell us: that your house phone wasn't in your mom's room when the storm hit, and the tetherball was gone too." She paused. "Good news or bad news first?"

Jeffrey rolled his eyes. "The good, I guess."

"Okay. Those charts you made? Turns out, they were spot on."

"Meaning what?"

"Remember the three things you tried to match to each text?

Where each phone clue was at each scene, where the bad stuff actually happened, and where each weird exclamation point was?"

Jeffrey nodded. "Yeah, and most didn't match."

M smiled. "Until the ace detectives took over." She held up the chart she'd been hiding.

Jeffrey studied it, amazed at the level of detail, not to mention all the new matches.

Toy Store	Sam's	Santa Monica
↓	↓	↓
3 matches!	3 matches!	3 matches!
On Fire Hydrant!	In Storeroom!	On Albert!
↓	↓	↓
✓ text = 2247pearl	✓ text = 3235550199	✓ text = SMLGT14
✓ Crash Site	✓ Fire Site	✓ Caught Thief
✓ Excl. Point	✓ Excl. Point	✓ Excl. Point

"Wow, you guys raised chart-making to a whole new level. But how's that possible, everything now matching?"

"Because we found things we missed before. Like starting with the toy store. Remember how we thought the store's address—the clue in our first text—was only above the front door, which didn't match the fire hydrant where the actual crash and exclamation point were?"

Jeffrey nodded.

"Well, when I thought more about it, I remembered seeing the store's address somewhere else, on that city notice! The one they emailed us that was hanging on the hydrant. In the space near the top where they wrote in the hydrant's location. Which all three things you listed for the toy store match."

She tapped each line one by one. "The store's address on the hydrant. The car crashing into that hydrant. The weird exclamation point also on that hydrant."

She motioned to Diana to take over. Pointing to the second column labeled Sam's, Diana said, "Okay, for this one, the phone clue we got was the store's phone number, right? You thought nothing matched because the store's phones were in their front showroom, not in the back where the fire was, and that the funny-looking exclamation mark on their sign was outside."

Jeffrey nodded again.

"Well, we went back to Sam's last night and convinced the clerk to show us where the fire started. So guess what was in that burned-out back storeroom? *Another sign!* Exactly like the one outside only smaller, with that same silly bat-and-ball exclamation point.

"It was leaning up against a wall, half melted. The clerk said it got delivered the same day the big one outside did, and they originally planned to hang it up in the front showroom."

M butted back in. "Guess what was on the wall right above the sign?"

Jeffrey guessed that one. "A phone."

M nodded. "Exactly. So, again, three matches, all in that back burned-out storeroom. The store's phone, the fire, and the sign's weird exclamation mark."

She turned back to her chart and tapped the last column, labeled Santa Monica. "For this one, all we needed was that online newspaper photo, the one Diana used to find Albert's tattoo. When we zoomed in on Albert again, we noticed writing on his T-shirt. We didn't see it before because once Diana found the tattoo we stopped looking."

Diana nodded. "Plus, he was always wearing his windbreaker on the beach that day, until the photos at the end."

"But the printing on the shirt was too small to read," continued M. "So I called the lifeguard station."

When Jeffrey cocked his head in surprise, she shrugged. "Hey, we really got into it. Anyway, get this... turns out each lifeguard gets assigned to the same tower for the whole summer. So their shirts have their tower number on them! Meaning, that clue from the phone text—S M L G T 14—was on Albert's T-shirt the whole time.

"Which makes three more matches, all on Albert! The tower number phone clue on his T-shirt, the weird exclamation point on his tattoo, and since he was the one who caught the thief, he was literally where the bad stuff happened."

Jeffrey shook his head. "Wow."

Diana held up her hand. "Yeah, but unfortunately that's the good-news part. Now comes the not-so-good."

She reached for another chart and handed it to M. Before displaying it, M used a black marker to write something on it, then flipped it around.

Labeled Jeffrey's House, it looked nothing like the others.

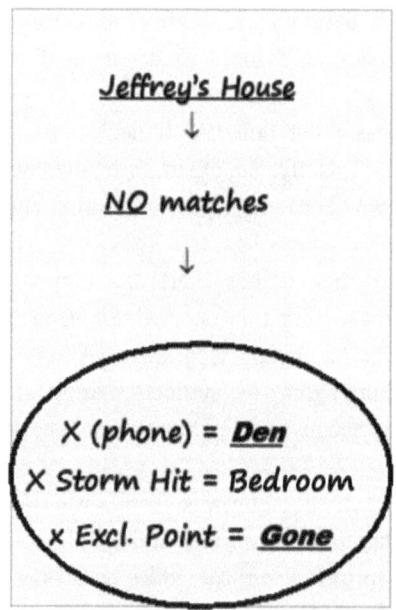

Right away, Jeffrey saw what M had written on it. After what he'd told them about the bedroom phone and tetherball, she'd added the words "Den" and "Gone" in the circled area.

"Okay," M began, "for that last text, the one I wrote out later with your home number on it..."—she tapped the word Den—"we now know the only phone in your house with that number on it was in your den, *not* in your mom's bedroom where the storm hit."

She tapped the word Gone. "And what we thought was a weird exclamation mark, that hanging-tetherball thingy, wasn't even there.

"That's zero matches. Storm hit bedroom. Phone in den. Hanging exclamation point gone."

Jeffrey stared at the chart. "So you're saying the storm—when and where it happened—was a fluke?"

M shrugged. "Hey, you live in Tornado Alley, right?"

"Close enough," he acknowledged.

He blew out a breath. "So that last text wasn't really a warning like the others?"

"Oh no. That's definitely *not* what we're saying!"

"Then I'm confused."

"It just wasn't warning about that storm," M said.

"Or that night," Diana added.

Jeffrey creased his forehead. "How can you know that?"

"Because of how that text ended," M replied.

"Huh?"

"Well, that's where things get interesting. Remember what I wrote down, the part *after* your phone number?"

"More numbers. When we thought the bad stuff would happen. '9-12' that night."

"Well, yes and no. More numbers, yes. But forget about that time range for a second. Think about those numbers. There were *two* of them, right? Nine, hyphen, twelve. But all the other texts ended with just a *single* number. A three, a twelve, a four. Third hour, midnight, fourth hour. Never two separate numbers with a hyphen in between."

"So?"

"So why not end with just a nine, or twelve? If it really was a time, either would have given us that same one-hour range like the others. Why totally change formats this time to a *three-hour* range?"

165

Jeffrey shrugged. "I'm sure you're gonna tell me."

M squinted. "What if it wasn't a time range? What else uses a hyphen between two numbers?"

Before he connected the dots, Diana whispered the answer.

"A date."

It took him a moment to process. But once he did, he stammered. "Wait… a date? You mean like 'nine-twelve' as in…

"September twelfth? Tomorrow? My birthday?"

Chapter 41

Jeffrey

W hat a great way to start off your big day.
Happy Birthday, Jeffrey! Enjoy it while you can!
After signing off Skype, I went to the den and dropped into my dad's leather recliner to reflect on it all. The girls were probably right about us misinterpreting that last phone clue. In fact, I'd been wondering the same thing during my flight home. But then we landed and more pressing things pushed that thought aside.

Now however, after seeing their new charts and hearing their latest theory, I realized what had been bugging me. All the other exclamation points we'd found were *actual* exclamation points. Each unusual in its own way, but still genuine punctuation marks—intended to emphasize something, like exclamation points were supposed to.

The one on the fire hydrant was big and bold to draw people's attention. The bat and ball on the Sam's sign emphasized the store's name. Even Albert's inked forearm wasn't random art. The tattoo artist clearly meant to draw an exclamation mark inside a circle.

But the thing hanging in my front yard wasn't like that. It had never been a real mark. *It was a tetherball on a rope.* It might've *looked* a little like one—to three kids with active imaginations—but it wasn't.

So we had to forget about that tree-hanging distraction and focus on the text itself. And if it really was a warning—just not about that tree, or the storm, or that night—then it had to be pointing to this den. Where our only home phone was. The only thing in our house with the same number M saw in that text. The big problem, of course, was that if doomsday was tomorrow, I didn't have much time to figure out why my den got picked.

I looked around the room. Before Dad moved out, this was his hang-out. He'd watch sports and old war movies, and read books, in this very chair. I looked over at the desk where the phone was, sweeping my eyes from one side to the other. But nothing stood out. Ordinary desk stuff. The phone, a green banker's lamp, a family photo in a plastic frame, a box of envelopes, a magnetic block with paperclips, a corkboard behind the desk with some bills tacked on, and pens and pencils in a black plastic cup with writing printed around it reading: *When Nothing Goes Right, Go Left.*

Unless one of those pens was an exploding James Bond device, nothing looked dangerous, unusual, or out of place. Nor did any strange-looking exclamation points pop out at me.

I moved on to the rest of the room. A floor lamp on my right, an end table on my left, the TV across from me on a stand next to a bookcase. All normal.

The only other things in the room were two wall shelves filled with knickknacks, the window by the desk, a heat vent over the door, and four poster-sized photographs—one on each wall—that my dad had taken.

I examined the wall photos. My dad loved photography and these four shots were some of his best. A snow-covered farmhouse, fireworks over the city, a downtown street on a rainy night, and a lake view at sunset. But none set off any red flags.

Shifting to the rest of the furniture, I stared at each piece, waiting for something to jump out at me, but nothing did. No weird punctuation marks, no spidey-sense tingles.

Running out of things to check, I got up, grabbed my phone, and snapped shots around the room. All four walls, each piece of furniture. Then I texted them to the girls with a message.

my den - c anything weird? i dont.

Fifteen minutes later they called back, asking for a video. "Your snapshots don't show much," M explained, "and we need more detail around the landline."

They said the quality would be better if I used my laptop webcam rather than my phone. It was kind of a hassle, holding it backward with the screen facing my targets, but I managed.

The girls guided me around on speakerphone. First panning the top of the desk, then across the corkboard behind it, then over the top shelf where two cubby holes were packed with more desk junk. Lastly, they moved me to the center of the room and had me spin around slowly for a final full-circle shot. After I confirmed it was all on my computer, they showed me how to use a service called YouSendIt to send it to them.

Before hanging up I remembered about tomorrow. "Hey, I almost forgot. We might not have to worry much about all this '9-12' stuff after all, since we're leaving on a road trip in the morning. So we won't be here for a good part of the day."

I explained Mom's plan about shopping in Maple Falls for new bedroom stuff, at a place called The Couch Potato, one of her favorite stores. "It's a two-hour drive, and we'll probably celebrate my birthday afterward."

But they still wanted to check the video since we'd be home before "9-12" ended. They promised to call if anything interesting came up and signed off.

Over the next hour, I re-inspected the entire room to make sure I hadn't missed something. But the more I looked, the more I doubted anything bad could happen in such an ordinary den. At least nothing like the things that happened in California.

Scanning it all one last time, a surprising wave of emotion hit me. Everything reminded me of Dad. The wall photos, the knickknacks, this recliner.

I missed him.

I thought about what the girls said out by the pond that day, about not staying mad. They were right. It was time to man-up and get my dad back in my life. Mom had mentioned he was stopping by on Monday to drop off a birthday present. So I thumbed him a text.

sorry i missd ur calls, how bout a b-day din monday somwhr?

Before touching Send, I added a heart emoji. Then I sunk back in the recliner, angling it as flat as it would go, and began

169

browsing the den shots I'd taken.
       That's all I remember.
       Phone propped against my chest, swiping through photos.
       The girls never called back.

Part IV

Angels Pass

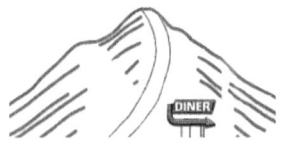

"Apparently there is nothing that cannot happen today."

Mark Twain

Chapter 42

Saturday, September 12

Jeffrey

A voice invaded my flying-tetherball dream.

"Rise and shine, Birthday Boy!"

Blinking my eyes open, sunlight instantly slammed them shut again. Inching away from the glare, I squinted to get my bearings.

I was in the den, the morning light bleeding through the curtains. I looked toward the voice I'd heard. Mom peered back at me from the doorway.

I looked down at myself. I was still in the recliner, still in my clothes, my phone still on my chest.

I checked the time. 9:20.

Whoa. Mom wanted to get an early start.

As she disappeared down the hallway, she called out that we needed to get going asap. I jumped up and stumbled into the bathroom, letting the scalding shower ease me back to life.

*   *   *

Iowa may not be as flat as Dorothy's Kansas, but it's darn close. Thus, most road trips in the state offer zero excitement. The one we were taking, for instance—Des Moines to Maple Falls—was basically a straight line with one right-hand curve where boring highway A merges into boring highway B.

Except for one part: *Angels Pass.*

Halfway between Maple Falls and Des Moines, Angels Pass climbed up and over the second-tallest peak in the state. According to the sign at the top, it's one thousand three hundred twenty-five feet above sea level (where they found sea level to measure from, I have no idea). Not exactly Mount Everest, but for people living in Flatland America thirteen hundred feet up might as well be outer space. And the views from the top were great, at least for Iowa.

The only negative was the Pass's horrible reputation for nasty accidents, especially on the much steeper eastern slope (the far side from Des Moines). In fact, that section had a pretty frightening nickname—*The Dark Side*—a label earned from one particularly ugly crash decades before I was born.

On a foggy morning in 1979, six cars and three trucks collided midway down, causing one of the worst chain-reaction crashes in state history. Two cars and one truck actually flew off the cliff and five people died.

It became known as The Crash on the Pass. They even covered it in my state history class. But for kids like me, with no personal memory of it, it was more of an urban legend. The few times I'd been on the Pass had been fun, even down The Dark Side. A nice break from an otherwise dull Iowa highway.

Of course, I didn't have to do the driving.

Once we'd passed the last remnants of Des Moines city limits, I re-adjusted my seat, stretched out my legs, and began spacing out my window. But it didn't take long for the endless telephone poles and miles of nearly identical farm plots to start melting my brain.

Itching for a distraction, I reached in my pocket for my phone —and realized that, in my rush to get ready, I'd left it at home.

No worries, though. Mom had hers.

So I closed my eyes and took a nap.

Chapter 43

Not long after Jeffrey faded out, Karen spotted a sign announcing a gas station at the next exit. The gauge showed half full, but she always filled up on road trips.

The tick-tocking turn signal woke Jeffrey up. As Karen slowed for the stop sign at the end of the off-ramp, he heard a soft thud. Possibly from under the car but he wasn't sure because it was gone by the time they stopped.

He looked over at his mother. She apparently hadn't heard it, and since it lasted only a split second, it wasn't worth mentioning.

A half block down the side road they pulled into the gas station and, as Karen rolled up to the pump, they both heard a different noise, a clink this time, like running over a key.

"You heard that, right?" Jeffrey asked.

Karen shut off the engine and listened. The only sound was the engine tapping as it cooled. She shrugged. "Probably ran over some trash, or loose change."

Jeffrey looked out his window. The station lot was pretty messy, so maybe she was right.

They both got out. Karen walked to the pump while Jeffrey peered under the car, then behind it. Seeing nothing unusual, he headed for the mini-mart to buy two water bottles.

*   *   *

Back in Brentwood, M leaned away from her computer and exhaled loudly. For the past hour, they'd been reviewing the pictures from Jeffrey's den. With laptops positioned side-by-side on the dining table, Diana was scanning the still shots, M the video clip. Last night's review had turned up nothing, but maybe after a good night's sleep they'd find something they missed.

M checked the time. 8:15 a.m. They still had two hours left

before they needed to get ready for the Saturday horseback-riding lessons Diana had convinced M to sign up for. After one last stretch and some finger-jiggling to get the blood flowing, she leaned back in to resume the video, this time in slow motion.

For six minutes the room stayed quiet.

Until M saw something and nudged Diana.

M's screen was frozen on a shot of the corkboard behind the desk in Jeffrey's den. She'd zoomed in on a piece of paper tacked to it, a bill of some kind. She pointed to it.

"Check that out."

Diana strained to read it, slowly mouthing the words printed at the top. "East... something... Village... Auto... Repair."

M nodded. "It's for their Honda Accord, dated five days ago, Monday." She tapped the bottom of the bill labeled Work Performed. "And look what they worked on."

Diana's eyes widened as she read the words.

Brake job.

*　　*　　*

By the time Karen topped off the tank and was back behind the wheel, Jeffrey was buckled back in, playing with her phone. "What's up?" she asked, starting the engine.

"Forgot mine at home," he told her. "But yours isn't much better. Only one percent juice left." He opened the glove box. "Where's your charger?"

Karen shook her head. "Darn. Forgot to plug it in last night. Too many things going on. And no car charger. The wire broke last week, sorry." Releasing the parking brake, she shifted into Drive and headed out.

He sighed, returning the phone to the glove box.

Karen looked over. "Wait. Power it all the way off first. That might re-juice it enough to at least check messages later."

He took it back out, held the off button until it powered down, then crammed it between the seats.

When Karen got to the gas station exit and stopped, Jeffrey

heard that clink again. "It's back," he said.

They sat there for a while, listening for strange sounds. But all they heard was the engine idling. Finally, Karen turned onto the frontage road, driving slowly so they could listen for new noises, but they heard none.

As she veered onto the highway on-ramp her expression suddenly lifted. "Ah, I know what that must've been. While you were in school Monday, I got the brakes done, for this trip. And last time I did that, they squeaked for a while till they got worn in. That's gotta be it."

Picking up speed, she merged into traffic.

*   *   *

Brake job.

Staring at those words, Diana took in a sharp breath. She turned to M. "I'm guessing that's the car they're driving now?"

M shrugged. "Far as I know."

Diana looked up at the ceiling. "Wait a sec. That can't be right."

"What?"

"Didn't we agree that their *den* was Ground Zero? Where their only landline with the phone number from the text is? So isn't *that* our target area? Not their car, or them on the road."

But M wasn't listening. She'd scrolled back up to the top of the auto repair bill, her eyes wide. "Wow," she whispered.

"What now?"

M looked away from the screen, gathered her thoughts, looked back at the bill, then at Diana.

"That last text, the one with Jeffrey's home number on it, remember the way I wrote it out that day? The blanks I left?"

Diana nodded. "Yeah, you said something about those first few numbers getting covered up. But we knew it was Jeffrey's area code because he confirmed the rest was his seven-digit landline."

M's eyes darted back and forth. "Or so we thought."

"What's that mean?"

M pointed to the screen. "Read the auto shop's phone number at the top."

Diana read it but didn't see M's point.

"And?"

"I know Jeffrey's area code, it's in my contacts. So why's this auto shop's different from his?"

"Huh?"

"Wouldn't you think they'd get their car worked on somewhere close by their house? So why different area codes?"

"I could think of a few reasons."

"Yeah, but what if it's because that covered-up area code we assumed was Jeffrey's *wasn't?*"

Chapter 44

With everything else going on since he got back home—wrecked house, construction workers everywhere, school starting, his mother getting sick before this trip—Jeffrey hadn't had much time to share his vacation adventures. But now, with miles of emptiness to fill, he got his chance.

He began at the beginning, describing his lucky seat placement and enchanted plane ride next to the Goddess of Brentwood. And for the next forty miles, the stories flowed. Ty's limo, M's guesthouse, Diana's mansion, their trips to Zuma, and his first-ever horseback ride.

Karen was loving every minute of it.

He did leave out a few minor details—the text messages, the car crash, the fire at Sam's, criminal activity in Santa Monica, and the whole hanging-tetherball drama. No point giving his mom any reason to rethink letting him return to LA. (After that last hug at the airport from you-know-who, he definitely couldn't risk that.)

At the one-hour mark, as raindrops began dotting the windshield, they passed a sign announcing sixty miles to Maple Falls, seven miles to Angels Pass, and four to the next food exit (a knife-and-fork doodle).

Karen asked, "Hungry?"

"Starved."

"Good. Me too. Let's grab breakfast at the next exit."

Through his window, Jeffrey could finally see the outline of Angels Pass, where the highway they were on linked with US Route 20. A little further east, he noticed thick bands of dark clouds. Hopefully, that stormy stuff wouldn't drift any closer. The Dark Side of the Pass was sketchy enough without a summer storm adding to the mix. Still, his mom was an excellent driver so he wasn't too worried.

Turning off at the food exit, Jeffrey heard the faint moan of a train whistle in the distance. He loved that sound. It stirred dreams of other places he hoped to explore someday. Shifting his gaze toward the sound, he caught the tiny silhouette of a long stream of freight cars inching toward Angels Pass, then disappearing behind it.

They traveled down a stretch of side road before turning into the restaurant's driveway. A large sign on the exterior of the building read Angels Pass Diner.

Despite its out-of-the-way location, the parking lot was almost full. But once Jeffrey thought about it, it made sense. He didn't remember seeing any other food exits since leaving Des Moines and when you're the only game around, people find you.

Karen saw someone leaving their parking spot two rows from the diner's front door and pulled in. As she came to a stop, Jeffrey heard that thud again—same as at the off-ramp—only this time Karen heard it too.

Shifting into Park, she killed the engine, then pumped the brake three times. After a few seconds, she turned to Jeffrey and shrugged. "Feels fine. Like I said, new brakes."

"You sure?"

She unbuckled her seat belt. "Remember, I was sick all week and the car's been in the garage that whole time. This is the first time out since the brake job. They've gotta wear in."

"If you say so."

They got out and headed for the entrance. The light drizzle felt good. When Jeffrey opened the diner door for his mother, the sweet smell of sizzling bacon made his stomach growl, melting away all thoughts of car noises.

Once seated by their hostess—her name tag said Sophie— Jeffrey couldn't take his eyes off the mesmerizing view out the diner's back window. Angels Pass, looming large and majestic, stood perfectly centered in the floor-to-ceiling glass spanning the entire length of the dining area, leaving no doubt where the place got its name.

Framed by the window's wide chrome borders, the view could've been a museum mural. The storm clouds now fully blanketed the mountain peak, so the cars and trucks climbing and descending all had their lights on. Red dots going up, white ones coming down. The swirling colors through the drizzle looked like pulsating blood vessels pumping life into the mountain.

Karen jostled her menu and cleared her throat to remind Jeffrey why they were there. Minutes later, their waitress, Francine, arrived. She was quite the talker and, as she and Karen chatted, Jeffrey scanned his menu for a suitable birthday breakfast. Until Karen mentioned it was his birthday and Francine roared, "Well, All Rightee Now!" drawing the attention of everyone in the restaurant to the Birthday Boy, who sank as low in his seat as he could.

By the time Francine left with their orders, Jeffrey knew more about her than anyone should know about their server: her son's name (John); John's career goal (architect); her husband's name (Ian); Ian's workplace (Iowa Highway Patrol); and how many years she'd worked at the diner (fourteen).

Returning his attention to the big window, a bright red patch off to the right caught Jeffrey's eye. Leaning forward, he saw the corner of a large umbrella, a whole row of them actually, sheltering a crowd milling around a dozen or so booths. Some kind of farmers' market, set up between the diner and the railroad tracks, packed with customers despite the rain (which also explained the nearly full parking lot).

After consuming possibly the largest breakfast of his life (even bigger than Brentwood), they were finally ready to leave. But only after Francine brought out two candle-lit birthday cupcakes and led the entire diner through an embarrassingly off-key rendition of the Birthday song.

Since the rain was coming down hard now, Francine "loaned" them an umbrella from the diner's lost-and-found for the trip out to their car. Outside, they sheltered under the awning while Karen tried to open the umbrella. It was stuck, so Jeffrey tried, eventually working the metal slider until it opened. After untangling the strap from his coat sleeve, he handed it back to his mom.

They waited for a break in the rain, then eventually just made a mad dash for the Honda.

Once in the car, Jeffrey shoved the wet umbrella behind his seat as Karen started the engine and flipped on the wipers and defroster. Waiting for the windows to clear, Jeffrey thought about the girls. He hadn't heard from them since last night. If they'd found anything strange in his den he needed to know. But as long as he and his mom were away from the house, there was no big hurry. He'd call them from the furniture store in Maples Falls.

Chapter 45

Diana checked her phone's contacts list. Sure enough, Jeffrey's area code was 5-1-5, not the auto shop's 6-4-1.

She turned to M. "If you're saying we might've assumed the wrong area code, that opens the floodgates. There's *hundreds* of area codes all over the country we'd have to check."

M shook her head. "I don't think so. If that '9-12' at the end of the text really is a date, Jeffrey would've been home by then. So any warning would've more likely been pointing to something around him *then*—in Iowa."

Opening a new browser window, she typed *iowa area codes* in the Google box, clicked the search button, and selected the first image on the results page. A map of Iowa area codes appeared. "Look. There's only six codes for the whole state."

She started punching keys on her phone. "Let's plug in Jeffrey's home number after each one and see what happens."

First, she tried the auto shop's 6-4-1 code, adding Jeffrey's seven-digit landline number after it. It rang twice, then a disconnected-number recording kicked in, so she hung up.

Next, she tried a bordering area code—7-1-2—but a recorded message told her it was an online business, presumably with no physical address, so a safe bet to ignore.

Next, she tried the code covering the northeast section above Des Moines—3-1-9. After three rings, a cheery female voice answered.

"Thank you for calling the Angels Pass Diner. This is Sophie, how can I help you?"

M hadn't planned this far ahead, so she clicked on speakerphone and winged it.

"Hi. I'm from out of town and was wondering where exactly you're located."

"We're just off Route 20."

Studying the area code map on her computer, M asked, "So if we're driving to Maple Falls from Des Moines, will we pass you?"

"Absolutely. We're about halfway between the most direct route."

M gave Diana a thumbs-up and, in as calm a voice as possible, explained she was actually calling from California and trying to locate her cousin. After providing a brief description of Jeffrey and Karen, Sophie remembered them, describing how the whole restaurant had sung the birthday song to the boy. But they'd already left.

"Any chance of catching them?"

"Not likely. They were trying to beat the storm over the Pass."

"The Pass?"

"Angels Pass—the name of our diner."

"What is that exactly?"

"You've never heard of it?" She snickered. "Of course you haven't, forgot you're in California. Anyway, it's a few miles up and I'm sure they were going that way because they talked about it while I rang up their bill."

"So it's like a section of highway?"

"Well, sort of. A mountain pass actually. Kinda famous, or I guess you'd say 'infamous.'"

"Infamous?"

"Yeah. Up here they call it 'the deadliest road in the state.'"

M hung up and turned to Diana whose gaze was frozen on her own computer screen. She'd pulled up an article about Angels Pass. A detailed history that included "The Dark Side" and "The Crash on the Pass."

Suddenly everything made terrible sense.

That last text had never been about Jeffrey's den.

It had been pointing them to this diner.

By "the deadliest road in the state."

Where Jeffrey and his mom were now headed.

On 9-12.

After someone had played with their brakes!

M's fingers flew over her phone, dialing Jeffrey's number. But after ringing four times it went to voicemail. She left a message and re-dialed. After four rings it went to voicemail again. "This makes no sense!" she muttered. She left a new message and tried a third time, but got the same result. "Why isn't he answering? He never leaves his phone off. That thing's his favorite new toy!" Desperate, she switched to calling Jeffrey's mom. "Come on, Aunt Karen, pick up!" she pleaded. This time it went to voicemail before even ringing. She left a new message, her voice quivering with tension.

Meanwhile, Diana tapped out texts, first to Jeffrey, then asking M for Karen's number and texting her too, begging them to call back. She turned to M. "Maybe they're in a dead zone."

M quickly googled *iowa cell phone coverage map*—which showed decent coverage in the area. Shaking her head, she looked at Diana. "Why are their voicemail prompts different? Jeffrey's rings four times first, but my aunt's doesn't ring at all."

"I think her phone's dead," Diana said.

Not allowing herself to consider what that might mean, M tried Jeffrey again, mumbling, "Okay, cuz, time to pick up!"—and leaving another shaky message when he didn't.

But what else could they do? They were out of time and options. Their calls and texts were going nowhere and they'd just missed them at the diner.

So Diana did the only thing she could think of.

Racing out the back door, she yelled for her "rock."

Chapter 46

Iowa State Patrol Officer Ian Lane was a twenty-two-year veteran of the department. For the past nine years, he'd worked the graveyard shift, three in the morning to eleven, covering a fifty-mile stretch of US Route 20 on both sides of Angels Pass.

The last few hours had been busier than usual, thanks to a big concert scheduled that afternoon in nearby Cedar Rapids. He checked his dashboard clock. 11:05. His shift was officially over, which explained the unsettling noises erupting from his stomach—likely the result of the low-carb diet his wife, Francine, had put him on to stop his belt from cutting him in two.

So his new routine, especially on Saturdays, was to starve himself through the end of his shift, then stop by the diner when Francine's lunch break began, where he'd be rewarded with a "healthy meal." Translation: no pancakes or pie. But even if he wasn't thrilled with most of the dishes Francine served him (lemon juice was *not* salad dressing), he did enjoy their lunches together.

Turning into the diner parking lot, he pulled up to his usual spot—the red no-parking zone ten yards from the entrance. The rain was coming down strong and steady now. Reaching for his radio mic to close out his shift, he noticed a lady and boy, probably mother and son, fiddling with an umbrella near the diner entrance.

As he made small talk with Bea, his dispatcher, he watched the pair struggle with their umbrella, taking turns trying to open it. Finally succeeding, they ran to their car, a blue Honda Accord.

After signing off with Bea, he buttoned up his plastic parka, donned his official Iowa State Patrol hat, and exited his vehicle. Approaching the diner's front door, something shiny on the ground sparkled. He reached down, picked it up, and wiped it off. It looked expensive.

He thought about the mother and son he'd seen fiddling with their umbrella. He looked where their car had been but the space was empty. Then, in the far corner of the lot he caught a glimpse of it pulling onto the frontage road, its taillights fading toward the east highway on-ramp.

His stomach growled again. He checked his watch. Francine was expecting him now. He peered into the diner's glass front door. The place was packed, as it always was on the Saturdays they held their "rain or shine" farmers' market. Meaning, his wife would be slammed with customers for a while.

He glanced at the object in his hand, then back out to the frontage road, then to his patrol car where he fixed on the three words printed on his driver's door. *Protect and Serve.*

Ah, heck.

He'd call Francine to let her know he'd be a little late.

Dropping the object into his breast pocket he jogged back to his car.

*   *   *

Somehow, Diana convinced Ty to call the police in Iowa. Although doubtful, he admitted that a normal-sounding grown-up might have a slightly better chance of mobilizing the cops than two wigged-out teens.

Unfortunately, it didn't work.

After patiently listening to his story of "a blue Honda with possibly bad brakes heading for Angels Pass," the policeman on the phone politely explained that they couldn't order a welfare check on a car. Nor could they pull one over without "probable cause"—which Ty's story wasn't.

Bottom line, the police had no legal basis to stop someone based on what Ty described, even if they could somehow find the right blue Honda out of the millions of them out there.

Hanging up the phone, Ty shook his head.

Diana turned to M. "We need to call back the diner."

"Why?"

"You got a better idea?"

*   *   *

As Officer Lane turned onto the side road toward the east on-ramp, his radio chirped. It was Bea, advising of a three-car pile-up five miles *west* of the diner—the opposite direction from where he saw the Honda go.

Darn. His special-delivery trip wasn't gonna happen. By the time he finished with this accident scene, they'd be long gone over the Pass. He'd have to ask Francine to put what he'd found in the diner's lost-and-found bin when he returned for lunch. Maybe the lady and her son would call once they realized what they'd lost. Or, if they paid by credit card, maybe the diner could contact them.

In any case, it didn't matter now. Duty called. Turning onto the westbound ramp, he flipped on his siren and light bar and raced toward the crash site.

*   *   *

The same hostess answered M's call. But this time M "embellished" the details—bad brakes, no phones, the deadliest road in the state—enough to get Sophie to put them on hold while she ran out to the parking lot to check if Jeffrey and Karen were really gone. Maybe they'd stuck around to use the bathroom, or wait out the storm in their car. Not likely, but she was more than willing to check.

When she returned with the bad news, she had one last thought. The husband of one of the waitresses at the diner was a highway patrolman who usually came in for lunch on Saturdays.

"I'll ask Francine to talk to him when he gets here. Maybe he can help."

M thanked her and disconnected. She turned to Diana whose expression said what both were thinking: By the time anyone reached them, it'd be too late. Looking down at the phone still in her hand, M thumbed in a new text, not mincing words.

STOP! ITS UR BRAKES! CALL US!!!

Too little, too late, she knew. But what else could she do?

Clicking the Send button, she whisked it off to Jeffrey's and her aunt's phones.

Chapter 47

The stretch of highway called Angels Pass was two lanes in each direction with an emergency shoulder on the right and guard rails on both sides. But unlike the steeper eastern face, the side Karen was now climbing was a gradual two-and-a-half-mile rise to the top, so traffic moved at a brisk pace despite the rain.

The good news was they hadn't heard any new noises since leaving the diner. The bad news was the weather. It had quickly turned nasty, the rain now pelting the car roof like a popcorn popper. Also, as Francine had warned, traffic was heavier because of a nearby music concert.

Leaning forward in his seat, Jeffrey peered out the windshield for a better view of the summit. There wasn't much to see. Storm clouds obscured most of it. As he sat back a bright flash lit the sky, followed by a low rumble. Oh great. Throw in a lightning and thunderstorm. It wasn't super-close, yet, but still.

A truck blew past in the fast lane, flooding their windshield with such force Karen nearly lost control. As the wipers worked to clear the mess, Jeffrey heard two loud thumps, followed by a new sound: a rhythmic slapping, like tires over back-to-back speed bumps.

He looked at his mom. Her expression hadn't changed. She'd surely heard this new sound but wasn't reacting, her eyes bouncing between the windshield and the rearview mirror.

Jeffrey turned to see what she was looking at. A big black tour bus was right on their tail, making it impossible for them to slow down. If Karen braked, they'd get rear-ended.

"Why won't it go around us?" he asked.

"Guess it's easier to bully us into going faster than for him to pull into the fast lane and upset more drivers."

The slapping noise suddenly stopped, promptly replaced by a clanking rattle that seemed to come from the engine area.

"Mom, we need to pull over and see what's up."

Karen nudged her chin toward Jeffrey's window. "Not possible."

He turned to look. Yipes. The emergency shoulder was wall-to-wall trucks, apparently doing their safety checks before descending down The Dark Side.

"Even if this bus let me slow down, there's nowhere to pull over." She forced a smile. "But we'll be fine. Once we get to level ground, we'll stop and check."

Jeffrey knew that a safety check *after* charging down The Dark Side made no sense. But why bring it up now? There was nothing they could do about it. Looking out the windshield, he tried to gauge how far they were from the summit. Maybe halfway. Still time to slow down before the plunge down. If only that bus would back off.

He needed a distraction. If he kept overthinking every inch of the road he'd go nuts. Looking around, he saw the tip of his mom's phone sticking out from between the seats. Maybe there was enough juice now to check messages.

As he grabbed it, it slipped further down. The space was too narrow for his hand so he squeezed two fingers along the side trying to wiggle it free, but it was stuck. Finally, he got his fingertips squished against its edge and slowly began sliding it up.

Without turning, Karen asked what he was doing. "Trying to get your phone out." Sliding it up millimeter by millimeter, his eyes stayed focused on the road while the windshield re-flooded with each passing truck.

Finally the phone popped out. He powered it up. The screen blinked on, then dinged. An incoming message.

A hard jolt—a giant pothole—ripped the phone from his hands, nearly catapulting him through the windshield. Thankfully, his seat belt did its job. As Karen worked to regain control, her right foot shot to the brake pedal. But an instant before stomping it, she stopped, recalling what she'd learned in high school Driver's Ed about braking in the rain.

Slow and steady wins the race, gentle braking keeps you safe.

Something about "hydroplaning," whatever that was. Plus, that bus was still on their butt. So she tapped the brake pedal lightly, keeping her eyes on her mirror.

But nothing happened. So she tapped again.

Still nothing.

Then again.

Watching her foot, Jeffrey's heart pounded. With each tap, he waited for the car to respond but felt nothing. Like the pedal wasn't connected. Swiveling toward the back window, he checked the bus. Still too close. Turning back around, he noticed his mom's phone on the floor mat in front of him, but it was too far to reach without undoing his seat belt, and after that last pothole, he wasn't doing that.

Then something began tickling his nose. A pungent smell, like smoke, but stronger, nastier. When he tried to clear his throat, he started coughing. He glanced at his mother. She had to smell it too, but her attention was clearly elsewhere. Eyes jumping between road and mirror, still tapping the brake, then more gas, then another brake tap. Trying everything to slow down without getting crushed from behind.

Yet nothing was working.

And the summit was coming.

Followed by The Dark Side.

"What's that smell?" Jeffrey finally asked.

But Karen didn't answer, her eyes and foot still fixed on road, mirror, brake pedal.

Jeffrey leaned over to check the speedometer.

Fifty-eight.

Too fast in the pouring rain this close to the top.

Then he remembered where he'd smelled that foul odor before. When their clothes dryer died, the repair man explained what it was: burning rubber.

*   *   *

A mile before reaching the three-car pile-up, Officer Lane's radio chirped again. It was Bea canceling the call-out. Another patrol unit was already on-scene and reported no injuries. Tow trucks were on route and he was no longer needed. He could clock out.

Whipping a U across the median, he headed back to the diner.

But the closer he got, the more he couldn't shake thoughts of that blue Honda. The sane side of his brain said it was too late—too much time had passed to catch it now. But the Good Samaritan side whispered what was the harm in trying? The diner would still be packed, his wife would still be busy with customers, and his patrol car was way faster than a Honda.

It took all of three seconds for the *Protect and Service* side to win the battle.

Checking his side mirror, he moved into the fast lane and punched the gas. If he didn't spot the Honda by Angels Pass, he'd head back to the diner, but maybe he'd get lucky.

About two minutes later, he thought he did.

Six or so car lengths ahead in the slow lane, a big bus with blacked-out windows and writing on the side—the kind politicians and rock bands use—was partially blocking what *could* be a blue Honda. Of course, there were more of those out there than pigs in Iowa, so he wasn't sure. Especially this far back, in the pouring rain, with a big fat bus blocking his view.

And now he was boxed in. A red SUV in front, a white van on his right. He squinted ahead at the possible-Honda. Even traveling in the slow lane, it was going too fast. Especially in these road conditions, this near the summit. Because once they crested, the trip down was *much* faster.

Then he realized why. The black bus was tailgating. But if he pulled it over, he'd lose the Honda. Plus, the shoulder was too crowded to pull anything over.

As he considered his next move, the red SUV in front of him flipped on its blinker and moved to the right lane. He smiled. Drivers hated police cars in their mirror.

He sped up, passed the SUV, then three more cars. Finally able to get a decent view of his target, he saw what looked like the outline of a decal in the possible-Honda's rear window.

He passed another car for a closer look.

There it was, in the lower-left corner. That same heart-shaped decal he'd noticed on the Honda in the diner parking lot.

He slipped into the slow lane behind the bus. Seconds later

the cop-in-mirror trick worked again and the bus began to slow down, finally giving the Honda some breathing room.

Checking his side mirror, he swung back into the fast lane, passed the bus, and slid directly behind the Honda.

He re-checked his speedometer.

They were still going too fast, over sixty now. In this downpour? No longer being tailgated? This close to the summit? *With a cop car behind them?* It made no sense.

But there wasn't much he could do.

There was nowhere to do a traffic stop here, not enough time to do it on the summit, and trying to pull them over on the way down was out of the question.

He'd have to wait until they leveled out at the bottom.

He lightened up on the gas pedal to give them more room. Hopefully, they'd see him in their mirror and at least slow down a bit.

Because it was a wild ride down.

Chapter 48

Jeffrey was terrified. They'd just hit the summit and were seconds from hurtling down The Dark Side—*way* too fast.

He checked the speedometer again.

Sixty-two.

Faster than the last reading.

He felt something at his foot and looked down. His mom's phone had slid against his shoe, close enough to finally reach. He leaned over and grabbed it. Overpowered by the burnt-rubber stench, his eyes were watering badly. He brushed his face with his sleeve to wipe away the tears, setting off a new coughing fit.

*　　*　　*

Officer Lane's phone was ringing.

Darn. He forgot to call Francine to tell her he'd be late. Had to be her. But he'd crested the summit now and was trying to keep pace with the Honda. He wanted to give it enough room to slow down, which required his full concentration, especially with his wipers barely keeping up with the pounding rain. No way he could reach his phone on the passenger seat. He'd have to call Francine back later.

He still didn't know why the Honda hadn't slowed yet. He'd seen a few flashes of brake lights earlier, but nothing now.

After seven chimes, his phone stopped ringing.

*　　*　　*

Karen's eyes were in full free-flow now, tears angling down both cheeks. But she couldn't take either hand off the wheel to wipe them. She tried blinking them away but that wasn't working. As she fought to stay in her lane, Jeffrey saw her lips moving, mouthing words to herself, the same ones over and over. He strained to listen, and then he heard them.

Grip Tight. Hug The Line.
Grip Tight. Hug The Line.

Pivoting her eyes from the road back up to the mirror, Karen did a double-take. Something had changed. The dark shadow shading her back window was gone. Or seemed to be, the glass too wet and foggy to tell for sure. Had the bus really backed off? If so, now was her best chance to try braking again. Even in the rain.

It'd take more than a tap at this point, she knew that. But not too hard or she'd lose control. Tightening her grip on the wheel, her knuckles stretched bright white, she carefully re-positioned her foot on the pedal.

Taking short breaths to fight the fumes, Jeffrey watched his mother's foot barely touch the brake—just as something lit up his hand. He looked down. He'd forgotten he was still holding her phone. The message icon was blinking!

Through watery eyes, he squinted to read it. Whoa. Twelve missed calls and texts.

He tapped the icon and an all-caps message flashed on.

STOP! ITS UR BRAKES! CALL US!!!

An instant later the screen went dark.

Turning to warn his mom, he stopped. What good would it do? The last thing she needed was a new distraction.

Besides, how could the girls know?

He watched his mother's leg tense, then push down on the pedal.

He waited.

Nothing happened.

She pushed harder.

Still nothing.

Water plumes splashed up both door panels as they careened down the winding lane. Quietly, Jeffrey began counting. A trick he used to stay calm. *One thousand one. One thousand two...*

Seconds passed. His mother's rigid leg kept pressure on the

brake, but nothing changed. The acrid smell finally forced him to crack open his window. Rain pelted the side of his head. Wiping it away, he powered the glass back up, then leaned over to re-check their speed.

Sixty-four.

The numbers still going in the wrong direction.

Another flash of lightning momentarily blinded him. He gasped, sucking in more fumes, triggering another coughing bout. Refocusing on his mother's brake foot, he tried breathing through his nose. Abruptly the road dipped, lurching the car forward. Stomach acid seared his throat as his breakfast rocketed upward. Struggling to hold it down, an avalanche of thoughts raced through his head.

His room, his calendars, his mom's laugh, his cousin. Diana.

He pushed them away and re-checked the speedometer.

Sixty-five.

More images flew by. His broken tetherball, Diana's tennis court, Spits. Was this how it ended? The fumes squeezed his throat shut. His eyes strained to stay open.

Then... blackness.

Chapter 49

They say you see bright lights when it happens.
Or leave your body and watch from above.

But neither occurred.

Because the blackness Jeffrey saw was the back of his eyelids, involuntarily slammed shut when his brain braced for impact.

Popping them back open, he was still in the car. Still plummeting down the Pass. Still going too fast.

But at least they hadn't crashed. Yet.

He turned to his mother. Her face was blank, tears streaming, eyes straight ahead, hands clutching the wheel, foot hard on the brake. The same pose as before his black-out.

Except... something was different.

Not with his mom. Not with the car. A sound?

He strained to listen, but heard only pounding rain and slapping wipers.

Yet it was something. If not a sound, a sensation...

A sharp twist in the road threw his mom's foot off the brake, flinging him against his door. Without missing a beat, Karen re-positioned *both* feet on the pedal this time and pushed down hard, arching her back for leverage.

Jeffrey squinted at the speedometer, then rubbed his eyes and looked again.

Sixty?

That sensation, or sound, or whatever it was, continued—now more a vibration. Soft. Low.

Slight pressure on his back nudged him forward.

Something about it felt vaguely familiar.

Then he remembered where he'd felt it.

His plane ride! The landing! Near the end of the runway, when the wings flipped up. Not as strong, but similar.

The vibration seemed to blend with a whoosh sound, almost

inaudible, but there—as the pressure on his back intensified.

He turned to his mother. Her expression hadn't changed—eyes forward, both feet on the brake, hands gripped so tightly he thought the steering wheel might crack.

Another speedometer check. *Fifty-five?*

The whooshing grew louder, higher pitched.

The pressure pushing him forward strengthened.

He looked out the windshield. Through the sloshing wipers, the car in front looked different. Smaller? Or were his eyes playing tricks on him? No, definitely smaller, further ahead actually, the space between them greater than before.

He blinked twice and looked again. Turning toward Karen's window, the passing cars were going faster. How could that be? He re-checked the speedometer.

Forty-eight.

His brain raced to catch up. Wait. The cars around them weren't speeding up; *they* were slowing down!

That was the whooshing noise.

That was the vibration.

That's what was pushing him forward.

The brakes engaging!

The pressure on his back increased. Reaching for the dashboard for support, he looked out his window. The landscape had shifted. No, not shifted; the ground was leveling.

He checked their speed.

Forty!

A smile crept across his face.

They weren't going to die.

They'd made it down the Pass!

A rainbow of lights lit up Jeffrey's side mirror.

A police car was pulling them over.

Chapter 50

Watching the policeman approach his side of the car, Jeffrey powered down his window. The cop appeared and squatted eye-level with Jeffrey. Water streamed off the rim of his hat as raindrops spattered Jeffrey's face.

The policeman nodded to both of them.

"Morning, folks. Officer Ian Lane, Iowa State Patrol."

Jeffrey glanced at his mom who gave him a quick shrug.

The policeman reached into his breast pocket and took something out. "The reason I stopped you... was because of this."

Extending his arm through the open window he displayed what he had. The boy's eyes bulged. Resting in the palm of the policeman's hand was Jeffrey's horseshoe charm bracelet.

Instinctively, Jeffrey reached for his left wrist where his lucky chain was supposed to be. It wasn't there.

"Figured one of you may have lost it?" the officer asked, though Jeffrey's reaction answered the question.

Pausing to find his voice, Jeffrey whispered, "Yes, sir. It's mine." He gently plucked it from the policeman's hand and re-clasped it around his wrist. "Thank you," he mumbled.

The trooper grinned. "You're welcome. Found it in front of the diner back there, and noticed you two playing with your umbrella in that same spot a few minutes earlier."

Leaning in closer, he wrinkled his nose.

"Whew," he groaned, scanning the car's interior. "What *is* that smell?"

It took Karen several minutes to relay the whole story, starting with when they pulled into the gas station outside Des Moines. The weird noises, the brake pedal problems, the horrible fumes, the Honda's recent brake job, and their terrifying ride down the Pass.

When she finished, Officer Lane offered to take a look under the hood. "But first you need to roll down your windows," he said, stepping back and coughing into his sleeve. "Don't worry about the rain. You can always wipe the water off your seats, but not the gunk from your lungs."

Karen rolled down the windows and unlatched the hood. Officer Lane strode to the front of the car, popped the release, and began poking around. A few minutes later he wrapped something in a handkerchief, slammed the hood shut, then circled the car, kneeling down by each tire for a moment. Finally, he returned to Karen's window holding a cloth-covered object.

He showed it to her. "Pretty sure this was your problem." Unfolding the oil-stained handkerchief, he revealed a small tool, about four inches long, black and charred, with bubbly stuff oozing on one end.

"Don't touch it, it's still hot," he cautioned. "It's a mini-wrench, for working on small bolts, like the ones on your master cylinder. That's the container they pour brake fluid into when they install new brakes. I'm guessing someone left it on top of your engine and forgot it. It didn't do any damage but likely made quite a racket bouncing around in there."

He pointed to the bubbly end of the wrench. "Then the rubber coating on the handle here melted to the hot engine." He made a face. "That's what that stink is. Fumes must've leaked through your firewall."

He re-wrapped the handkerchief and handed it to Karen. "Here, in case you need proof of your mechanic's stupidity. Ask for a refund. Tell 'em a highway patrolman found it melted to your engine block and said you should get your money back. Might work."

Karen handed the handkerchief to Jeffrey who stowed it in the glove box. The policeman continued. "But like I said, everything looks fine. The brakes were wet but no brake fluid leaks around the wheels or master cylinder, and all the bolts are tight. Though it wouldn't hurt to have someone take another look once you get home. Also have them check why fumes leaked into the passenger compartment. And please keep your windows cracked until they do."

He angled his head slightly. "Maybe use a different mechanic this time. One who checks his tools before closing the hood."

Karen nodded. "Got it. But if everything's fine, why'd the brakes act up like that?"

Officer Lane snickered. "Probably 'cause it's raining cats and dogs out here, in case you hadn't noticed." He removed his hat, shook it off, and re-positioned it on his head. Kneeling eye-level with Karen, he said, "Look, brakes don't work the same in these conditions, especially new ones on steep, slick, windy mountain roads. Plus, in a storm like this, every passing vehicle throwing off water is flooding your brakes even worse than your windshield. And once flooded, they don't work right."

"But they worked okay earlier," Karen explained.

The policeman nodded. "They dry out a little every time you engage them, as long as you don't push too hard. That's probably why things got better the further down the Pass you got." He stood back up. "Tell you what though. If you scoot over, I'll double-check them, dry 'em out a little more, make sure everything's good."

Jeffrey moved to the back seat, Karen scooted over, and Officer Lane sat behind the wheel. He pressed down on the brake pedal a half-dozen times, then drove up and back a few car lengths while braking several times in each direction. When he was satisfied, he exited the vehicle, wished them a safe trip, and turned toward his patrol car.

From the back seat window, Jeffrey called out. "'Scuse me, sir." Officer Lane turned. Jeffrey offered a weak smile. "I was wondering if you had a phone I could maybe borrow for a second? Ours is dead, and there's some pretty freaked out people waiting to hear if we're okay." He paused for a moment before adding, "Maple Falls is still an hour away. I'll be real quick."

The policeman stood there for a moment, a tiny trace of a smile forming. Then, without a word, he walked back to his car. Not sure what to make of that, Jeffrey returned to the front seat. A minute later Officer Lane approached Jeffrey's open passenger window and handed Jeffrey his cell phone.

Jeffrey nodded to the policeman, took the phone, and punched in M's number. She answered right away, clearly relieved to hear his voice. While Officer Lane hovered nearby, Jeffrey rapidly delivered his really-can't-talk-now mini-summary: forgot his phone, his mom's was dead, using a policeman's, he and Karen were fine, full report later.

Taking the hint to keep it short, M replied, "Okay. Later. Oh, and happy birthday." Jeffrey grinned slightly, disconnected, and handed the phone back to the smiling patrolman.

Fifty-five minutes later they arrived in Maple Falls, the rest of their trip gloriously uneventful. No fumes, no noises, no brake problems, no drama.

Chapter 51

It took Karen nearly two hours to pick out her new bedroom set at The Couch Potato. Shuttling back and forth between floor displays and catalogs, Jeffrey occasionally nodded when asked. Even if it took his mom forever, it was a great way to put the whole Angels Pass ordeal behind them.

By the time Karen finished making final delivery arrangements, most of the storm clouds had moved on, so they decided to stay in town to celebrate Jeffrey's birthday.

They lunched at a cute barbecue place. They explored local shops (Jeffrey picked out two presents at his mother's insistence: a winter coat and a three-book set of Nancy Drew mysteries). They even took in a movie at Maple Falls' only theater—*Lord of the Rings*—a three-hour blast-from-the-past (and the perfect film length for delaying their trip home—just in case). They ended the night with a delicious birthday dinner at a steak house recommended by their lunch waiter.

On the ride home, Karen found an alternate route that bypassed Angels Pass entirely, but added an extra forty-five minutes to the drive. So they didn't get back until after midnight. Which was fine with Jeffrey since it meant the day was officially over; they'd made it through "9-12" in one piece!

True, things had gotten a bit dicey there for a while. But in the end, nothing bad happened. No car crashes, no fires, no witch-flattening tornadoes. Just some anxious moments before a fun-filled day of birthday cheer.

Following his mom into the house, Jeffrey thought back over the last two days. How stressful they'd been—investigating, worrying, obsessing over yet another false alarm. Like that stupid hanging tetherball. If only they'd learned from that mistake and ignored the last text, they could've saved themselves a ton of grief.

He gave his mom a big hug, thanked her again for a memorable birthday, and went to his room. After putting away his presents, he collapsed on the bed.

Then he remembered his promise to the girls.

He checked the time. 12:25 a.m. Not that late in California especially on Saturday night.

He trudged into the den and found his phone right where he'd left it, on the arm of the recliner. Climbing into the soft leather, he keyed in his cousin's number.

M answered on the second ring and, still at Diana's for another night, put him on speaker. He apologized for calling so late, let them sing him one last happy birthday chorus (it was still his birthday in Brentwood), slid the recliner as far back as it would go, and launched into Jeffrey's Crazy Road Trip.

He left nothing out, detailing each nerve-racking, funny, mind-blowing moment as if narrating an adventure novel. The car noises, the stinky smells, Francine and the diner, getting caught in the storm, losing his bracelet, the roller-coaster death ride over the Pass, eventually seeing all their missed texts and calls, and of course how Iowa State Patrolman Ian Lane came to their rescue, returning his bracelet and even checking their brakes.

Then it was the girls' turn. They described finding the brake-job bill tacked to the corkboard in his den and figuring out it was the diner's phone number in that last text and not his. They told him about the hostess remembering them and trying to help, and all the scary stuff they'd read about Angels Pass. They even mentioned Ty calling the police in Iowa (Jeffrey was shocked and flattered).

By the time their stories ended, it was late in both time zones, so they said their goodnights and signed off, thinking the night was over.

*   *   *

Jeffrey changed into his Hawkeyes nightshirt, then went to the bathroom to brush his teeth. As he stared at himself in the mirror, a nagging thought re-surfaced. One that had bugged him most of the way home. A regret, actually. About the way he'd handled that whole encounter with the policeman. Rather, how *poorly* he'd handled it.

After all the trouble the man had gone through, way beyond what any normal cop would do, Jeffrey hadn't exactly shown an outpouring of appreciation. No, his only reaction had been a pathetic, barely audible, two-word thank-you.

He'd been more interested in borrowing the man's phone than showing any real gratitude.

Yes, he'd been pretty traumatized at the time, after that whole Angels Pass thing, added to the shock of suddenly seeing his bracelet in the policeman's hand. Still, that was no excuse for being an ungrateful brat.

Then a thought hit him. A way he could fix things. He'd email the man! Use his writing skills to compose a proper thank-you.

Except he didn't have an email address, only his name and job. But surely the highway patrol had contact information online.

He cleaned off his toothbrush, stuck it back in its holder, and returned to his desk. Turning on his laptop, he typed *ian lane, iowa state patrol* into the search box and tapped the Find button. The top link of the results page immediately caught his attention—a recent news story about that policeman. He clicked it.

By the time he finished reading, he could barely breathe.

*   *   *

The girls were not happy. It had nothing to do with Jeffrey. Of course they were glad he and his mom were home safe. No, they were unhappy with themselves. Still fuming over getting everything so wrong. For obsessing over that last text and all that stupid 9-12 stuff. For inventing more phony clues and letting their imaginations run wild. *Again.*

They were also embarrassed. All the needless worry their stupid actions had caused everyone. Jeffrey. His mom. Ty. The Iowa state police. Even that diner hostess. Not to mention the stress and anxiety they'd put *themselves* through.

And this time they'd been so sure. All the pieces fit together perfectly. The new brake job. The diner's phone number. "The deadliest road in the state." All of it happening on 9-12.

Yet they'd blown it. Again. Which explained their not-great mood when Jeffrey called back ten minutes later.

Except right away, they could tell something was wrong. No greeting, no jokes, Jeffrey babbling even faster than usual.

Something about writing a thank-you to the cop who'd rescued them. Then going online for his email address.

"So google him, right now!" Jeffrey insisted. "*Ian Lane, Iowa State Patrol.* Then click that first news article. I'll wait."

They did as instructed and soon had the same story up on their screen. It was a news report, posted hours earlier by a local reporter in Cedar Rapids. About an incident occurring that afternoon near the Angels Pass Diner. An incident that, judging from the times listed, happened minutes after that cop pulled Jeffrey and Karen over.

Disaster Averted, Diner/Market Saved
– 'Right Place, Right Time' Says Hero Cop –

Timing is everything. Just ask Iowa State Patrolman Ian Lane. A little past noon today, he was driving on a rarely used back road between Route 20 and the iconic Angels Pass Diner. A road he never should have been on. His wife worked in that diner and he'd postponed his lunch date with her to return a motorist's lost property and, running late, had used that road as a shortcut back.

Then fate stepped in. Nearing the diner, his patrol car's rear tire blew. Quickly determining the cause—a cracked railroad tie on the track he'd just crossed—he immediately recognized the danger. The Chicago oil run from Houston—forty-six tanker cars of high-explosive crude—was scheduled to pass over those very tracks within the hour, as it did every other Saturday. Making matters worse, the diner and attached farmers' market, both packed with weekend customers, sat just yards from those tracks.

Thankfully, Officer Lane instantly swung into first-responder mode. In less than two minutes he'd patched through to the railroad's emergency hotline, collaborating with their crew to safely re-route the train with a slim nineteen minutes to spare, thus preventing an almost certain human and environmental disaster.

The railroad later issued a statement commending the officer's heroism, noting that because the broken track was fresh, it had evaded the company's early warning system.

When advised he was being hailed a hero, Officer Lane shrugged it off. "Right place, right time is all—just hustling back to keep the wife happy."

When they all finished reading, no one spoke as the significance of those facts sunk in.

It had never been about Jeffrey's house, or den, or car.

It was a warning about a train wreck—a potentially massive one—by a diner, on a certain day.

Information they'd had all along.

In a single line of text.

One that began with the *where*—the diner's phone number.

And ended with the *when*—9-12.

But just as chilling was how the disaster had been averted. By two timely twists of fate: A lost lucky bracelet, and a cop's good deed returning it.

Later that night, after Ty finished his moon drills, the girls showed him the news story. He took his time reading it before handing the phone back and just staring out at the pool for a while.

After a long silence, he turned, gave the girls a tight smile, quietly mumbled "Sweet dreams, all," then strolled off toward his house without another word.

As they watched him disappear into the darkness, they could almost hear that *Twilight Zone* jingle playing in the background, though Ty wasn't humming it.

Chapter 52

Despite the bombshell news article, sleep came fast for Jeffrey. Not surprising when your birthday spirals into a seventeen-hour roller coaster ride—zigzagging from scary to fun to freaky—across half the state of Iowa.

Unfortunately, the deep sleep didn't last.

Twenty minutes in, Jeffrey's phone beeped. He tried to ignore it, but the light from the display wouldn't let him. Reaching for it, he expected to see a follow-up from the girls, but it wasn't.

Due to unauthorized activity detected on your phone,
it will be DEACTIVATED for your security
within 24 hours. We apologize for the inconvenience.
Please visit a service center for replacement information.

He massaged his eye sockets, trying to turn his brain back on. Was that bad news or good? On the one hand, how could they investigate a phone mystery without the phone? Then again, a new phone would at least stop the weird texts and related stress, probably.

Either way though, there was nothing he could do about it in the middle of the night. He'd run it by the girls in the morning.

Returning the phone to the nightstand, he stretched out one last yawn and went back to sleep.

The next morning his phone was dead.

Part V

The Only Child Club

"Growing up, we realize it's less important to have lots of friends and more important to have real ones."

Author Unknown

Chapter 53

Sunday Morning

Brentwood

M stood in her rock-star bathroom flossing her teeth. She'd grown used to the massive size of the room, so no longer paid it much attention. In fact, her only thoughts since waking had been about that news article.

Danger seemed to be following Jeffrey wherever he went, even to Iowa. Was someone tracking his phone? What else could explain the bad stuff trailing him around like that? Or that only *his* phone got those texts?

Except if that were true, someone would've had to plan that whole diner-train thing. Which was clearly impossible. Too many moving parts. They'd have to know about Jeffrey's road trip, and that they'd be eating at that diner, and that a particular train track was broken (or actually break it), and that a train with deadly cargo was due on that track, on that day, at that time.

No way.

Still, that sense of urgency she and Diana had been feeling even before Jeffrey's road trip was definitely on high alert now. What were they missing? More importantly, how could they avoid more bad things?

She rinsed her mouth and headed downstairs.

In the kitchen, she was greeted by Diana, Ty, and the housekeeper preparing another impressive morning feast: mushroom and cheese omelets, fresh-squeezed orange juice from one of Diana's fruit trees, applewood bacon crisped in the pizza oven, pineapple/strawberry fruit cocktail, and the final act: salted caramel gelato drizzled in hot fudge—because what's a palace breakfast without dessert?

Just another Brentwood morning.

*   *   *

Des Moines

Seventeen hundred miles away, Jeffrey and his mother were driving to the mall.

Karen had spent the morning shopping online for curtains, the last thing she needed for her new bedroom before The Couch Potato furniture arrived in three days. And once she'd found the perfect set in a store at the downtown mall, she'd bribed Jeffrey to come with her, promising him one last birthday present: a book he wanted—*Ten Secrets to Winning on Jeopardy!*—in stock at the bookstore there.

A few blocks from the house, Jeffrey used Karen's cell to text the girls about his phone's sudden death. A minute later, he got two shocked-face emojis back with a message saying they'd discuss it at their Skype session that night.

It was one of those rare, not-fatally-humid Midwestern summer mornings, perfect for a Sunday drive with the windows down. Not quite the California coast, but nice. Cruising down the main road to the mall, Karen was in a festive mood, singing along to her classic-rock station. Jeffrey, meanwhile, barely spoke, his thoughts still stuck on how his dead phone had basically torpedoed their investigation.

When they turned into the shopping center's main entrance, Karen was belting out the chorus to an old Eagles tune. As she headed down the ramp to the underground parking area, the car speakers began to sputter, so she clicked off the radio but kept humming the song.

After finding a parking spot two rows from the stairs, Karen cut the engine, paused, then turned to Jeffrey. "Hey Mr. *Jeopardy!*-Man, help me out here. What's the name of that song I was just singing to? For the life of me, I can't think of it."

Jeffrey shook his head. He hadn't been listening.

Karen reached for her purse and pulled out her phone.

Jeffrey looked over. "What're you doing?"

"It'll bug me all day. Maybe they've got a playlist online."

She tapped in the radio station's call letters, hit search, and waited. Making a face, she mumbled, "Darn, can't get through, have to try later." She dropped the phone in her purse and exited the car.

Jeffrey got out and caught up with her.

Ten steps from the stairs, he froze.

What had just happened? He wasn't sure but it seemed important. His mind raced back... Then the dots connected.

That 7-Eleven.

*   *   *

Brentwood

Twenty minutes after they finished breakfast, Susan arrived to pick up her daughter. As they headed back to the Valley, while waiting for a light a block from the freeway, they both noticed the detour signs ahead. Some kind of road work blocking the on-ramp, likely saved for the lighter traffic on Sunday.

M pulled out her phone to find an alternate route. But when she tapped her maps app an error message popped up.

Your phone's Locations setting is off.
Do you want to turn it on to enable GPS?

Strange. Her phone must've updated overnight and defaulted to that setting. About to tap the OK box, something stopped her. One word. She ran it through her head. Could it be that simple?

Why hadn't she thought of it before? Now it was too late. One day too late. With Jeffrey's phone dead, she could no longer check. Then an idea came to her and she speed-dialed her aunt.

*   *   *

Des Moines

Jeffrey was still in a daze, following his mom around the fabric store like a zombie. When Karen had asked about it—his

212

"moment by the stairs"—he'd played it down, claiming he'd thought of something he needed to do when he got home.

Which was mostly true, if not the full story. Because, meandering down the aisles, his mind was replaying each text, seeing if they fit with his new parking lot revelation.

After paying for the curtains and getting Jeffrey's book at the bookstore, they headed home. A few blocks from the house, Karen's phone rang. Jeffrey pulled it out of her purse, saw his cousin's name on the display, and answered it. M began talking before he finished saying hello.

"I know your phone's dead, but I need you to try something."

She explained what she wanted and how to get it—"maybe." He promised to try as soon as he got home. She hung up before he could share his new theory with her.

*   *   *

Burbank

M was out of the car the second Susan pulled into the driveway. She needed to prep before Jeffrey sent her what she'd asked for. Assuming he could.

Rushing to her room, she retrieved a notepad and pen from her desk, flopped down on her bed, positioned the pad on her bent knees, and got started.

First, she listed the seven days Jeffrey was in LA, from the Sunday he arrived to the Saturday he left. Under each day, she then added a short description of what they did that day. Lastly, next to each of the four days they received a text, she wrote the location where that text had sent them.

By Monday, she wrote "Malibu." By Tuesday, "Hollywood." By Thursday, "Santa Monica." And by Friday, "Diner/Iowa."

Then she closed her eyes and waited.

*   *   *

Brentwood

Staring out her bedroom window, Diana's mind was overloading. Breakfast had been a nice distraction, but alone now, a million questions raced by, all triggered by that news article.

How could everything that happened by that diner be a coincidence? How could its phone number end up in that last text? How could it be the same diner Jeffrey and his mom happened to eat at? Right before that train almost destroyed it?

And what about that whole lucky-bracelet thing? Jeffrey losing his, that cop magically finding it, then returning it right before driving over that broken train track "just in the nick of time"?

Really?

Listing all those things together sounded like some insane movie script no studio would ever buy because it was way too ridiculous.

With each passing day, their huge pile of questions just seemed to get bigger. And with Jeffrey's phone now toast, their chances of finding any answers had basically bit the dust.

What had started out fun and exciting had turned horribly frustrating.

No, beyond frustrating.

Hopeless.

Chapter 54

Sunday Night

O pening her Skype screen for their Sunday evening session, Diana
was totally unprepared for the expressions on her friends' faces.

Two kids in a candy store.

Jeffrey and M could barely contain themselves. Something
was definitely up.

Her eyes darted from one to the other. "Whoa, guys, what's
going on here?"

"Major stuff!" Jeffrey announced, like he'd just won the
lottery.

"Ditto that!" M beamed.

"Great. So who's first?"

With Jeffrey ready to explode, M nodded his way.

"Thank you," he said. "So cutting to the chase, I know what
triggered the texts!"

Diana cocked her head. "Do tell."

"Okay, but fair warning, it's not your cave. Not directly
anyway. First, though, you need to know *how* I figured it out…"

Both girls rolled their eyes.

"So this morning I went to the mall with my mom. And while
we were still in their underground lot, she tried to google a song, but
couldn't."

Diana cut in. "'Google a song?'"

He nodded. "Yeah. She couldn't think of the name of the one
she'd been singing to and wanted to see if the radio station had an
online playlist."

"Whoa. Quite the music buff."

"Oh, big-time. Major geezer-rock fanatic."

M brought them back on topic. "Couldn't what?"

"Huh?

"You said she tried googling a song but couldn't. What,

couldn't find a playlist?"

"No. Couldn't get through, to Google."

He paused a beat. "Now you're supposed to ask me *why* she couldn't get through? Remember, we were still in their underground lot."

Both girls chanted in unison, "No reception!"

"Exactly. Now think where else there was no reception."

Diana answered quickly. "Duh. The cave, which we already knew since I pointed that out on Day One."

He nodded. "Okay. But where else?"

They waited.

He leaned in, grinning like the Cheshire Cat. "In the underground lot of that 7-Eleven! Remember? On our way back from Zuma? We bought snacks for that last sleepover at M's before I left LA the next day."

M shrugged. "So?"

"So think about the timing of that last text. The one you later wrote out for us. It didn't show up in the cave that day and it didn't show up on our way back to the parking lot. But then a few miles later, after leaving that underground 7-Eleven lot, *boom*, it pops up."

"And that's earth-shaking why?"

"Because, as you pointed out, underground lots don't get reception. Every time we got a weird text—the *only* time we got one —we were always in no-reception areas. Yes, mostly in the cave, but also in that underground 7-Eleven lot. That's what triggered them— *dead zones*. It's the only thing that makes sense. Not some magical thing about the cave, or an evil villain stalking us. Just whenever we entered a dead zone."

He took a drink from his water bottle.

"Here's more proof of that: Besides those four texts we've been focused on, I got one other weird one that I almost forgot about. When I first landed in LA, in the airport parking lot. The only reason I remembered it was because it was my very first text on my new phone. I even showed it to M. But since it was just a single character —some odd slashed zero that disappeared as soon as I rebooted—we ignored it.

"But think about *when* I got it. Right after getting off the plane—where I was *thirty thousand feet in the air.* The biggest dead zone of all! *That's* what triggered it. Like the cave did later, and that 7-Eleven lot."

"Then why only a weird symbol that first time?" asked Diana. "Instead of a warning like the others?"

He made a face. "Not sure about that part yet—"

M broke in. "I think I know…"

But Diana wasn't done. "Wait. There's a bigger problem with your theory: You just reminded us about that last Friday at the cave—the only day we *didn't* get a text there that whole week. But the cave's a dead zone, so why no text there that day?"

Jeffrey smiled, ready for that one.

"Remember the weather? That was the only day that whole 'marine layer' thing hit. The beach was totally overcast. I think that thick cloud cover messed with my phone, the way bad weather screws up satellite reception. It was too cloudy for my phone to recognize the cave's dead zone.

"But as soon as we got back into clear weather, and hit that underground 7-Eleven lot, that last text appeared. Plus every other time we got a text in the cave, the weather was clear, so my phone always knew it was in a dead zone."

He stopped, waiting for their next question. But none came. Instead, both girls thought about it a while longer, then slowly began nodding.

Jeffrey's theory actually made sense.

After allowing sufficient time for them to fully absorb his masterful detective skills, he smiled at M.

"Okay, cuz, your turn."

Chapter 55

E ver wonder why we got sent to such random places?" M asked.
After waiting a moment, she explained.

"I mean, first to a toy store in Malibu? Then forty miles south to Hollywood? Then back to the coast to Santa Monica? Then clear across the country to Iowa?"

She lifted an eyebrow. "Why such weird locations? That always bugged me. No rhyme or reason."

No one responded.

"So my big ah-ha moment came while we were driving back from Diana's today. We hit this detour and when I tried to check my Waze app for the best way around it, I got an error message. My 'locations' setting was off. Which got me thinking about *Jeffrey's* location settings. Except, with his phone bricked, it was too late to check... until I got a brilliant idea. Putting his SIM card in his *mom's* phone—and it worked!"

"Whoa, you're losing me," moaned Diana.

"Sorry. All that's important is Jeffrey was able to access his dead phone's memory logs—locations and calls—for the seven days he was in LA. Then once I showed him how to make screenshots, he sent them to me and I plotted it all out—where we went and when we went there. And when I compared that to our four texts, everything matched!"

"Okay, now *I'm* lost," Jeffrey said.

M smiled. "All four places we got sent to—Malibu, Hollywood, Santa Monica, and the diner in Iowa—were in your phone's memory *before* we got sent there. *That's* why your phone picked those locations."

She found an entry in her notes. "Take that first one, the text sending us to the Malibu toy store." She ran a finger down the page. "Your logs show your phone pinged off a Malibu tower... sixty-one minutes before that text arrived."

Jeffrey nodded. "I remember driving by that 'Welcome to

Malibu' sign on our way up to Zuma that first day."

"Exactly. Same with the second text. The one sending us to Sam's in Hollywood. Think back to where we ate lunch the day before we got it. At that In-N-Out *in Hollywood!* So there's a Hollywood ping in your memory before that text sent us there."

She glanced at her notes again. "Same for Santa Monica. There's a Santa Monica ping recorded after that Hollywood ping."

Diana agreed. "Yeah. We drove through Santa Monica right after leaving that In-N-Out."

"Yep. Then a few days later, that text sent us to the lifeguard station there."

Jeffrey shook his head. "But that doesn't work for the last text, the one we now know was pointing to Angels Pass. Me and my phone were never anywhere near there that week. We were in LA."

"Correct. No Angels Pass pings. But it *was* still in your memory. Just not a ping, a *call.*" She checked her page again. "That diner's number is listed in your Call log on the same day you arrived in LA."

"No way. They never called me, I never called them. I'd never even heard of the place back then."

"Well, someone using your phone did. It's listed right before you called your mom." While Jeffrey considered that, she added, "Don't forget, the diner's number is the same as your landline except for the area code."

That jogged Jeffrey's memory. "Ah, okay, I remember now. While we were in your kitchen drinking hot chocolates, I tried calling my mom but misdialed." He chuckled. "Still getting used to those tiny keys, I guess. So I hung up and redialed. I must've blown the area code and got the diner that first time."

M nodded. "Then a few days later that same number pops up in that last text. The one we thought was your home number because I couldn't read the area code. Only later, while you were on your road trip, did we figure out it was the diner's number."

She thought of something else. "Oh, and that very first text you were just talking about? The one you got in the airport parking lot? Here's what I think happened:

219

"Your phone was brand new then, right? Nothing in its memory yet. So when your plane's dead zone triggered that text, it just spit out a random symbol because it had no locations to pull from. It was only *after* that first day—when your phone began storing calls and pings—that we started getting warnings about specific locations."

A thoughtful pause followed as they quietly considered her analysis.

Everything she said about the locations made sense.

As did Jeffrey's account of dead zones triggering the texts.

Gradually, each began to smile. After so many false alarms, it slowly started to register…

They'd just solved two big pieces of their puzzle!

Chapter 56

U nfortunately, their excitement didn't last. Because the real world has a way of dragging you back into mind-numbing daily life.

Another day, another week.

On Monday, Karen drove Jeffrey to the phone store after work and bought him a new phone with a new number. (They wouldn't take back the dead one though; it had to be returned to Amazon.)

Tuesday was packed with school quizzes and too much homework.

On Wednesday, Karen's new bedroom furniture arrived.

On Thursday, Jeffrey went on a lame field trip to a nearby "geological site" with no gooey dinosaur bones and too many wasps.

After school on Friday, Diana picked something up at the *Brentwood Times* offices that she and M had ordered for Jeffrey's belated birthday present.

Saturday was the girls' horseback-riding day.

And then came Sunday.

When their mystery abruptly sprang back to life.

During a football game.

*   *   *

It was late morning. Ty was watching the Patriots-Jets game on TV. Born and raised in Boston, he'd been a diehard New England fan practically since birth. It was the middle of the second quarter and Brady and the Pats were winning.

At a commercial break, the network aired a promotional ad for the new season of its popular TV series, *Subject of Interest.* The previous year, Ty had snagged a small role in an episode of the show. So when he saw the promo, it brought back nice memories. Not just about the episode he'd been in, but also because Larry Armstrong, the show's creator, happened to be a dear friend of his.

Back in the day, Larry and Ty had attended film school together. And though their careers had veered in totally different directions—Ty with his Internet ventures, Larry blossoming into a successful TV writer and producer—they'd remained good friends. In fact, Ty always suspected Larry had secretly helped him get that part, putting in a good word when he heard Ty was auditioning.

When the next commercial came on, Ty's thoughts were still on the show, but had shifted to its storyline. Something about that theme—what the whole series was about—seemed important, or familiar, or… he wasn't quite sure what it was.

Then, as the game resumed and New York scored, the connection finally dawned on him.

Now he really needed to talk to Larry.

Before the next commercial break came on, he'd set up their lunch date: the Rusty Pelican in two hours.

*   *   *

On a good day, the drive from Brentwood to Newport Beach takes at least an hour, usually more, even in light Sunday traffic. Unless you're rolling in a red Ferrari F430—a sweet ride with a powerful V-8 (and Ty's favorite freeway cruiser)—in which case it takes exactly forty-six minutes.

The Rusty Pelican overlooks the Newport Beach Harbor, a mile from Larry's house. When Ty arrived, Larry was waiting at a corner table with a postcard view of bobbing boats and pale blue water. Over clam chowders, they caught up on each other's lives since their last meet-up. But by the time their fish plates were served, Ty had steered the conversation to Larry's television show.

Nearly two hours later, they were the last lunch guests to leave, promising to meet again soon, next time in Brentwood.

As Ty waited for his Italian Stallion by the valet station, he smiled to himself. No question, the trip had paid off. His friend had been generous with his information, giving Ty more than enough to work with.

On the drive home he called Larry with one last request. And by the time he pulled into his garage, twelve PDF pages of Larry's original research notes were waiting in his email inbox.

Guided by those notes and his lunch conversation, Ty spent the rest of the day at his computer, deep-diving into subjects he barely knew existed.

A full bag of pretzels, two water bottles, and half a pastrami sub later, he finished.

Leaning back from his computer, he twisted until he felt his back crack, then took in a breath and blew it out slowly. Just one more thing to do. He made two short calls (actually, the same number twice), then checked the time.

9:15.

Whoa. He'd been at it far longer than he realized. But the timing was good. The kids usually held their Sunday Skype sessions around now.

After sending off a quick text, he gathered the pages he'd printed, arranged them in workable order, and with a satisfied smile, slid them into a folder.

His original hunch had been right.

He *had* been on to something.

And now it was showtime.

Chapter 57

They were ending their group session when Diana's phone chirped. She looked down, read the text, looked back up.

"It's Ty. He says to stay put, that he's on his way." She shrugged.

Four minutes later, Ty appeared in Diana's Skype panel. Sitting down beside her, he flashed his signature smile, then got right to it. "Okay, sorry for the unusual entry, but this is important. It's about the texts. Actually, it's about me solving your mystery."

Which naturally got everyone's full attention.

His next question also took everyone by surprise. "Ever watch a TV show called *Subject of Interest*?"

"Yeah," M answered. "That day out by the pool eating fish tacos. All three of us watched it."

Ty smiled. "Well, I'm not sure if Diana mentioned it, but I had a small part in an episode last year, so I had to learn the show's storyline. Does anyone remember what it's about?"

Jeffrey answered. "Wasn't it some guy with a special computer rescuing people?"

"Pretty much. The main character invents a computer that tells him when someone's about to get in trouble before that person knows about it, so the good guys can rush in and save the day."

Diana stopped him.

"Wait a second. Not to slow your roll, but where's this going? I mean, you're talking about a *science fiction* show, right? Not real. Nothing like our little mystery—which was obviously *very* real. No 'fiction' about it. Each text, each incident, definitely happened."

Ty chuckled. "Patience, child. I promise this has nothing to do with make-believe." He took a sip from the Coke can he'd brought.

"Okay, so while watching football this morning, they aired a promo for the show, which got me thinking about its storyline again. Particularly, how close it was to our own little mystery. I mean, 'a computer that predicts people's fate' sounds an awful lot like 'a phone that predicts bad things coming.' To me, anyway.

"And here's where it gets good: I know the guy who created the show. Larry and I go way back. We went to film school together. So I met him for lunch today, to ask him more about that theme. Not sure what I was after. Guess I was just hoping it might give us a new direction to consider."

He grinned. "And boy did it ever."

He sat back in his chair, now fully engaged.

"I knew I was on to something the second Larry started talking about his secret to writing good sci-fi stories. Because he threw out this one line that basically stopped me cold. He said that to make the stories more believable you always needed to mix in some 'real science' with the fiction!

"So I asked him the next logical question: If he'd used that technique when developing his TV show. And, surprise surprise, he did! He said that whole 'knowing-things-before-they-happen' theme *was* based on real stuff; that he'd just taken actual things he'd read about and exaggerated them! He even gave me a mini-lecture on it all, plus copies of his original research notes.

"Then once I got home, I dove in deep, using his notes and our lunch discussion as my starting points." He chuckled. "Been at it for hours—read a million articles, tech journals, historical pieces— slowly piecing it all together. So let's get to it!"

He picked up a sheet of paper sticking out of the folder beside him, then looked back into the webcam.

"The more I dug in, the more I kept seeing the same two words." Clearing his throat, he began reading from the page he was holding:

"*Predictive Analytics… The advanced branch of data analysis that employs a variety of techniques—including statistics, data sorting, artificial intelligence, and machine learning—to make predictions about future events.*"

Diana made a time-out T-sign. "Translation, please."

He smiled. "Yeah, it didn't mean much to me either, at first." Pulling out another paper from his folder, he skimmed it quickly before looking back up.

"This predictive-analytics stuff is all the rage now. And once you get past the technical terms, it's actually pretty simple. Basically, it's just a modern way of using past events to predict future ones. Which, if you think about it, is how *all* predictions get made.

"For instance, say M wants to predict if a basketball player's gonna make his next free throw. And she knows he's missed his last ninety-nine out of a hundred shots." He arched his eyebrows. "She's gonna predict he'll miss it, right? See? Past events helping to predict future events."

Diana shook her head. "But that's just common sense. How about something less basketball-ish?"

Ty smiled. "Sure." He thought for a few seconds.

"Okay, you know how the CDC announces when next year's flu season will probably start? How do you think they do that? They look at past years. Analyze patterns, take averages, stuff like that. Again, past events predicting future ones."

Jeffrey shook his head. "Yeah, but that's not nearly as specific as the texts we got."

"True. But before I get to that, you need a little background." He fiddled with his papers, read something, then looked back up.

"Best I can tell, this prediction stuff started centuries ago, back in the 1600s, when this French dude named Pascal came up with what became known as his 'probability theory.' And once it started circulating, others began tweaking it, using names like *Numerical Forecasting, The Law of Large Numbers,* and my personal favorite, *The Wisdom of the Crowd.*

"But they all had one thing in common: The more data they used, the more accurate their predictions got. I'll get to why that's important in a second, but first here's a simple example."

He moved to another sheet of paper.

"This is one of the earliest examples I could find of the one called *The Wisdom of the Crowd.* They filled this big jar with thousands of jelly beans, then asked two hundred people to guess how many were in the jar. Most guesses, as expected, weren't that close. But... when they *averaged* all two hundred answers, that average was *very* close. Much closer than most of the individual guesses."

He smiled. "See? The more data they used, the more accurate the result."

Diana cut in. "But what's guessing jelly beans have to do with predicting a crash, or fire, or crime at the beach?"

"Or train wreck," added Jeffrey.

"*Computers!*" Ty shot back. "That's where I'm going with this. Imagine dumping these ancient prediction theories into the twenty-first century. Where we've got all these nifty little gadgets called computers, capable of crunching mega loads of data in microseconds.

"Which brings me to The List…"

Chapter 58

T y pulled out another page.

"Okay, this is from an insurance company's website. Comes out once a decade. The top insurance claims for the past ten years. How much was paid out for injuries, property damage, things like that, grouped by category."

He spun the page around so Jeffrey and M could see it while Diana leaned in from the side.

"This is the most current one, listing the top loss categories." He gave them time to look. "So check out four of the six listed."

He pointed to each one as he spoke.

"Motor vehicles. Fires. Mass transit. Crimes."

He stared at them, waiting, his eyes moving from one to the other. When no one spoke, he said, "Those are the *identical* categories for the texts you got. 'Motor vehicles' for the crash in Malibu. 'Fires' for the one at Sam's. 'Mass transit' fits what almost happened at the diner in Iowa with that train. And 'Crimes' matches your purse snatch in Santa Monica."

"Why's that important?" Jeffrey asked.

"Because if it's on this list, it happens a lot. And if it happens a lot, that means there's tons of data out there on it. And if there's tons of data available, then there's gotta be modern-day computers capable of crunching all that data."

Talking faster, his excitement grew. "Especially when you consider how *much* data's out there. Everything you can possibly think of. Dates, descriptions, locations. You name it, it's available. Collected every second of every day by these shadowy creatures called 'data miners.' Everybody's doing it. Search engines, news departments, cities, police, social media, insurance companies. All of which makes finding anything you want super easy. Most of it for free, some for a few bucks.

"Heck, you wouldn't believe what someone like me, with zero experience, was able to find in minutes. Every detail imaginable.

Car crashes—down to cities, streets, even what they ran into; a tree, a car, a hydrant. Commercial fires—even the one at Sam's was in a fire department database. Ditto for crimes—every police agency publishes the stuff, by types, times, locations, and ages.

"There's even enough data out there to predict a train wreck, like what almost happened at the diner. Maintenance records, local temperatures, hazardous-cargo routes. Cross-reference them with the proper computer power and—presto—you've got what you need to predict a train derailment."

His expression turned serious. "Now do you see what I'm talking about?"

Diana winced. "Not really."

He held both hands palms-up like it was too obvious.

"Once we know that predictions get more accurate the more data you have, there's only one way those texts could've been as specific as they were: major computing power crunching huge reams of data! They've got plenty of names for it: machine learning, supercomputing, artificial intelligence. But whatever you call it, what it's *not* is some evil demon with a crystal ball conjuring up the future."

He stopped to let them absorb that before continuing.

"The truth is, and I hate to be the bearer of bad news, but given all this new info, it's pretty obvious that the 'clues' we've been chasing haven't been real. All the wonderful charts, the dozens of photo comparisons, the very weird exclamation marks—they've all been red herrings. I'm sure Jeffrey can tell you that's what mystery writers call false leads that take you down empty rabbit holes.

"And once you start following red herrings, 'tunnel vision' kicks in. It's only natural. Trying to force things to fit our latest theory, whether they actually fit or not. Like a store sign, or a fire hydrant notice, or a tattoo. All of them seemingly connected in very creative and clever ways, but all of them totally *not* related.

"Because once you get past the smoke and mirrors, there's only one possible explanation for everything that's happened: No doubt about it, it's a tech thing! *A computer did this!* A very powerful, very sophisticated one."

A long silence followed as they chewed on that.

Finally, Jeffrey spoke. "You honestly think 'a tech thing' could be that advanced? Make the kinds of detailed predictions we got? Days, times, places?"

Ty nodded. "Absolutely. Check this out." He picked out another page. "This is from a law enforcement site called *American Policing*. An article about cops using this computer-prediction stuff right now. Here in California, also in New York. Trying to predict when and where actual crimes might happen—neighborhoods, even times of day. So no, Dorothy, this ain't Oz, baby. This stuff's real!"

They all smiled at that. But Ty wasn't done.

"We've all heard how technology doubles every few years. So don't you think there's computers out there *right now* capable of tackling even bigger numbers than what these police are using? Mega machines capable of analyzing tons of data almost instantly?

"Oh, and here's another little detail that confirms this is some kind of computerized intelligence." He addressed Jeffrey. "Remember when you told me about that first weird text you got? Some random mark I think you described as a zero with a line through it?"

"Yeah, in the airport parking lot."

"Well, I checked that too, and guess what? Turns out a 'slashed zero' is *computer code!* It's called an 'empty set symbol' and shows up when a computer doesn't have enough data to process." He pulled out another piece of paper.

"This is from an IT site I found. 'The empty-set symbol typically indicates a computer error where essential data is missing or inaccessible.'"

M cut in. "Hey, that's exactly what I thought last week. His phone's memory was too new to have any location data in it yet."

Ty nodded. "More proof that your texts were computer-generated. I don't know why, but I'm sure of the *how:* a super advanced version of this predictive-analytics stuff!"

He could tell from their expressions they were disappointed. Even if it's not your fault, being told you've been going down empty rabbit holes, and that your carefully crafted theories were all bogus, is tough to take.

"Hey, don't feel bad about it. Even ace detectives chase red herrings and get tunnel vision. Happens all the time. What's important is that you did a remarkable job with what you had! Remember, until today none of us had ever even *heard* of 'predictive analytics.' So feel good about all the things you *did* accomplish.

"I mean, think about it. Figuring out that dead zones triggered the texts? And why you got sent to the places you did? Not to mention rescuing a little old lady and saving Jeffrey's mom from... well, you know." He flashed his big white smile. "You definitely made ol' Nancy Drew proud!"

Jeffrey's expression lightened a bit. "Well, thanks for that. I guess we did do pretty good with what we had."

"You bet. And now that we know how the predictions got made, most of your puzzle's been solved. Something that seemed pretty impossible a week ago."

Jeffrey nodded. "You're right. But still, before it died it would've been nice to know why it only happened to *my* phone."

Ty shrugged. "Look, it'd be nice to know why M's brain does what it does. But, hey, life's full of loose ends, and at least we've tied up most of them now. So let's be happy with the ninety percent we got, and the fun we had getting there."

He held up a finger. "Oh, and speaking of your dead phone, one last question. You said it got shut down last week, right?"

"Yep."

Ty shook his head. "Then you must've got the zombie model. Because before I came over, I called it. And it's apparently risen from the dead!"

Chapter 59

Jeffrey

Ty described how, after finishing his research, he was still curious about my supposedly dead phone so he'd dialed the number to see what would happen. And, as expected, after two rings it disconnected—just like a dead phone would. But when he thought more about it, that didn't make sense. If my phone had recently been deactivated, why hadn't he heard a no-longer-in-service message?

So he'd called it back, and this time got a completely different result. After four rings it stopped, but instead of disconnecting he heard a short burst of static, then a full twenty seconds of what he described as "unusually patterned clicks," before a robotic voice mechanically declared "Program Aborted" and disconnected.

He didn't know what it all meant, other than something was still fishy with my "dead" phone. So I promised to bring it back to the service center and this time pay to have it thoroughly examined before returning it for Mom's refund. Though that never happened.

*   *   *

It was nearly midnight by the time our Skype call ended. A long but productive night. Between last Sunday's discoveries and tonight's, we'd solved three major pieces of our puzzle: what triggered the texts, why locations were picked, and how the predictions got made. Not bad for three—make that four—extremely amateur detectives.

Before going to bed, I went in the kitchen for a glass of water. When I turned on the light, I saw the package. A UPS box sitting by the sink with a note on top in my mom's handwriting.

Mrs. Langley brought this over (misdelivered again).
Didn't want to bother you during Skype. Mom

The Langleys sometimes got our deliveries since their address was one number different from ours.

The first thing I noticed was the big bow drawn in black marker on the side of the box. From that, plus the Burbank return address and my now-proven superior detective skills, I cleverly deduced it was the belated birthday present the girls said was coming.

Taking it to my room, I set it on my bed while I went to the bathroom and brushed my teeth. After changing into my nightshirt, I sat down beside it, peeled back the packing tape, and opened the top flaps. Stuffed between crumpled newspapers were three items: a book, a plaque, and a framed picture.

I took out the plaque first. It was a rectangular piece of dark wood, a foot wide and half as high, with the words *Santa Monica Police Department Commendation* etched across the top. Below that, our three names were printed on a bronze square with a four-line description of our "extraordinary services in citizen crime prevention."

How cool was that? *Jeffrey James, Caped Crusader.*

It'd be up on my wall tomorrow, next to my Cali-calendars.

I set it down and pulled out the book next. It was a journal of some kind with a black leather cover. A sticky note on it read: *For the Writer...* A gold horseshoe was embossed in the center, similar to the one on our bracelets, encircling five words:

Very classy.

I flipped it open. On the inside cover, at the very top, two hand-printed lines read:

The Only Child Club
Founding Members: Jeffrey, M, Diana

Across the top of the page on the right, the first real page, they'd written: *Chapter One...* The rest of the page was blank, as were all the other pages.

I had a lot of writing to do.

I set the journal down and removed the last item from the box: the framed photograph. An eight-by-ten of M, Diana, and me in front of Lifeguard Tower 14, but not the same as the one in the newspaper. This one showed just "the three young heroes"—no Sylvia or Albert. The photographer had taken several poses that day, which meant the girls had special-ordered this one for me.

I could see why they'd picked it. The three of us couldn't have looked happier. Broad smiles, arms draped around each other, the tower in the background, surrounded by sparkling sand. It reminded me of another favorite from my *Oz* book. Dorothy arm-in-arm with her three friends, skipping down the Yellow Brick Road.

Before my trip, the closest I'd come to a moment like this photo was through the pages of a book. Until one magical week in paradise changed everything.

I turned the picture over. Two messages had been penned on the cardboard backing. The one on the left read:

> *Who needs flying monkeys*
> *when your cousin's from Iowa?*
> *Happy B-Day, Corn Man!*
> *– MM*

And the other one read:

> *Sibs you're stuck with,*
> *but friends you choose.*
> *Happy Birthday, Mr. Smooth!*
> *– WW*

234

Ha! MM. WW. Mega-Mind and Wonder Woman.

Re-reading both messages, a goofy smile spread across my lips. I pulled out the thing that keeps the frame from falling over, set it on my nightstand facing my bed, and sat down in front of it, studying those three happy faces.

What an awesome team indeed. Tirelessly tackling—and *solving*—most of what had seemed unsolvable, all while having the times of our lives.

But it was more than that. And more than falling in love with California. We'd talked about it in the cave. That only-child thing. That longing to connect.

Near the end of the book, the Wizard tells Dorothy, "It's not where you go, it's who you meet along the way." And that's where my own Yellow Brick Road had taken me. Down a path where friends are measured by how they treat you, not by looks or money or where you live. Where a trio of unlikely misfits—a bookworm, a loner, and a fairy princess with ducks in her backyard—could join together to make their "whole" so much better than its three oddball parts.

So three cheers for The Only Child Club!

The Brentwoodian, the Mega-Mind, and Me.

Chapter 60

Jeffrey

Clearing off my bed, I set the plaque and journal on my desk and began stuffing the crumpled newspapers back into the empty box.

That's when I noticed the tip of something wedged between the flaps at the bottom. Pulling it out, I immediately broke into a grin.

Your Simple Guide to Using Your New Phone.

I'd completely forgotten about taking it on my trip.

Another sticky note in M's handwriting was stuck to the front: *Found this in your sock drawer...*

I got into bed with the handbook and stared at the cover. It felt like years since I lay in this very spot, re-reading these pages, trying to get my new birthday present to work right. The same phone that now sat two feet away on my nightstand, supposedly dead to the world. Who could've guessed the wild and crazy adventures it would bring.

I opened the manual to the first page, scanning the Table of Contents on the right. I smiled, thinking back to how many times I'd read this page that first night.

Then for some reason, my eyes drifted left, to the inside front cover. I'd never looked there before, my attention had always been focused on the Table of Contents on the right. And for the first time I noticed printing on that side too. A small box of text titled: *Battery Installation.*

Staring at those words, a tingle crept down my back. I'd never installed a battery. It was built-in, right?

So why battery-installation instructions?

I hopped out of bed and rushed to my closet. Digging through a pile of dirty clothes, I found the box for the phone and pulled out the Amazon gift receipt inside. I scanned it, looking for the "sold by" line to see where the phone came from.

I expected to see a name I'd recognize, a big phone seller like Nokia, Best Buy, or Amazon. Instead, it was one I'd never heard of before: "4C Technologies."

I returned to my desk, turned on my laptop, and googled it. Nothing. What kind of business sells a brand-name phone on Amazon without a website? But the better question was *why include battery instructions if the battery's built in?*

I crawled back in bed, grabbed my dead phone off the nightstand, and slid off the back cover.

The battery was easy to spot, the biggest thing in sight with plus and minus signs on top. I popped it out, set the cover and phone back on the nightstand, and examined the battery. Nothing looked weird, just a normal battery.

Until I flipped it over and saw the label.

The goosebumps hit before I finished the first sentence.

Thank you for testing our revolutionary 4C Technology®—a unique blend of proprietary algorithms and cutting-edge AI analytics. Your phone was randomly selected, with all activity channeled through anonymous servers to ensure privacy. Notifications were limited to inactivity periods.

I kept staring at the words. Then re-read them.
I had no idea what any of it meant.
But it creeped me out and my heart was pounding.
Two more lines were printed below that.

Link life: *initial charge + 7 days*
Ionization: *battery removal + 3 hrs*

More gibberish.
Then I thought back to the first time I'd charged my phone.
The Saturday before I left for LA.
And I returned that following Saturday—*seven days later.*
Link life: initial charge + 7 days.
Was that why the weird texts stopped?

Though I had no idea what "ionization" meant.

Another line of smaller text was written below those lines.

4C Technologies Inc. — 4C-ing the Future®

I re-read that tagline. Clever little word-play.

I looked away. I needed time to think.

I set the battery on the nightstand and turned off the light. As I closed my eyes, snippets from the label began streaming through my head, filling in more pieces of the puzzle.

Phone randomly selected.

Why only my phone was affected?

Cutting-edge AI analytics.

Ty's prediction research?

Notifications limited to inactivity periods.

Dead zones triggering the texts?

At that point my brain felt like it was about to explode, so I forced out the label snippets and filled the space with happy thoughts.

Of waves crashing at Zuma. Ocean air in my face. Sand between my toes.

And, thankfully, that worked…

*   *   *

I woke to sunlight streaming through my bedroom window. When I turned to check the time, I learned what *ionization* meant.

The battery was there, but the label was gone.

I squinted to make sure I was seeing things clearly, then reached over and ran my fingers across where the label had been.

Smooth. No glue bumps. No rough spots.

What was happening? Had it all been a dream? The label, my trip, the cave, the texts?

Like Dorothy's return to Kansas?

Instinctively, I touched my left wrist—and felt my lucky bracelet, securely locked in place. My eyes then drifted back to the nightstand—where those three happy faces smiled back at me from their photo.

With a sigh of relief, I sunk back in my pillow.

It hadn't been a dream.

It had all been very real.

My trip. My friends. The best week of my life.

I checked the time. I still had twenty minutes before my alarm went off. So I shut my eyes and quickly slipped into a real dream.

Of a bright yellow pickup truck cruising up the coast on a gorgeous summer day while a solitary pelican glides gracefully overhead.

And as the truck gently fades into the horizon, its bumper sticker sparkles in the sunlight with the perfect ending to my story.

All Good, No Worries.

Epilogue

W eeks later, they were still marveling over all the seemingly trivial, unrelated things that helped solve their mystery *and* prevent a major train disaster: googling a song, a road detour, a lost bracelet, a cop's lunch date with his wife, a TV show, a stupid phone manual.

True, there was no "big bang" ending like in the movies. No heart-pounding, do-or-die climax that mystery writers love to end with. But that's not how most real mysteries end. More often it's much less dramatic. Just some dedicated, hard-working folks (even young, quirky ones) with clever minds and never-give-up attitudes, unwilling to leave any stone unturned.

Then, just when they thought nothing more could surprise them, M stumbled on another stunner. While working on a crossword puzzle one night, the clue was two letters for "the 3-1 postal code." Of course M guessed it right away: CA—the postal code for California, since C and A were the third and first letters of the alphabet.

Which got her thinking about *other* initials, mentally numbering them by their place in the alphabet. Jeffrey's were the coolest: "10-10" for JJ. But then another name popped into her head. That policeman, the one who'd returned Jeffrey's bracelet—Iowa State Patrolman Ian Lane, a name forever burned in her brain.

And that's when she nearly fell out of her chair. Because his initials—I L—were the ninth and twelfth letters of the alphabet.

Yep, 9-12.

The last two numbers in that final text. The date of the near-disaster at the diner. Jeffrey's birthday. And now the hero-cop's initials.

When she told the others about this latest "coincidence," they didn't know what to make of it either, but Jeffrey said he was definitely adding it to his journal.

*   *   *

As summer slipped into fall, life began returning to normal. Or as normal as can be after starring in your own sci-fi drama.

In Iowa, Francine and Ian Lane wasted no time planning their fantasy vacation. After such a close call at the diner, life's joys could wait no longer. Within days of their near-disaster, they booked their dream cruise: a one-month adventure along the coast of Australia.

So in late November, while their neighbors hunkered down for another brutal Midwestern winter, they visited scenic ports, basked by the pool in summer-like weather, sipped drinks with little umbrellas on top, and danced the nights away in the ship's three nightclubs. Francine even gave Ian permission for a once-a-day slice of pie at the buffet. (Not as good as the diner's, but close enough.)

A few weeks before their trip, Ian received a thank-you postcard at his State Patrol offices from the boy whose bracelet he'd returned. A real shock considering no one sends postcards anymore. Naturally, Ian wrote back, reminding the boy of the vital role *he* played that day:

> *"If not for your bracelet, Francine and I would've been eating lunch in the diner, waiting for that next train to roll by."*

*   *   *

Out in California, Ty kept to his normal routines—tinkering with his cars, cruising around town, enjoying the Brentwood good life. Well, actually, there'd been two major changes to those normal routines: a job and a woman.

The job came out of the blue. It started the day he dropped the kids off in Santa Monica to meet with his agent. That meeting led to an unexpected audition that blossomed into a recurring role in a new HBO series called *Mustang Medical*. About an LA doctor practicing medicine for the poor out of her medically-customized Mustang convertible. No surprise, Ty played the doctor's driver (and personally customized the car they used). And, yes, old buddy Larry Armstrong was the show's executive producer.

JOSH EBER

And the new woman in his life? You guessed it. Aunt Susan. After keeping his promise to meet M and her mom for dinner once school started, things progressed quickly. On their third date, he confessed to owning four courtside Lakers season tickets, and when he invited Susan and M to the season opener, they both nearly passed out. Even Diana, the world's worst basketball fan, tagged along to round out the foursome.

* * *

Back in the Valley, M had never been busier, or happier. Since starting high school, she hadn't heard a single negative nickname. She was also enjoying Saturday horseback riding with Diana. And, after some coaxing from Ty and Jeffrey, she'd even tried out for—and *made*—the after-school basketball team at the rec center.

As the new point guard for the Burbank Bisons, she was the only girl on the team and its second-highest scorer. One of her teammates had even started flirting with her.

What more could ex-loner and Girl-Formerly-Known-As-Margaret ask for? Boys, basketball, a new Brentwood BFF, a long-lost cousin from Corn Country, Ty around the house to shoot hoops with, and her mother had even started calling her M.

* * *

Across town in Brentwood, Diana was also doing well. School wasn't horrible; not one bratty classmate had upset her the entire first month, a personal best. She'd even begun volunteering on Sundays at a homeless kitchen a few blocks from M's animal shelter. Every Sunday, instead of Ty and the limo, she took the bus into Hollywood where she'd meet M for their joint bus ride downtown.

She'd also adopted a new kitten from M's animal shelter, naming it Drew in honor of Ty's childhood crush.

* * *

As for Jeffrey, he still read a lot, wrote a lot, and kept in regular touch with the girls. His new phone worked perfectly—not one crazy text to report—and he got his mom her refund on the old one.

He did occasionally wonder about *everything* that happened—the texts, the events, that label. Until he realized it really didn't matter. Whether real, imagined, or somewhere in between, their adventure was so much more than a cool mystery. It was a powerful lesson on how true friendship can indeed change lives.

Of course, he also daydreamed a lot about those glory days in California, though the memory that stood out most surprised him: *the pelicans.* Their gorgeous formations and that one flying alone. Nature's perfect balance—using the support from your flock to build the confidence needed to take care of business.

And that's what he'd used to finally have The Talk with his parents—which, as the girls had predicted, went well. He was now an active part of the family conversation, happily splitting time between both worlds. Bike rides, photo tips, and weekend adventures with Dad. Movies, music, and all that cringy advice he secretly loved from Mom. He had two loving parents and that's all that mattered.

Dad was even coming over for Thanksgiving, so who knows? And on Halloween they'd both surprised him with an early holiday present: a round-trip ticket to visit his cousin over winter break!

Christmas in California. He was already counting the days. And this time he wouldn't miss the Tar Pits.

Now if the post office would just deliver his *Jeopardy!* invitation, life would be perfect.

*   *   *

Somewhere Near Another Valley

High above the hills overlooking Silicon Valley, in a darkened penthouse on the top floor of one of his many properties, the man sat in front of four massive computer screens, soaking in those beautiful blinking lines of data.

The last few months had been extremely productive, all eight test subjects validating his experiment. The algorithm wasn't yet perfect, but it was getting there. He'd used self-destruct labels as added layers of protection in the event his secret project leaked. But despite the slight delay with that last phone shut-down, the ionization process had erased all remnants, so leakage was no longer an issue.

Although he never appeared in published wealth lists (flying under the radar was his specialty), the man had quietly amassed the largest net worth on the planet, controlling interests in all major sectors: technology, transportation, energy, social media, finance, health, consumer goods, general media, even outer space.

Which left one final frontier: *The Future.*

And with final testing now complete, that would soon be his as well. Because *knowing* the future meant *controlling* it. And all that flowed from it. Property values, company profits, all Next Big Things.

So yes, Dorothy, there really was a man behind the curtain, pulling all the strings and mining all the data.

Meet the *real* Boogeyman, boys and girls.

Hiding in plain sight, you never saw him coming.

And likely never will.

The man checked the time. If he left soon, he'd be home before his daughter went to bed. This time of night, the Bell chopper would be faster than the Lear. For now though, he'd savor the moment a bit longer, the thrill of global domination finally within reach.

He picked up the silver paperweight from his desk, absently running his thumb across its textured surface. One of his most prized possessions, it had been a gift from his daughter, his very special good luck charm.

Leaning back, he looked down at it and smiled.

She'd always had a thing for horseshoes.

#

Author's Notes

The cool thing about writing fiction is you get to make stuff up. So while most of the cities, beaches, highways, and landmarks in the story are real (the Kodak Theatre was renamed The Dolby in 2012), I did take some liberties.

Some of the directions have been adjusted and you won't find Pearl Street in Malibu, Sam's in Hollywood, Riverside Stables in Burbank (a tribute to the late great Pickwick Stables), or Maple Falls or Angels Pass in Iowa (although there's an even taller peak in Northwest Iowa called Hawkeye Point).

And while I spent my high school years living in my family's backyard guesthouse in Burbank, and many summers on the beaches of Santa Monica and Zuma, I never found a sea cave as described in the story. But there are some nice ones further south in La Jolla.

As for predicting the future, if you think the concept is pure fiction, think again. A lot has happened since 2009 when the story takes place. Predictive Analytics—the power of computers to predict future events from historical data—is now very much front and center.

The Department of Homeland Security has tested predictive algorithms to help identify potential terrorists hidden among airline passengers. Hundreds of police departments—including Chicago, Santa Cruz, Los Angeles, and New York—regularly employ some form of "predictive policing" to help pinpoint possible criminal activity. Even the inspiration for the fictional TV show in the story, CBS's *Person of Interest*, employed an exaggerated form of predictive analytics called statistical learning.

Meanwhile, data-mining has drastically intensified. Besides all the available data Ty mentioned in the story, literally every measurable metric in the world is now readily available. From weather, traffic, and finance, to energy, ocean currents, even outer space activity—to name just a few.

Add to that all the *personal* data collected from your phone, online activity, apps, smart appliances, and cameras everywhere, and the potential for making accurate predictions of future accidents or incidents could be closer to reality than you think—if not already here.

And with the recent explosion of artificial intelligence and chat bots, many believe that predicting disasters, or even personal events, could someday be as common as googling a song.

So while you shouldn't expect predictive phone batteries at your local 7-Eleven anytime soon, the sci-fi plot of this story may soon be less *fi* and more *sci* as computers and data-mining operations grow more powerful, and those controlling them find new ways to evade regulation.

Lastly, a few more absolutely true facts from the story:

- M's condition, H-SAM—also known as Hyperthymesia or "perfect recall"—is real. Researchers have discovered about sixty people who have it, though they have no idea why, or whether all brains have that potential.

- Home to one-third of the country's entire hog population (at last count), the great state of Iowa is indeed the self-proclaimed Pig Capital of America.

- Spits, the legendary, saliva-flinging training horse, lived a long and happy life in the San Fernando Valley, both terrorizing and charming his riders for many years.

- And there really was a guy on the beach offering free onions.

- Josh Eber, La Jolla, CA

About The Author

Josh Eber

Josh Eber is the pen name for a San Diego writer, lawyer, and businessman who prefers keeping his fictional world separate from his real one (though the former grounds the latter). He's authored multiple books across multiple genres under various names.

To contact him or be put on his mailing list, please email him at:
josheber@smartphonethebook.com.

AND IF YOU ENJOYED THE BOOK…

… please consider writing a short review. It could help more readers find it and encourage future installments. Just use the link or QR code below, then look for "Write A Review" in the lower review section of the page.

https://amzn.to/3N4wmYm

www.ingramcontent.com/pod-product-compliance
Lightning Source LLC
Chambersburg PA
CBHW031716170626
46808CB00005B/1778